Both Rosie and Eli had been unaware of the sudden silence that had befallen the rest of the patrons at first sight of the ominous stranger when he walked into the dining room. Lean almost to the point of looking gaunt, he wore a flat-crowned hat pulled low, but still not low enough to cover the vicious scar that ran like a lightning bolt across his face. Forks were suspended halfway between plates and mouths as all eyes fixed on the dark messenger of death as he approached the table by the kitchen door, rifle in hand.

Eli looked as if he had seen a ghost, for in his mind that was exactly what had appeared before him. The silver chain and heart dropped from his hand as he struggled to get up from his chair, at the same time reaching for his pistol. In his panic, his efforts succeeded only in tangling him in the chair and resulted in causing him to go over backward on the floor. Terrified by the grim figure standing over him, with his unblinking, almost paralyzing gaze, Eli could not wrestle his gun from his holster as Ben's rifle barrel pointed at him like an accusing finger. The first shot sent some of the patrons scattering for the door. It was followed by five more rounds, cranked methodically one after the other until there was no uncertainty on whether or not the man was dead. . . .

LEFT HAND OF THE LAW

Charles G. West

BERKLEY
New York

BERKLEY

An imprint of Penguin Random House LLC

penguinrandomhouse.com

Copyright © 2011 by Charles G. West

Excerpt from *Outlaw Pass* copyright © 2011 by Charles G. West

Penguin Random House supports copyright. Copyright fuels creativity, encourages diverse voices, promotes free speech, and creates a vibrant culture. Thank you for buying an authorized edition of this book and for complying with copyright laws by not reproducing, scanning, or distributing any part of it in any form without permission. You are supporting writers and allowing Penguin Random House to continue to publish books for every reader.

BERKLEY and the BERKLEY & B colophon

are registered trademarks of Penguin Random House LLC.

ISBN: 9780451234025

Signet mass-market edition / July 2011

Berkley mass-market edition / February 2022

Printed in the United States of America

13 15 17 19 21 20 18 16 14 12

For Ronda

Chapter 1

Ben Cutler looked up and smiled when his six-year-old son, Danny, appeared at the barn door carrying a Mason jar half filled with cider. Ben knew that his wife, Mary Ellen, had no doubt put the thought in the boy's head to fetch the cider from the spring box in the creek and surprise his father with it. He wouldn't let on that he suspected as much, because Danny was very proud to be the bearer of the cool refreshment on this hot summer day in the southeast corner of Kansas.

"Well, bless my soul," Ben exclaimed. "I was just this minute wishin' I had a drink of cool cider. How'd you know that's what I was thinkin' about?" Danny's answer was a delighted giggle and he thrust the jar out for his father to take. "Why don't you have a little drink yourself?" Ben suggested. It wasn't really hard cider; he hadn't let it ferment that long, so it wouldn't hurt the boy. Eager to accept the offer, Danny gulped a few swallows down, smacked his lips loudly, then extended the jar toward his father again. He stood back to watch as Ben took a long draw from the jar and smacked his lips in turn to show his appreciation.

"Somebody's comin'," the boy suddenly announced, and Ben turned to follow his son's gaze to the head of the lane, where he saw a lone rider coming toward the house.

Ben put aside the harness he was in the midst of repairing and got up to stand beside Danny. The rider looked familiar, and when he was halfway to the yard, Ben recognized Eli Gentry, a deputy sheriff from Crooked Fork. Ben could not say he knew the man very well, and what little bit he knew didn't impress him very much. He had what Ben would describe as a weasel face with dark eyes that seemed too close together on each side of a long, thin nose. The thing that set him apart was the cutoff sword he liked to wear on his side. In a scabbard like a long hunting knife, it had once been a cavalry sword until about a third of the blade had been broken off. Sheriff Jubal Creed's other deputy, Bob Rice, struck Ben as a much more mature lawman. He had to admit that he knew very few people in the settlement at the forks of the Neosho and Lightning rivers, some fifteen miles away from his place on the Neosho. Curious, he walked out to meet Gentry. "Howdy, Deputy," he called out in greeting. "What brings you out to this part of the county?"

Pulling his horse to a stop when he was hailed from the barn, Gentry turned to meet Ben and his son. "I swear, Ben Cutler," he replied with a genuine look of surprise. "Is this your place?" Ben responded with no more than a smile, since the answer seemed obvious. He was amazed that the deputy knew his name. Gentry continued. "You got a right tidy little place here, looks like. I didn't think you knew much about farmin'." He looked around him at the barn and the corral. "Looks like you're more into raisin' cattle."

Ben shrugged. "Well, I guess I do know a little more about horses and cows than I do about raisin' crops, but that's what happens to a man when he meets the little woman who's gonna run his life." He placed an affectionate hand on Danny's head. "Mary Ellen got tired of havin' me gone so much of the time, and wanted us to have a place of our own. Have to admit, she was right." He waited for the deputy to explain his appearance this far from Crooked Fork, but Eli continued to look around him as if evaluating the progress Ben had made. "Step down," Ben invited, "and get a cool drink of water, or some of this sweet cider. You didn't say how you happen to be out this far. Are you on sheriff's business?"

Gentry took another look toward the house before dismounting. "Yeah, that's right," he answered. "There's been some raidin' of some of the farms and ranches in the county, and Jubal sent me and Bob out to look around. He thinks it might be Injuns from down in the Nations."

"Is that a fact?" Ben responded. "Well, I haven't seen or heard of any trouble like that around here. If it's Indians, I doubt if it's any of the Cherokees. I talked to Jim White Feather a couple of days ago, and he didn't say anythin' about any raidin' around here."

"Huh," Eli snorted. "I doubt he'd say anythin' if there was. He mighta been one of 'em doin' the raidin'."

"I reckon I'd have to disagree with you there, Eli," Ben said. "Jim's a good man. He's been a friend to me ever since I started to build this place."

Gentry did not reply to Ben's statement. Instead, he affected a thin smile and abruptly changed the subject. "You are mighty close to the Nations. I expect you're about the only white family down the Neosho this far."

"Where are you headin' from here?" Ben asked.

"Back to town, I reckon. I've got a long way to ride ahead of me, too long to get home tonight, and I'm short of supplies as it is. But I expect I'll make me a camp somewhere along the way."

Knowing common courtesy called for it, Ben said, "It is a long ride into Crooked Fork from here, and the afternoon's about played out. You'd be welcome to take supper with us, and you can sleep in the barn if you want. Then you can start back to town in the mornin'."

"Well, now, that's mighty neighborly of you, Cutler." Gentry was quick to accept the invitation. "That sure would make it a lot easier for me. You sure that pretty little wife of yours wouldn't mind?"

"I expect she'd most likely invite you yourself," Ben replied, then turned to Danny. "Run to the house, son. Tell your mama we've got company for supper." Turning back to Gentry then, he said, "Come on. I'll help you put your horse in the barn." He led the way to one of four stalls in the barn, hoping that his irritation at piling this on Mary Ellen with no warning wasn't too evident.

"Yessir," Eli commented as he stood between the stalls and looked around him, "you fixed yourself up real fine here." He cocked his head back to look Ben in the eye and grinned. "Musta cost you a little money, from the looks of the barn and house."

"Well, I guess I had a little money put back from my cattle, but I built the house and barn myself, like everybody else in the county, I expect." It struck him as an odd conversation to have with Eli Gentry, but he supposed that it was just the deputy's way of trying to make polite talk.

"If you've still got some of that money put aside, I hope you've put it away somewhere safe, like a root cellar or someplace where Injuns ain't likely to look."

Not wishing to pursue a subject that he considered his private business, Ben switched to another. "Like I said, you can sleep here in the barn. I can get you an extra blanket if you need it, but I doubt you will, hot as it's been." He waited for Gentry to pull his saddle off and spread his blanket on the hay. "We might as well go on up to the house and see how long it'll be before Mary Ellen has supper on the table."

"You know Deputy Gentry, don't you, Mary Ellen?" Ben asked when they walked into the kitchen.

"Evenin'," Eli offered while making no attempt to disguise his thorough study of Mary Ellen's body.

"Why, of course I know *of* the deputy," Mary Ellen said, with a forced smile, turning her attention to Gentry. "We've never met, but I'm pleased to meet you now. Welcome to our home." When Gentry shifted his gaze to see what was on the stove, she glanced at her husband and rolled her eyes, registering her annoyance. He shrugged and made a helpless gesture. When Gentry returned his gaze to concentrate on her again, she said, "Why don't you two go ahead and wash up for supper, and I'll have it on the table by then? You go along, too, Danny. I know your hands could use some scrubbing."

Eli stood by while Ben and his son washed up at

the pump on the back porch, feeling no compulsion to do likewise. "You know," he commented, "a drink of likker would go good before supper. You must have a bottle around here somewhere. Ain'tcha?"

"Sorry," Ben replied. "I ain't got anythin' stronger than cider, and it ain't even hard cider, but you're welcome to that." It was not the truth. He had a bottle of rye whiskey that he took a nip from every once in a while, but he figured supper was enough to waste on the likes of Eli Gentry. It could be, he thought, that he was judging Eli too harshly, but he had heard a few stories about the bullying tactics of the deputy. He guessed it boiled down to the fact that he just didn't like the man. It was a gut feeling.

Eli curled his lip in a show of disgust. "I reckon I'll pass on the cider."

Supper was a silent affair for the most part. Mary Ellen and Ben tried to engage in some polite conversation at first, but there was no response that amounted to more than a grunt from Gentry. His attention was focused strictly on his plate as he stuffed his face with food.

"Well, I reckon I've put you folks out enough," Gentry finally said. "I'd best get out to the barn and hit the hay." He looked at Mary Ellen, who was already clearing the table. "Thank you for the supper, ma'am. I ain't et that good in a while." Then he smiled at Ben and said, "You're a lucky man, Cutler."

Ben grinned. "I reckon I'm aware of that." He winked at Mary Ellen. "She won't let me forget it." He got up from the table then and walked Gentry to the door. "I don't know how early you're thinkin' about startin' out in the mornin', but you're welcome to some breakfast with us if you want."

"Just might do that," Eli replied, casting a quick gaze in Mary Ellen's direction. "Just might do that," he repeated, then stepped out the door.

"I'll send Danny out to get you when breakfast is ready," Ben called after him. He turned back to find Mary Ellen facing him.

"I'll be glad to see that man gone from here," she said. "He's got a look about him that makes my skin crawl."

"He ain't what you'd call housebroke, is he?" Ben replied, shaking his head as he thought about the awkward mood around the supper table. "I reckon he's all right. I guess we can stand him for one night and breakfast in the mornin'." He clasped his hands together over his head and took a good long stretch. "I guess I'm ready to turn in. I've got a big day tomorrow if I'm gonna get the lower field plowed." He winked at his wife and shifted his eyes toward his son, who was emulating his father's stretching. Mary Ellen smiled and nodded her head.

Ben had already gone into the bedroom by the time Mary Ellen had finished cleaning up her kitchen. The evening had already faded from twilight to make way for the deep darkness that would soon follow when she paused at the back door before hurrying across the yard to the outhouse. Ben would probably laugh at her, but she didn't feel comfortable with Eli Gentry in the barn. Although she was sure he was not up and about, she still felt as if his eyes were somehow on her. As soon as her business in the outhouse was finished, she almost ran back to the house. Once inside, she quickly barred the door and made straight for the bedroom, never feeling at ease until she was snuggled up against her husband's back.

In spite of her sense of concern, the night passed as other nights before it, and she woke at first light and slipped out of bed. She would start the fire in the stove and put the coffee on to boil before waking Danny. Ben would already be awake. He was always aware when she left the bed. She rolled out her dough and formed her biscuits to be ready when the oven was hot enough. While they baked, she sent Danny to the henhouse to gather eggs while she cut strips of bacon. A thought occurred to her that it might not be a good idea to prepare such a big breakfast. It might encourage Eli Gentry to visit again. *But then he might tell everyone in Crooked Fork that Ben Cutler's wife was a sorry cook.*

Ben came in when she called to him from the kitchen. He poured himself a cup of coffee and sat down to await breakfast. He was into his second cup when Mary Ellen sent Danny out to tell Gentry breakfast was ready. Baked biscuits, a large bowl of scrambled eggs, and a plate piled high with bacon were all on the table and in danger of getting cold when Mary Ellen paused and looked toward the back door. "Where in the world is that boy?" she exclaimed. "How long does it take to walk to the barn?"

Ben chuckled. "Probably forgot why you sent him out there. I'll go get 'em."

Gentry was standing near the barn door when Ben walked in. "Mornin'," Ben said. When there was no sign of his son, he asked, "Where's Danny? He was supposed to tell you that breakfast is ready."

"He did," Gentry said. "He's over in that back stall."

"Danny!" Ben called. "What are you doin', boy?" When there was no answer, he walked back to the stall to see what the rambunctious boy might be up to. "What are you do—" he started to repeat, but was stopped cold by the sight of the boy lying facedown in the middle of the stall. "Danny!" he uttered fearfully, and rushed to drop to his knees beside his son. Only then did he see the blood-soaked hay beneath Danny's head. "Danny!" he cried again, forgetting all else in his panic, his only thought to save the boy's life. The horror of the discovery sent his mind reeling with a paralyzing jumble of thoughts. He turned Danny over and started to pick him up, but was staggered by the sight of his son's neck gaping from a bloody slit from ear to ear. Still, in an effort to save him, he struggled to his feet, his only thought then to get to Mary Ellen, praying she could tell him what to do to save Danny's life. With Danny's body in his arms, he turned to be met with the full force of Gentry's half sword across his face. The blow rendered him unconscious. Dropping to his knees, and still clutching the still body of his son, he fell over on his side.

Confused, still dazed, he returned to consciousness, aware of a searing pain that seemed to clutch his entire body. Gradually, he began to remember the events that took place before his brain blacked out, and he tried to get up on his feet, but he could not move his arms or legs. Unable to see clearly in the darkness of the barn, he started to call for help, but immediately started choking as soon as he drew breath to shout. *Smoke!* He realized then that his barn was on fire and he was helpless to move because he was tied down. As he struggled against his bonds, he was struck with devastating pain in his chest that forced him to lie back and surrender to his obvious fate. In a matter of moments, he could feel the flames as they swept through the barn, closer to him, pushing a wave of black smoke to sweep over him. Calling on all the force he could summon, he strained against the ropes that held him, but his bonds were too secure, and he knew that in a very few minutes he would be helpless to save himself. He thought of his wife and son, and prayed that Mary Ellen had somehow escaped the evil deed that had claimed Danny and him. He lay back then to wait for the end.

As the smoke began to fill his lungs, he began to slip away from consciousness again with the smoky image of a dark form hovering over him. Then suddenly, he felt his body being jerked and dragged over the hard dirt floor of the burning barn. The last sensation he felt before drifting away from reality altogether was a rush of cool air in his lungs.

Finally, he woke again, this time to a world of stinging pain, but the choking smoke was gone from his lungs. He heard a voice then. "Damn, partner, I wasn't sure you were gonna make it." Though his vision seemed hazy, he was able to recognize Jim White Feather, his closest neighbor.

He blinked several times in an effort to clear his vision before realizing that his head was bandaged with one eye completely covered. "Jim?" he questioned, confused. Then, in a moment, he remembered and tried to get up. "Mary Ellen!" he cried, but the pain in his chest caused him to drop back on the bed.

"You've got to lie back and keep the strain off your chest," Jim said, "and let them wounds heal."

"Jim!" Ben pleaded. "Mary Ellen, Danny!"

Jim shook his head sadly. "They're gone, Ben—both dead. I'm sorry I didn't get there in time to help either one of 'em. But they're gone and I was almost too late to get you out of that barn."

The memory of that most horrible moment in his life returned as details came rushing back to him. He saw Danny lying lifeless in his arms. The image caused an agonized moan to slip from his mouth. He remembered his panic to get to Mary Ellen, and the great loss struck him like an arrow in his heart. Mary Ellen was part of him. He could not live without her. The gentle moan increased in intensity until he roared out his sorrow. Standing beside her husband, Little Swan took a step backward, afraid Jim's friend was going to explode uncontrollably.

Feeling exhausted from the violent eruption deep inside him, Ben fell back on the bed again, drained of the will to live. Then he remembered Eli Gentry and the brief flash of the sword seconds before everything went blank in his mind. He reached up to feel the bandages on his head, and in a voice suddenly calm, he asked, "My eye?"

Relieved to see Ben calmed down again, Jim answered, "You got a pretty bad wound across your face—cut to the bone across your forehead. Little Swan stitched it up as best she could, but your eye's all right. She just had to cover it when she wrapped them bandages around your head." That still didn't explain the severe pain Ben experienced in his chest, and he strained then to look down at it. Understanding, Jim continued. "That feller shot you. Thought he'd finish you off, I reckon. Little Swan tried to dig the bullet out, but she couldn't. It's lodged in there against somethin', and she was afraid she was gonna kill you if she kept at it."

"Where's Mary Ellen?" Ben asked, his emotions still under control.

Misunderstanding, Jim was quick to repeat, "Mary Ellen's dead, Danny, too."

"I know," Ben replied. "Where are their bodies?"

Worried that Ben might become violently stricken with grief again, Jim explained, "They're buried, Ben, already in the ground. You wouldn'ta wanted to see them like that, so I buried 'em right away, just as soon as the fire died out." When Ben seemed to accept that without protest, Jim was at once relieved, for both bodies had been burned beyond recognition, and would only have created lasting memories of his family that might haunt him forever. Now that Ben appeared to have his emotions under control, Jim was anxious to ask the question that had been on his mind from the beginning. "Who did this thing to you, Ben?"

"Eli Gentry," Ben answered, his voice soft and calm.

The answer surprised him. "The deputy sheriff from over in Crooked Fork?" Ben slowly nodded. "Damn," Jim swore. "You sure that's who it was?" It was hard to believe a lawman had been responsible for the massacre.

"It was him," Ben confirmed. Then he went on to tell Jim that the deputy had eaten supper with him and his family, and spent the night in the barn. Jim knew without asking that his friend had found a new incentive to live, if only for one purpose. Had he been able to read Ben's thoughts, he would have seen that his friend wished only to live long enough to avenge his family.

After hearing as much of the details as Ben could remember before turning to be met with a sawed-off sword in his face, Jim could make a pretty accurate guess about the rest. "I was followin' a little herd of antelope all the way up from Dry Creek, tryin' to get close enough to get a shot at one of 'em. I wasn't but about two or more miles from your place when I saw the smoke. I studied on it for a while, but decided it was too much smoke for you to be burnin' hedgerows or somethin', so I figured I'd better take a closer look. When I got to your place, the whole house was in flames, just about gone, and the barn was goin' pretty steady. I knew it wouldn't be long before it went up like the house. I didn't see nobody around—no livestock, either. The thought that first struck me was that you'd got sick and tired of tryin' to grow somethin' in this soil and you packed up, burned the place down, and left. I don't know what gave me the notion to look in the front of the barn before it caught, but it's a good thing I did. I saw you, tied to a post, and the fire wasn't far away from you already. When I was dragging you out, I looked back and thought I saw a body—small, had to be Danny—lying in a big circle of fire. Wasn't no way I could get to him, but he wasn't movin', so I figured I was too late, anyway."

Ben listened to Jim's accounting of the massacre in thoughtful silence, trying to answer all the questions in his mind while struggling to hold his emotions in check. He almost sobbed when he pictured his son, innocent little six-year-old Danny, and the horror that had awaited him in the barn. Gentry had slit the boy's throat, then waited for Ben to come looking for him. A bullet would have been easier, but Gentry likely didn't want Mary Ellen to hear the shot in the house and react in time to defend herself. He tried not to think about the circumstances of Mary Ellen's death, knowing it would drive him insane if he allowed his mind to dwell on it. Gentry had left him tied to the post to burn up in the barn. He must have come back afterward to finish him off with a bullet. Why he hadn't made sure he was dead was something of a mystery. Maybe the fire had been getting too close and he'd decided to get out of there before the roof caved in. Maybe because Ben hadn't moved when shot, Gentry had figured he was already dead. *Who knows?* he thought. *But that was the mistake that sealed Eli Gentry's death warrant.*

His healing was slow at first. The wound in Ben's chest did not seem inclined to improve. The time spent lying in a corner of Jim White Feather's log cabin was a grinding hell, filled with dreams of his wife and child and their horrible suffering, and he felt responsibility for their deaths. *How could I have seen it coming?* He asked the question a thousand times, unable to discard the guilt he felt. He should have reacted immediately when he found Danny's body. Maybe if he had, if he had been quicker, he might have at least prevented Mary Ellen's death. Finally, he decided that he had wallowed in self-pity long enough and it was time to heal physically in order to avenge his family's death. No amount of regret for his slow actions was going to bring them back. Eager to regain his strength, he improved rapidly from that point, causing Jim to remark, "We was worried about you for a time there. Looked to me like I was gonna have to dig another grave." A few days after that, Ben got up from the bed, and in three weeks he felt fit enough to pronounce himself ready to leave their care.

"What are you aimin' to do?" Jim asked as he helped Ben saddle the horse he loaned him.

"The same thing you would do, I reckon," Ben answered. "But first, there's a lot I have to do before I pay a visit to the deputy sheriff. I'm headin' back to see what's left of my place. I guess Gentry ran off with all my stock, but I'll return your horse and saddle as soon as I can get my own. I've got money from the two cattle drives I brought up from Texas. I was savin' it to buy five hundred acres next to my land." He gave Jim a sorrowful glance. "I ain't got no use for that land now. But if nobody's found where I buried that money, I reckon I'll be using it to buy a horse and a saddle." He hesitated for a moment, thinking to himself before adding, "And a rifle and some clothes, and everythin' else I need, plus some for you and Little Swan for all the grub I ate."

"You don't owe us nothin'," Jim said. "You know that."

Little Swan walked out of the cabin to join them. "When you coming back? You not well yet." She reached up and touched the long scar that extended from his hairline, across his brow and the bridge of his nose. "It still pink, but look pretty good."

Ben chuckled. He knew what it looked like, and it wasn't pretty. "Yeah, it looks fine. You did a good job."

He stepped up in the saddle then. "I'll be back before dark if you're sure you ain't ready to kick me out."

"Hell," Jim snorted, "you know you're welcome here. You want me to ride over with you?"

"No. I'll be all right. Besides, you've got your own work to do. That plowin' ain't gonna get done by itself."

Jim and his wife stood watching Ben as he rode out of the yard. When he had disappeared from their view, beyond the line of cottonwoods, Jim looked at Little Swan and shook his head, concerned. He feared that his friend was setting himself up for a world of trouble if he went after Eli Gentry. He would have tried to persuade Ben to go directly to Sheriff Creed and let the law take care of Gentry, but he knew it would have been a useless endeavor. In the time he had known Ben Cutler, Jim had found him to be a man of strong but gentle disposition. Men like Eli Gentry ran roughshod over men like Ben. "I've got to get to work," he finally announced to Little Swan, and started toward the barn. He gave Ben one last thought. *Every man has a path to walk. It's not for me to question the wisdom of it.*

Even though he had tried to prepare himself for the worst, his insides were suddenly paralyzed by an icy grip on his spine at first sight of his home. He paused on the ridge above the ruins of his barn to give himself time to control his emotions before nudging Jim's horse to descend into the yard. Jim White Feather had been right. There was nothing left but a pile of charred timbers, leaving two great black circles where once his house and barn had stood. Thoughts of Mary Ellen, and what torture she might have suffered, threatened to send him into a wave of hopeless despair, and he fought hard to resist it. Dismounting, he walked into the midst of the burned rubble that had been his and Mary Ellen's dream. Already, weeds were pushing their heads up through the blackened earth where his parlor had been. He stirred through the ashes with the toe of his boot, searching for anything that might have survived. Broken dishes, scorched cups, pieces of sooty rags, and all that remained of their clothes were strewn about. Footprints he found bore evidence that someone had been there before him. Judging by the prints and the number, he guessed a hunting party of Indians was the likely answer. Turning toward the kitchen, he saw the only thing that might have survived the fire, the iron stove. But in keeping with his bad luck, it was destroyed, broken by the heavy ridge pole that had collapsed upon it.

There was nothing to salvage from his home, so he walked over to the ruins of the barn. He didn't spend much time there, only long enough to search for any tools that might have survived. Anything with a wooden handle bore signs of the fire's intensity. Some of his tools were missing, giving further evidence of prior visitors. Spotting a handleless shovel lying near the tack room, he picked it up and carried it with him. Deciding then that there was nothing to keep him longer in this melancholy place, he walked halfway up the ridge where he had cleared off a family cemetery. This was where Jim had buried his wife and son, alongside a small grave that he had dug soon after he settled his family there. It was marked with a carved board that read SHEP—MAN'S BEST FRIEND—APRIL 18, 1877.

He stood over the two fresh graves for a long while. Jim hadn't left stones or anything to mark them, and

Ben decided that he'd prefer to leave them that way. He had never been a praying man, but he asked the Lord to take care of his wife and child, and he apologized for being angry with Him for the evil that had befallen them. When he had finished, he moved over to stand before the smallest grave and studied it for a few minutes. Then he dropped to his knees and with the piece of shovel he had found in the barn, began to dig up the grave. It was not easy, for the ground had packed hard over the last couple of years, but he continued to work at it until, finally, he uncovered the rusty metal container that held the money he had saved to buy land. It was more than enough to outfit him with a horse and weapons, and he would acquire what he needed at Lon Bridges' trading post on the Grand River in Indian Territory.

Finished with his grim task, he picked up the board that had marked the fake grave and the rusty container, then walked back down to the ruins of his home, where he tossed them into the middle of the charred timbers.

Chapter 2

"I'm pretty sure they all perished," Eli Gentry replied in answer to the sheriff's question. "All I know is there wasn't no sign of any of 'em when I rode by there, and there was three graves up on the side of the ridge. Ain't much doubt who done it. Some of them Injuns slipped over there from the Nations, I expect." His story was not a total lie, for when he had ridden back two days later the bodies had been removed and there were three graves on the ridge. Someone had happened upon the scene right after he had left.

It had been several weeks since Gentry reported the attack, and the sheriff rode over to look for signs that might tell him if there was any possibility for more Indian raids to threaten his town. What he found was consistent with what Gentry had said. The only thing that puzzled him was the fact that one of the graves, the smallest one, had been desecrated, and the body apparently removed. He assumed that the child had been buried there, but who would have dug up the kid's body? He might have blamed it on a coyote or wolf, but he doubted that either could have used the shovel blade found beside the grave. Possibly Eli was correct in blaming Indians, although there were really no other signs that would confirm it. This was the second such raid on a remote farm in the last month. Both had been discovered by Gentry, not surprising to Jubal since Eli was more of a rakehell and more inclined to range farther from town than his other deputy, Bob Rice.

Jubal was reluctant to send for help from the army, since there had been no trouble from either the Osage or the Cherokees for quite some time, but he supposed that he should at least report the two recent raids. "I reckon we'd best send word to Fort Gibson and let 'em know what we've found up here."

Eli hadn't really thought things through to that possibility. His thinking had been to knock off a farm here and there once in a while and blame it on the Indians. Having a detachment of soldiers patrolling the country was definitely not to his advantage. "I don't know, Jubal," he was quick to reply. "It might be the wrong thing to get a bunch of soldiers comin' in here to tell us how to run our business. I just said it looked like somethin' an Injun would do. More likely, it was an outlaw that struck that farm, and he's probably long gone now. We don't know where that Cutler feller came from, anyway. I've heared some talk that he mighta made some enemies down in Texas. A man like that mighta had somebody lookin' to square things with him." He paused when it appeared that Jubal was giving his words some consideration. "Too bad about that wife of his, though. She was a real looker."

"Maybe you're right," the sheriff allowed. "Might be best to wait for a while to see if there's any more trouble." He wagged a finger at his deputy then. "You see that you stick close to town. If I need you in a hurry, I don't wanna have to go lookin' for you."

"Whatever you say, Jubal. You're the boss." Pleased to have diverted Jubal from sending for the army, he got up from the chair beside the sheriff's desk and stretched. "I think I'll go on over to Thelma's now and get me some supper."

Thelma White managed the dining room in the Crooked Fork Hotel, an establishment owned by her husband, Harry. Under an arrangement with Jubal Creed, Harry had agreed to serve the sheriff and his deputies one free meal a day. Jubal and Bob Rice were fine with Thelma, but she was never pleased to see Eli walk in the door. She just didn't like the man, in particular his habit of undressing every woman in the place with his eyes. Her only waitress, Rosie MacDonald, was especially vulnerable to his malicious scrutiny as she walked back and forth from the kitchen, carrying bowls and pitchers to the tables. Depending upon his mood, Eli would sometimes attempt to make physical contact. Rosie had learned to treat him with the same respect one would have for a wolf on a tether, making sure to always keep just out of his reach. Thelma had complained about the man's behavior to her husband, but Harry was reluctant to talk to Jubal about Eli, so she and Rosie resigned themselves to putting up with Eli's lewd glances and suggestive comments.

"Make sure all your buttons are buttoned," Thelma called out to Rosie when she looked out the window to see the deputy crossing the street. "Here comes Eli." There were no other ladies in the dining room, so Rosie would receive all of Eli's attention.

Rosie rolled her eyes heavenward. "I wish my husband paid as much attention to me," she said. "I guess he'll set himself down at that table by the kitchen door." She and Thelma had come to the conclusion that he always sat there for a longer view of Rosie's behind as she walked out into the dining room.

As expected, Gentry swaggered into the room and paused to look over the patrons seated at the tables before proceeding to the small table he favored by the kitchen. As soon as he was seated, he picked up the heavy coffee mug at the place setting and started rapping it loudly on the table, a mischievous grin on his narrow face. Failing to be amused by his thoughtless behavior, Thelma strode quickly over to ask him to control his juvenile exhibition. "We don't need that racket in here, Eli. You're disturbing the paying customers."

"Is that so?" Eli retorted, the smirk still firmly in place. "Well, I reckon they can get up and leave if they don't like it, can't they?"

He was obviously in one of his hellish moods, Thelma decided, so she softened her approach. "Now, Eli, these are law-abiding citizens who came in here to have a quiet supper. They're the folks who pay your salary."

"Hell, I don't need no lily-white citizens to pay my salary," he responded. "Anyway, where's Rosie? I need to give her my order."

"I can take your order for you," Thelma said. "You want your usual steak?"

"I said, where's Rosie?" Eli flared up. "I got somethin' to show her."

Coming from the kitchen with a pot of coffee, Rosie said, "I'm right here." She stepped nimbly aside to avoid the hand reaching for her. "You're gonna make me spill this coffee in a minute," she scolded. "It just mighta landed in your lap."

"I'd druther have you land in my lap," Eli replied, the malicious grin still in place.

Rosie glanced at Thelma then and said, "Go on, Thelma. I'll take care of Deputy Gentry." Turning her attention back to him, she ordered, "Put that cup down, so I can pour some coffee in it. Then just play like you've got some manners, and I'll get your order in."

Grinning like a naughty schoolboy, Eli watched her fill his cup as Thelma walked away. "I got somethin' to show you, now that that old bitch is gone. This is somethin' just for you to look at. It ain't none of her business." She started to leave, but this time she was not quick enough to escape his hand on her wrist. "Down here," he said, motioning below the table. Thinking it another of his lewd attempts, she tried to pull away, but could not. "It ain't nothin' bad," he implored. "It's somethin' pretty." He pointed to the ever-present half sword on his belt.

At first glance, she didn't see what he was trying to show her. Then she saw the delicate silver chain looped over the hilt of the crude weapon and the silver heart attached. She could not help exclaiming, "Where did you get that?"

"I bought it," Eli lied, satisfied that she was properly impressed. "As soon as I saw it, I said to myself, 'that little heart would look good on Rosie.' Course you're gonna have to do a little somethin' to earn it."

Rosie pulled her hand free of his grasp. "I don't reckon my husband would be too happy about it, even if I did want it—which I don't. So, do you want your usual supper? Or did you just come in here to show us you don't have any manners?" She never told her husband about the ongoing mission Eli carried on to get her into bed. William was a hardworking man of gentle nature, and she feared he might call Eli out if he knew of the deputy's advances toward his wife. And Rosie was afraid that might result in her husband's death. He was happy in his work at the livery stable. There was no need to place him in danger.

Her rebuke caused only a lascivious grunt from the leering deputy. The foolish grin on his face extended as he lifted the chain from his sword hilt and held it up for her to see. "It's a mighty fine little doodad—solid silver, worth a lot. Your husband don't have to know what you did to get it, and you might enjoy it a helluva lot more to do it with a real man."

He had gotten way too far out of line as far as Rosie was concerned. This was an outright proposition, and more than she intended to tolerate. For a brief second, she considered pouring the contents of the coffeepot she was holding in his lap, but restrained herself, knowing how fearful of the sheriff and his deputies her boss was. Instead, she took another step away from the table and in her most businesslike voice asked, "Are you going to eat?"

"Yeah, I'm gonna eat," he replied, then held the chain out toward her again, gently swinging it back and forth in an effort to entice her. "Somebody else is gonna get it. You sure you ain't interested?"

"I'm interested." The voice, deep and without emotion, came from behind them.

Surprised, both Rosie and Eli had been unaware of the sudden silence that had befallen the rest of the patrons at first sight of the ominous stranger when he walked into the dining room. Lean almost to the point of looking gaunt, he wore a flat-crowned hat pulled low, but still not low enough to cover the vicious scar that ran like a lightning bolt across his face. Forks were suspended halfway between plates and mouths as all eyes fixed on the dark messenger of death as he approached the table by the kitchen door, rifle in hand. Rosie was startled by the wild look of fear that suddenly appeared on Eli's face. Turning to see the cause, she almost dropped the coffeepot when she encountered the dead blank stare of the figure behind her. Too frightened to speak, she backed quickly away.

Eli looked as if he had seen a ghost, for in his mind that was exactly what had appeared before him. The silver chain and heart dropped from his hand to land on the floor as he struggled to get up from his chair, at the same time reaching for his pistol. In his panic, his efforts succeeded only in tangling him in the chair and resulted in causing him to go over backward on the floor. Terrified by the grim figure standing over him, with his unblinking, almost paralyzing gaze, Eli could not wrestle his gun from his holster as Ben's rifle barrel pointed at him like an accusing finger. The first shot sent some of the patrons scattering for the door. It was followed by five more rounds, cranked methodically one after the other until there was no uncertainty as to whether or not the man was dead. When the explosion from the vengeful man was over, the dining room had emptied except for one. Rosie MacDonald had trapped herself between the table and the wall, and was left with no escape without having to pass by the sinister executioner.

Ben stood over the bleeding body of the man who had destroyed his life and everything he held dear. There was no feeling of justice served, only a deeper melancholy for all he had lost. He reached down and picked up the silver chain and heart, a present he had given Mary Ellen on their wedding day, formed a fist around it, and squeezed it tightly in his palm. Only then taking note of the quivering girl pressed against the wall, he turned to speak to her. "You can go if you want to, miss. I've done what I came to do." The calmness in his voice struck her as eerie after what he had just done. She would tell Thelma later that his gaze was not that of a mad killer, but rather mournful. She quickly slid by him and ran out the door to the hotel lobby.

He had not really given much thought as to how he was to effect his escape. The thought that had been foremost, to the point of excluding all others, was to end the life of Eli Gentry. Once that was accomplished, he had no other plan than to simply leave town, and Kansas as well. He knew that he could not remain in the place where he had lived and loved Mary Ellen Lytle, so he turned then and followed the frightened waitress.

With no urgency, he calmly walked into the hotel lobby to be met by Jubal Creed and Bob Rice. Both lawmen were waiting with shotguns aimed directly at his face. "Drop it right there!" the sheriff commanded. Then, astonished to recognize the killer, Jubal blurted, "Ben Cutler! What the . . . I thought you was dead."

"So did your deputy," Ben replied stoically, "but he didn't stick around to make sure." Glancing from Jubal to an equally confused Bob Rice, Ben attempted to state his case. "Eli Gentry murdered my wife and my son, burned my house and barn down, and left me for dead. All I came here for was to kill him for what he did. I don't mean any harm to anybody else. I'm aimin' to leave this part of the country now."

Dumbfounded by Ben's startling accusation, Jubal could only stare at the wicked scar across the young man's face for several long moments, unable to believe what he was seeing and hearing. If what Ben said was the truth of the terrible massacre of his family, he might be inclined to accept an eye for an eye and let Ben go, but his sense of responsibility reminded him that he was the sheriff. "Wait just a damn minute," he exclaimed, taking charge of his emotions once more. "You can't just walk into town and shoot somebody down and say he had it comin'. Drop that damn rifle, like I told you to." Seeing that he had little choice, Ben carefully laid his rifle on the floor. In control again, Jubal said, "I don't know if what you claim is true or not. We'll let a judge decide that, but you don't take the law in your own hands in this town. If Eli was the one that killed your wife and son, I expect we'd have arrested him and hung him."

"What's the difference?" Ben replied. "Seems to me like I saved you the trouble."

"It might seem to you that way, if Eli *was* guilty," Jubal came back. "But there ain't nobody's word on it but yours. There ain't no witnesses." He wasn't sure but what Ben might have thought the killer looked like Eli. He was faced with the loss of a deputy sheriff. He couldn't forget about that. Even though he knew that Eli was thought of as a rogue lawman, he would have to take time to think about this. Rogue or not, Eli deserved a trial before his execution.

"Here's a witness," Ben said, pointing to the long scar across his face. "I got a good look at him when he did this."

"I'm sorry about your wife and kid," Jubal said, "but we're gonna wait for the judge to decide on this. It's the law in this town. Pick up that rifle, Bob." He nodded toward the front door then and ordered Ben to start walking. "Harry," he said to the hotel owner, "send somebody to get Doc Jensen to come get Eli's body."

Two thoroughly shaken women walked back into the dining room to stand gawking at the bullet-rid-dled body of the late Eli Gentry. "God, what a horrible sight," Thelma uttered with a shiver in her voice. "You suppose he really did what that man said?"

"I wouldn't doubt it," Rosie answered. "I wouldn't doubt it one bit. Where do you suppose Eli really got that necklace he was showing off? Ben sure acted like that necklace belonged to him."

"I've only seen Ben Cutler a time or two, when he was in town with his wife and boy," Thelma said. "But I swear, I didn't recognize him when he walked in here a few minutes ago—that scar and all, I guess. But he sure looked different. He had a right pretty little wife."

Unable to remove her gaze from Eli's body, Rosie was inspired to say, "He made sure ol' Eli was dead, didn't he?"

They stepped back out of the way when Doc Jensen walked in, and Thelma whispered to Rosie, "It sure ain't no big loss to the world, is it?" She sighed then. "I guess we're closed for the rest of the day. We don't have a cook, anyway. Jesse went out the back door when the shooting started, and I don't know when he'll show up again. In the meantime, we've got a mess to clean up."

The Crooked Fork jail consisted of only two cells in the rear of the sheriff's office. At this time, Ben Cutler was the only occupant, and Jubal was frankly in a bit of a quandary over the killing. Ordinarily he would have no sympathy for anyone taking the life of an officer of the law, especially considering the blatant, execution-style murder that Ben was guilty of. But if Eli was the man who slaughtered Ben's wife and boy, and left him for dead, then he could understand Ben's desperation for revenge. He was forced to confess that he might have done the same thing if it had been his family. It would be three weeks before a federal judge could make it down to their little town just north of Indian Territory, and from experience Jubal knew that Judge Lon Blake liked to come back with a conviction to justify the long ride from Topeka. It was difficult to think that Eli could have done what Cutler accused him of. There was little doubt that Eli had been wild, and sometimes out of control, the kind of man that rubbed a lot of people the wrong way. But Jubal had never seen evidence of any actual breaking of the law on the part of his deputy. His remaining deputy, Bob Rice, walked in at that moment, carrying the prisoner's noon meal, so Jubal decided to get his thoughts on the issue.

"Bob, let's talk a minute about Eli," Jubal said when Rice returned from the cells.

"All right," Bob replied, although with little enthusiasm. He plopped his lanky frame down in the chair beside Jubal's desk. "Whaddaya wanna talk about?"

Jubal paused to study his deputy for a moment. Bob Rice was as much an opposite of Eli Gentry as God could have made, he supposed. Quiet, always serious, Bob took his responsibility as a lawman to heart as a guardian of the citizens of Crooked Fork. "Do you think Eli could have done what that man in there says he did?"

Bob shrugged. "If you askin' me if Eli did it or not, I ain't got no way of knowin'. Could he have done it? It's hard to say." He paused to think about his next statement before continuing. "But it wouldn't surprise me none if he did." There had been more than a few occasions when Bob had been suspicious of Eli's motives, especially those times when he insisted that he needed no help in going after certain outlaws. It had seemed to Bob that Eli preferred to work alone, and he could remember occasions when Eli was unsuccessful in apprehending a villain, but seemed to be flush with spending money afterward. Eli always boasted that he was unusually lucky playing cards. In spite of this, Bob didn't think it his place to report his suspicions on a fellow officer, and as long as Eli had not attempted to involve him in any of his under-the-table activities, he had decided to keep his silence. Now that Eli was dead, it didn't seem to matter, so he told Jubal about some of Eli's past activities.

"That don't really surprise me none," Jubal responded. He knew that he had looked the other way on more than a few occasions when it came to Eli, only because the unruly deputy inspired enough fear in the wilder citizens of the town to keep them under control.

"How do you reckon Judge Blake will rule on this?" Bob asked.

"Whaddaya mean, whether he'll find him guilty or not?" Jubal responded. "Well, hell, there ain't no doubt he's guilty. Half the town saw him do it. What you mean is whether or not he was justified in killin' Eli. Judge Blake will find him guilty, all right, but he might not hang him if he believes his story."

Bob thought about that for a minute or two, and then expressed what he really believed. "They ought not send that man to prison for coming after a damn animal that did that to his family."

"Well, it ain't up to nobody but the judge," Jubal said, but he tended to agree with Bob after having talked about it. "I reckon we'll have us a visitor for two or three weeks, though."

"Yeah, I was gonna tell you about that," Bob said. "Rosie said she'd bring his meals over—save Grover the trouble of goin' after 'em."

Jubal looked surprised. "She ain't ever done that before." He looked to Bob for further explanation. "She a friend of Ben's?" he asked.

"Don't ask me," Bob said. "It oughta tickle Grover, though." He had to grin when he pictured the ever-grumpy countenance of Grover Atkinson, who usually came in the sheriff's office a couple of hours every other day. It was Grover's responsibility to clean the office and the cells, and do any other odd jobs necessary. Rosie's offer to deliver the prisoner's meals would save Grover from having to come in every day, three times a day, to pick them up himself.

"What oughta tickle me?" Grover asked, just catching the end of the conversation as he came in the door. When Jubal explained, the old fellow's response was typically straightforward. "You oughta give Ben Cutler a medal for riddin' the town of that no-good trash you called a deputy."

"Damn!" Jubal exclaimed, somewhat surprised. "That's a helluva way to talk about a law officer just shot down. I never heard you talk that way about Eli before."

"Hell." Grover shrugged. "I got better sense than to thump a rattlesnake on the nose. I didn't need him to come after me with that damn sawed-off sword he was so proud of."

Another thought struck Jubal then. "Eli ain't got no kin around here that I know of. I reckon the town's gonna have to pay for his buryin'."

"Hmmph," Grover grunted. "I reckon there'll be three folks at that buryin', them two fellers Doc has to dig the grave, and the undertaker." He cast an accusing eye at the sheriff then. "If you ask me, you shouldn'ta made him a deputy in the first place."

"I didn't ask you," Jubal retorted. He was in no mood to submit to a lecture from the grouchy old man, but he knew Grover was right. Jubal was aware that Eli had possessed a mean streak. He just didn't think it was that wide. There really wasn't any doubt in anyone's mind that what Ben Cutler said Eli had done to him and his family was true. And Jubal was beginning to feel the guilt for having hired the rogue deputy. It did no good to tell himself that Eli would have slaughtered Ben's family whether he was a deputy or not. In retrospect, he halfway wished he had not sent for the judge.

Chapter 3

During the days leading up to his trial, Ben Cutler came to know a few citizens of Crooked Fork better than he would ever have imagined. His treatment by Jubal and Bob Rice was fair, and they both did all they could to make his stay in their jail as tolerable as possible. Grover came by periodically to play a game of checkers, and Rosie MacDonald continued to bring his food every day. He was aware of the efforts of these people—folks he had never really known before he walked into the dining room and shot Eli Gentry—to make his incarceration comfortable. He appreciated their concern, but there was little they could do to ease his mind of the terrible sense of loss that would not release its hold on him. In addition, he was reluctant to enter casual conversation with Rosie at first. He felt self-conscious, knowing the menacing facade created by his scar. In time, however, he began to think that the young lady had become accustomed to it, and paid it no further mind.

It was Rosie who told him what had become of the buckskin horse he had ridden into town. His mind had been so laden with grief that he had not bothered to even ask about the horse and saddle he had just bought three days before the shooting. One day at mealtime, she told him that her husband managed the livery stable for the owner. "William said to tell you that he's taking good care of your horse," she said, "and he'll be in good shape when they let you out of here after the trial."

"Tell him I'm much obliged," Ben said. "And I also appreciate the trouble you go to, bringin' my food over for me. I've never been in jail before. I didn't know they treated a prisoner so good in this town."

Rosie smiled. "They don't usually," she said, "but you're a special prisoner. I think everybody in town thinks you shouldn't even be in jail, and the jury won't waste much time in deliberating your innocence."

Her assurance that the whole town was on his side caused a change in his fatal attitude and his indifference to whether he lived or died. Maybe Mary Ellen would not have wanted him to give up on life. He began to think more and more about moving out across the high plains to see what lay beyond the mountains, far away from civilization. Maybe that would heal his empty heart and give his tortured mind some peace. She would probably want him to do that. They never talked about it, but he was sure she knew the sacrifice he had made, to leave the open prairie and the trail herds and try to become a farmer. In his mind, however, no sacrifice had been too much just to be with her and Danny. Now, without her in his life, there was nothing to heal his sorrow, and he felt he might

eventually kill himself if he did not find peace somewhere away from this place.

The day finally arrived when Judge Lon Blake rode into
town on a mule, with another trailing along behind
him on a lead rope. His accommodations having been
arranged in the hotel by Jubal, His Honor wasted little time in setting the wheels of justice in motion and
scheduled Ben's trial for first thing the following morning. After setting everything up with Jubal that evening,
Judge Blake paid a short visit to the cells to get his first
look at the accused. Lying on his bunk, Ben suddenly
sensed that he was being watched and turned to face
the cell room door. There were no words exchanged
between the prisoner and the somber-looking judge, as
Blake continued to stare at Ben, a fixed frown in place.
After a long moment, the judge turned to Jubal. "He
give you any trouble?"

"No, sir," Jubal answered with no hesitation, "no
trouble at all."

"All right, then," he said brusquely, "we'll try him
in the morning. I've got other places to cover before I
head back to Topeka."

Everyone in town crowded into the River House
Saloon the following morning to attend the trial of
Ben Cutler. In fact, it rendered the rest of the town so
deserted that Jubal instructed Bob Rice to patrol the
main street in case some opportunistic robber decided
to take advantage of the lack of vigilance. There were
more than a few willing men to volunteer for jury duty,
all in support of the man who had come back from
the dead to avenge his family and rid the town of its
bullying deputy sheriff. There was a general show of

disappointment, however, when Judge Blake called the meeting to order and announced that this was not to be a jury trial. Owing to the attitude he had witnessed in the short time he was in town, he decided that a jury could not render a fair verdict. Consequently, he decreed that he would judge the evidence as presented and rule according to the laws of the state of Kansas. "The prosecutor will now open with the charges," he ordered.

There followed a long silence while everyone looked around them to see who stepped forward. Finally Jubal stood up and said, "There ain't no prosecutor, Your Honor."

Judge Blake tilted his head down and peered over the top of his spectacles in order to fix his gaze on the sheriff. "Are you telling this court that no one is prosecuting this case?"

"I'm tellin' you that we ain't got no prosecutor," Jubal replied. "We ain't never needed one before."

"Is there no lawyer in this town?" Blake asked.

"No, sir. There was one, but he moved his family back to Kansas City."

This disturbing bit of information was obviously disconcerting to the judge, and it was obvious to everyone in the saloon that his patience was near exhaustion. "Sheriff, what is the reason I was dispatched all the way down here from Topeka?"

"Well, sir," Jubal replied, "the prisoner here, Ben Cutler, shot my deputy. That was the reason we wired Topeka, but after thinkin' it over some, we ain't so sure he wasn't justified in doin' it."

Blake was amazed. He continued staring at Jubal for a long moment before issuing his orders. "Let me tell you how this is going to work," he said. "You are the prosecutor in this case, representing the town of Crooked Fork." Now that that was taken care of, he looked around the room at the people crowding up to the front. "Who is defending the accused?" he asked. When his question was met with yet another silence, he threw up his hands in frustration. Tiny beads of perspiration appeared at his temples and traced their way down to disappear in his heavy gray beard, while he continued to shift his gaze across the assembly. "All right," he finally decreed, "we're going to dispense with formality. Sheriff, suppose you tell me what happened?"

"Like I said," Jubal replied, "Ben, here, walked into the hotel dinin' room and shot Eli Gentry six times in the chest while he was settin' at the table."

"Why?"

"Because Eli murdered Ben's wife and son and left Ben for dead, and burned his house and barn down," Jubal said.

"Were there witnesses who saw Gentry do this?"

"Well, no. There weren't no witnesses except for Ben, but there ain't no doubt that Eli did it."

A look of amazement spread rapidly across Judge Blake's face as he observed the nods of agreement from those in the crowd. "So what I'm asked to try is a crime of murder, witnessed by at least a half dozen people in the hotel dining room, by a man who said the victim killed his family. No witnesses, just the accused said that Gentry committed the murders. Without any evidence that Gentry actually did it, except for his murderer's word on it, I have no choice but to rule that the defendant is guilty of the murder of Eli Gentry, according to the laws of the state of Kansas." His verdict triggered a wave of growls of disappointment, but he went on to further decree that, because of the lack of evidence concerning Ben's family's deaths, he was not going to recommend the death sentence. "But, by God, the laws of this state demand to be respected," he stated while wagging a finger at the crowd. "We can't have folks taking the law into their own hands." Turning to Ben then, he said, "I sentence you to serve ten years in the Kansas State Penitentiary in Lansing for the crime of murder. You are to remain in jail until federal marshals are sent to pick you up and transport you to Lansing."

He might as well have issued the death sentence as far as Ben was concerned. He did not think he could survive ten years locked away in a prison cell. He had worked outdoors all his life, on a horse, with nothing fencing him in but the horizon. His initial reaction was to escape, or die trying, but when he looked into the apologetic faces of Jubal and Bob Rice, he knew he could not bring himself to do violence against the two lawmen. They were plainly dismayed by the judge's decision, so he made no attempt to resist when Jubal took him by the arm and led him out of the saloon.

Back in his cell, he sat down on his bunk to think about the future that awaited him. He still had every intention of escaping, but he decided to wait until the marshals picked him up, so there would be no involvement with Jubal or Bob. He glanced up to find Jubal still standing there, looking as if he wanted to say something, but was having trouble choosing the proper words. "It's all right, Jubal," Ben said. "You and Bob did the best you could for me, and I'm much obliged. How long do you figure it'll take 'em to come after me?"

"I don't know," Jubal answered. "I don't know where they'll be comin' from, Topeka or Lansin', but it'll most likely not be for a week or more. We'll try to make your time here as comfortable as we can."

"Thanks. I appreciate it."

The next few days saw several of the town's residents drop by the jail to wish Ben luck and offer their opinions that he had done the town a favor when he put a stop to Eli Gentry's bullying. Rosie was still a regular visitor, and even Thelma stopped by. Jubal joked that it was like having the governor in his jail. One of the visitors was Jim White Feather. He stayed to talk for two hours before heading back home. Ben told him the approximate number of cattle he had left, and that most of them could be found across the river from his wheat fields. "Take 'em, Jim, and sell 'em for whatever you can get. They're yours. I'll see if I can have the sheriff give you that buckskin gelding I just bought, too. I'll have to wait till those marshals get here, though, or I'd see if you could take him with you now. I might have to ride him to prison if they don't send one of those jail wagons." When Jim got up to leave, Ben shook his hand. "I'll be sayin' good-bye, friend, 'cause I don't plan to go to that prison." Jim nodded, understanding; then he wished him luck and left for Indian Territory.

Jesse had finished cleaning up the kitchen at the Crooked Fork Hotel and gone home. The tables were all set up for breakfast in the morning, except for one, where four people sat, finishing off the last of the coffee. "Hell, this is crazy talk," Bob Rice commented. "You ought not even be telling me stuff like that. If Jubal knew what you're talkin' about doin', you'd all be in jail and I'd lose my job, or worse."

"I'm not suggesting that you do anything but take a walk down the street," Rosie said. "You were the one who said it was wrong to send Ben Cutler to prison. Jubal feels the same way. He's just not in a position to do anything about it. You talk to anybody in town, and they'll all say Ben did the right thing."

"Oughta give him a medal," Grover said.

"I did say it was wrong," Bob confessed, "and I meant it, but, damn, I don't know . . ."

Rosie looked at her husband for support. He nodded his reassurance. "You're right, Bob," Rosie went on. "You don't know." She looked around the table. "I don't know, William doesn't know, and Grover doesn't know. All you have to do is to check the stores like you're hired to do. You don't need to know anything else."

Bob exhaled forcefully before relenting. "All right, but damn it, you folks better be careful."

Rosie smiled. "Why? We're not gonna do anything."

The following day was a long one for Ben. It seemed that his incarceration was harder to take since Judge Blake had sentenced him to prison. He knew that his intention to flee the town and the territory was further from his reach, and would call for a generous portion of luck if he was to effect his escape. He gained some small relief from his melancholy when Rosie came in with his supper.

"I swear, look at that plate," Jubal exclaimed when she walked by his desk. "I wish Doris fed me that well." He delayed Rosie for a minute while he looked it over. "Big piece of cake, too. What is it, Ben's birthday or somethin'?"

Rosie laughed. "I brought you and Bob a piece, too." She took a cloth from her apron pocket and unfolded it to reveal two slices of cake. "Don't tell Doris I spoiled your supper."

"She'll never know about it," Jubal said, then took one of the pieces and handed the cloth to Bob Rice while Rosie went into the cell room to deliver Ben's supper.

Having heard the conversation from his cell, Ben was on his feet awaiting Rosie when she walked through the door. "I see what Jubal was talkin' about," he commented when he saw the plate piled high with food. "Is today a holiday or somethin'?"

"No, it's no holiday," Rosie replied. "We're just celebrating today because it seems like a good day to." She studied his face as he sat down to eat. Once a pleasant, almost handsome face, it was now grotesque after his encounter with Eli Gentry's saber. *The poor man's paid enough for what he did*, she thought. She sat beside the bars and made light conversation with him while he ate, making sure he took time to finish his meal. When he had eaten the last of it, she took the empty plate he passed back through the bars and said, "I wish you luck, Ben Cutler."

"Thank you, Rosie," he replied, somewhat puzzled by what seemed to him a more solemn attitude than her usual high spirits.

"Jubal already gone home?" Rosie asked when she

walked back into the office. When Bob said that he
had, she said, "I wanted to make sure you got a piece of
cake before you started making your rounds. I expect
you're about ready to do that now, aren't you?"

A cold shiver of uncertainty ran the length of Bob's
spine, for he realized that something was about to happen that shouldn't, something he didn't want to know
about. He hesitated. "I don't know," he stammered. "It's
a little bit early yet. And Jubal don't like to leave the jail
unguarded when there's somebody in the cells."

While he stood undecided, Grover walked in the
door and announced, "I didn't get a chance to clean
the place up this afternoon, so I'm gonna do it now.
I'll be here to watch things if you're wantin' to do your
rounds. Sounded like some rowdy noise when I came
by French's Saloon. You might wanna take a look."

"Evening, Grover," Rosie offered cheerfully as she
made for the front door. "See you tomorrow, Bob."

Then she was gone, leaving a nervous deputy to
stand fumbling before the withering stare of the old
man. Reluctantly, he forced himself to don his hat and
move toward the door. Purely in an effort to appease
his conscience, he said as he went out, "You be careful
around the prisoner."

"Yeah, I will," Grover replied drily. He stood at the
window watching Bob until he was sure the deputy
wasn't going to change his mind and return to the
office. Then he grabbed the ring of keys from the desk
drawer and went into the cell room.

"Evenin', Grover," Ben greeted the old man. "What
are you doin' here so late? You lookin' for a game of
checkers?"

"Ben." Grover returned the greeting. "Nah, I ain't in

the mood for checkers right now." He went directly
to the corner where he kept his cleaning supplies and
grabbed a broom.

Just noticing the key ring in Grover's hand then,
Ben asked, "What are you fixin' to do? You ain't supposed to clean up my cell when Jubal or Bob ain't here."
Sometimes the old man seemed to suffer a little
absentmindedness.

Without answering, Grover proceeded to insert a
key in the lock and open the cell door. Astonished, Ben
could only stand and watch, until Grover admonished,
"I swear, you're as bad as Bob." He walked into the cell
and handed the keys to Ben. "If I ain't mistaken, that
one right there is the one to the gun rack. You're gonna
need that fancy new rifle you bought yourself. Best
you go down the back alley to the stable. William Mac-
Donald won't be there, but your horse will be saddled
and waitin'."

Staggered by the realization of what was happening,
Ben could not find sufficient words to acknowledge the
risks being taken to free him. "I don't know what to
say," he finally blurted, aware that Rosie, her husband,
Grover, maybe even Bob were all in this plot together.
For a moment, he was almost overcome with emotion.

"This ain't the time to talk," Grover retorted. "This
is the time to get goin'." He went over and sat himself
down on Ben's bunk.

In control of his senses at last, Ben wasted no more
time. "I'm obliged," he said, "to you and everybody
else in this with you. You're takin' a helluva chance,
and I'll never forget any of you for this."

He started to leave then, but Grover stopped him.
"Hey, lock the cell door and hand me my broom there."

Then his perpetual frown reversed itself into the first smile Ben had ever remembered seeing on the grizzled old face. "Good luck, son."

"Thanks, Grover."

Moving as quickly as he could, he unlocked the gun rack and withdrew the new Winchester and his handgun and holster. He then locked the rack again and returned the keys to the desk drawer. Taking only a moment to make sure no one was outside, he then ran beside the jail to the alley behind and headed for the stables, where he found the buckskin, saddled and waiting with all his possessions in the saddlebags. Still finding it hard to believe that he was free to ride out, he led the buckskin out to the stable door and paused there for a few moments to look back up the street toward the sheriff's office. He halfway expected to see Jubal and Bob suddenly appear to block his escape, but the street was deserted. He climbed up in the saddle and nudged the buckskin to a brisk walk, unaware of the man watching him from the shadows behind the blacksmith shop next to the barn. It was good-bye to Crooked Fork and the friends he didn't even know he had until his trial. When he had disappeared around the bend in the road, Rosie's husband emerged from the shadows and stood there for a moment looking after him before turning to go to the hotel dining room.

"Grover, what the hell?" Bob exclaimed when he returned to find the grizzled old man sitting comfortably on the bunk inside the cell. "How did you get in there? Where's Ben?" He had known when he left to make his rounds that Ben would most likely be gone when he got back, but now that it was a fact, he tried to forget that he had had a hand in it.

Grover shrugged. "I reckon I got careless and let him grab the keys when I started to clean his cell. He'd been so peaceful, I didn't think he would make a run for it, but before I knowed what was happenin', he'd done turned the tables on me and I was on the inside and he was on the outside."

Bob stood there for a long moment, studying Grover's face as if he really didn't suspect his story. "I told you to be careful," he said, "but I reckon it ain't your fault he got the jump on you." Continuing to play his part, he asked, "How long has he been gone?"

"Long enough to get away," Grover answered, puzzled by the deputy's question.

"All right," Bob said. "You run on up to get Jubal. I expect I'd best get down to the stable. That's most likely the first place he headed, to get his horse." Jubal would have a lot of questions, and he wanted to be able to answer that he had taken the obvious steps to pursue the fugitive.

Across the street in the hotel dining room, Thelma walked up to stand beside Rosie, who seemed intent upon something she had seen out the window. "What are you staring at?" she asked.

Rosie turned and gave her a smile. "Nothing," she said, "just Bob Rice walking down the street toward the stable." She surmised that Bob was probably playing a game with himself to ease his conscience. Rosie wasn't concerned because William had already stopped by to tell her that Ben was long gone. The thought brought another smile to her face, and she spun about and declared, "Time to finish cleaning this place up and head for home."

Still standing at the window, Thelma called after her, "There's Jubal running back to the office. Wonder what he's in such an all-fired rush about."

"Hard to say," Rosie answered. "Could be anything, I guess." The smile would remain on her face for a few minutes yet.

Chapter 4

Deputy marshals Graham Barrett and Ike Gibbs rode into the little settlement of Crooked Fork late on a Sunday afternoon. Heading straight for the sheriff's office, they found Bob Rice on duty. Bob had heard of both lawmen, especially Graham Barrett, although there had never been occasion for either of them to have visited his town before. He saw them out front as they were tying their horses at the rail, and knew immediately that they were the marshals sent to escort Ben Cutler to prison. "Damn!" he cursed under his breath as he stared out the window. "Why the hell did they have to show up when Jubal ain't here?" He walked over and opened the door.

He had heard tales of Graham Barrett that almost placed the lawman in a superhuman category. He was said to have the tracking ability of an Indian and the patience of a coyote on the prowl. Jubal said that he had heard that Barrett had once tracked a group of four train robbers all the way from Wichita, across

Nebraska, and halfway to Montana before running them to ground near Fort Laramie. It was said the outlaws chose to make a stand in the Laramie Mountains since the odds were in their favor, four to one. After the gun battle that ensued, Barrett was the only man standing, and he delivered the fugitives tied across their saddles. Upon first meeting the man, it was not difficult to believe the stories.

Bob stepped back as the two deputies entered. Both men were big, but Barrett had to bow his head to keep from knocking his flat crowned hat off when he came in the door. Wearing a black jacket, even on this late summer afternoon, open to reveal a pair of Colt .44s with the handles facing forward, he studied Bob with eyes that appeared lifeless. "Sheriff Creed?" he inquired quietly.

"Ah, no, sir," Bob was quick to reply. "The sheriff ain't here right now, but he ought to be back any minute." He hoped that was a fact. He preferred to have Jubal inform the two marshals that they had lost the prisoner.

Ike Gibbs remained silent, content to let Barrett do the talking while he stood in the middle of the tiny office and looked around him as if inspecting the room. "Well, it don't really matter," Barrett said. "My name's Barrett." He nodded in Ike's direction. "He's Ike Gibbs." He reached in his inside coat pocket then and produced a folded document. "I've got a paper here that says you're to transfer a prisoner to us to escort back to Lansing." He handed Bob the paper.

"Yes, sir," Bob stammered as he accepted the court order, trying to delay as long as possible. "There's been a little problem on that."

Barrett's bored expression never changed. "What kind of problem?"

"Well," Bob started to explain, but was saved by the sudden appearance of Jubal in the door. "Here's the sheriff now. I'll let him tell it."

Not any happier to see the two marshals than Bob had been, Jubal, nonetheless, had hurried over to his office when Harry White came into the dining room to inform him that two strangers had pulled up before the jail. His Sunday afternoon ritual of coffee and a slice of cake at the hotel was interrupted without hesitation, because he had a pretty fair idea who the strangers were. Both Thelma and Rosie had hurried to the front window as Jubal went out the door. "I'm Sheriff Creed," Jubal said upon entering his office.

"Sheriff," Barrett acknowledged. "We'll take that prisoner off your hands." He nodded toward the document Bob Rice was still holding.

Jubal took the paper from Bob and pretended to study it while he formed the words for the explanation for the empty cell in the next room. Finally, he looked up into the expressionless face of the deputy marshal and said, "The prisoner's gone." The statement only served to raise an eyebrow on Barrett's stony countenance, and forced the first sound from his partner.

"Huh," Ike snorted.

"Whaddaya mean, he's gone?" Barrett demanded gruffly.

Jubal shrugged helplessly. "He's gone, escaped. I telegraphed the U.S. Marshal's office, but you fellers were already on the way."

Barrett walked over and peered through the door at the empty cell room. "How the hell did he escape?"

Jubal explained that Ben had gotten the best of the old man who had carelessly opened his cell to clean it, then made his escape on horseback. Barrett listened to the explanation without interrupting, with only an occasional glance at Ike Gibbs. When Jubal finished, Barrett asked, "Did you go after him?"

"Well, sorta," Jubal answered, realizing as soon as the words left his mouth what a poor choice they had been.

"Sorta?" Barrett responded, and exchanged bemused glances with Ike.

"I tried to raise a posse to go after him," Jubal explained, "but nobody volunteered to go."

"Is he that dangerous?"

"No," Jubal replied. "See, that's the problem. Most ever'body in town thinks Ben Cutler ought not have to go to prison for killin' Eli Gentry, and they were kinda glad he got away." Jubal went on then to explain Ben's motive for killing Gentry. "Oh, I went after him by myself, and it was plain he'd started out the road toward Wichita, but I had to give up after about ten miles. He had too big a head start."

The two marshals listened to Jubal's story without even a scant show of sympathy—in fact, with little emotion of any kind. When the sheriff had finished, Barrett informed him that Cutler would be brought to justice. "I don't give a damn about whether Ben Cutler was a sinner or saint. That ain't for me to decide. I've got a court order to bring him in, and I'll by God do that if I have to chase him to Canada. I ain't never come back without the man I was sent to get, and Ben Cutler ain't gonna be the first."

"I don't know," Jubal said, scratching his chin whiskers as he considered the marshal's boast. "I can't see you havin' much of a chance of trackin' him. On the Wichita road, there ain't no way of tellin' which tracks are Ben's and which ones are somebody else's. And there ain't no way of tellin' where he's got it in his mind to go."

"So you're sayin' just let him go," Barrett replied. "Is that it?" He didn't wait for Jubal to answer. "Well, it don't work that way with me. The judge sentenced him to ten years, and so he's gotta do ten years—maybe more now, since he's decided to run." He turned to Ike then. "Whaddaya say we get us a good supper and start out early in the mornin'? Is that all right with you?"

"Suits me," Ike replied, and both men looked at Jubal expectantly.

"Hotel dinin' room," he said. "Best in town. They'll be servin' in about an hour."

"Well, Creed was right about the food being good here," Ike said as Rosie came to the table carrying the coffeepot. He shoved his cup to the edge of the table to make it easier for her.

She filled his cup, then gestured toward Barrett's, but he waved her off, saying he'd had enough. When she hesitated for a moment beside the table, looking as if she wanted to ask a question, he gazed up at her with dead man's eyes and waited. "I guess since Ben Cutler got away, there's nothing you marshals can do but go back to Topeka," she said.

The corners of Barrett's mouth twitched slightly when he responded. It was the closest he ever came to a smile, "Now, why do you think that? Don't you think murderers oughta be caught and punished?"

"Well, yes," Rosie answered, "most of them, but Ben Cutler isn't like them. He was only going after the man who killed his family. Eli deserved what he got."

"Why, then, I reckon we don't need any judges or courts at all," Barrett retorted sarcastically. "Just let the people decide when it's all right to murder somebody." He waved his hand in a gesture of impatience. "Is this whole town crazy? The feller down at the stable talks the same way you do—hell, just let him go."

"Ben Cutler's a good man," Rosie insisted as she turned to leave.

"I don't care," Barrett declared. "The law's the law." He pushed his chair away from the table. "Let's get the hell outta here before the good folk of Crooked Fork decide we need to be executed for doin' our jobs." Ike laughed and downed the rest of his coffee. It always amused him to see Barrett get frustrated. It happened so seldom.

Outside on the street, Ike suggested they should walk up the street to French's Saloon for a drink before turning in for the night. Barrett shrugged. "Why not?"

When they walked into the noisy barroom, the room went suddenly silent, for everyone there knew who they were. Ike laughed and commented, "Makes you feel kinda warm and cozy, don't it? Maybe we're on the wrong side of the law." In the next instant, the saloon returned to its raucous noise and the drinking resumed. The two lawmen made their way through the crowded room to stand at the bar. "Whiskey," Ike ordered, and watched while the bartender poured.

When he stopped pouring, Ike motioned with his hand until the bartender poured a few drops more to fill the glass to the rim. "Just gonna spill it on the bar," he groused.

"If I do, I'll lick it up," Ike replied, and tossed it down. He set the glass down and motioned for it to be filled again. "I'll bet you think we oughta let Ben Cutler go free," he said while watching the bartender again.

"If we'd had a jury trial like they were supposed to do, I guarantee you he'd be free." He started to fill Barrett's glass again, but was waved off. Barrett never had more than one drink when he was working.

They remained at the bar for a while, discussing the road ahead of them. Ike nursed his second drink along, sipping instead of belting it down in one shot. Barrett had many years trailing fugitives, and he was thinking this one was like no other before. According to what they had learned, Ben Cutler was not a hardened criminal. To the contrary, he had always been a hardworking, law-abiding citizen. He'd just had a streak of bad luck. Barrett had been truthful when he told Rosie he didn't care. He was interested only in what his experience had taught him about men caught in similar circumstances. Vocalizing his thoughts, he said, "Cutler doesn't know where he's headed. Creed was probably right when he said Cutler headed for Wichita, 'cause that was the easiest road to take. Chances are, right now he don't know what to do or where to go. If we're lucky, we might catch up with him around Wichita while he's tryin' to decide."

"Maybe," Ike said, "but it's a three- or three-and-a-half-day ride from here to Wichita. You think it'll take him that long to make up his mind?"

"It might, but even if he doesn't, we might be able to

pick up his trail, anyway. With a face scarred like they say his is, somebody's bound to remember seein' him. We'll catch up with him somewhere along the line. I wouldn't be surprised if he follows a crowd of other folks and heads up toward the Black Hills. He's got to find a way to make a livin', and if he's as honest as these folks claim, he ain't likely to take up killin' and stealin' as a pastime." He glanced at a man weaving his way toward them, obviously having had too much to drink. "I'm ready to hit the hay—get an early start in the mornin'. Let's go before another one of Crooked Fork's citizens tells us to go back to Topeka."

They had lingered a moment too long, for the drunk cut them off before they reached the door. Stepping up to block Barrett's path, he demanded, "Why the hell don't you sons of bitches go on back to where you came from and keep your nose outta our business?" Without replying, Barrett stepped to the side and started to walk around him. "Hey, I'm talkin' to you," the drunk slurred, and grabbed Barrett's arm. The marshal's reaction was so fast that many in the saloon were not sure what had happened. In one quick move, Barrett drew one of his .44s and slammed the barrel across the side of the drunk's face, dropping him in a heap on the floor. With no show of emotion, he holstered the weapon and continued toward the door.

Behind him, Ike grinned at the bartender and commented, "Barrett don't like for nobody to lay their hands on him." Reading the shock in the bartender's face, he said, "Maybe you oughta call a marshal. There goes one yonder." He pointed at Barrett's broad back, already at the door. He followed his partner then, still laughing at the joke he had made.

In a show of courtesy for the local law, they stopped back at the sheriff's office before retiring for the night. They found Jubal talking to Bob Rice and an older man whom Barrett presumed was the one who had allowed the prisoner to escape. His guess proved to be true, and it was Grover who identified himself as the culprit even before being asked. "I'm the old fool that let your prisoner get away," he volunteered.

It struck Barrett that Grover almost seemed to be proud of it. "Is that a fact?" Barrett responded, not really interested. He had already put two and two together and come up with what he was confident was the right answer. "From what I've heard since we've been in town, that oughta make you a hero."

Grover could not avoid the grin that appeared on his scruffy face, but quickly tried to remove it. "He got the jump on me. It was my fault, though. I got careless. But it wasn't Jubal's or Bob's fault. I guess I should oughta be more careful."

Concerned that the marshals might want to charge Grover with aiding and abetting, Jubal jumped in to change the subject. "You boys are welcome to sleep here tonight. There ain't nobody in the cells, and them bunks are fair to middlin' comfortable."

"Thanks just the same, Sheriff," Barrett replied, "but I expect we'll bed down with our horses, so we can ride out of here early in the mornin'."

"It's a long ride back to Topeka," Jubal said. "You oughta stay around long enough to have you a big breakfast in the hotel dining room before you start out."

"Sounds like a good idea," Barrett said, "but we're headin' for Wichita, and we need to get an early start."

Jubal looked surprised. "That man's long gone," he said. "There ain't no way you'll ever catch up with him."

"I've been told that before," Barrett replied, "more than once."

It had been quite some time since Ben Cutler had seen Wichita. The last time had been in 1877 when he had partnered with Sam Ingram to drive a herd of cattle up from Texas. He had kept his promise to Mary Ellen then that it would be his last drive. It was with bitter chagrin that he remembered his search for land he could buy to build their homestead on which his family would be safe from the scattered bands of renegade Indians that still raided in some parts of the territory. Realizing that he was once again heading down that path of sorrow, he immediately tried to bring his mind back to the present.

He could readily see that Wichita was a thriving town, although it had changed since his last visit when it was still referred to as *Cowtown*. Settlers had moved in and fenced off the prairie and the old Chisholm Trail with barbed wire. A store owner on the edge of town had told him that Wichita's days as a railhead for cattle were over and most of the drives had shifted west to Dodge City. This was bad news to Ben, for he had toyed with the idea that he might hook up with a trail boss who was heading back to Texas. On the run with no future, he couldn't think of anything else he could do. Although he planned to watch his money carefully, he knew it would not last indefinitely, and cattle and horses were things he knew very well. So he decided the best thing for him to do was to ride west to Dodge City to see if he could hire on with one of the Texas outfits. At any rate, he had to get out of Kansas.

He skirted Wichita on the south side, aiming to head toward Dodge, assuming it risky to ride into town. The federal marshals were bound to have telegraphed every town around, advising them to be on the lookout for him, so he crossed the river and rode on into the afternoon, until time to start thinking about finding a campsite. *I should have camped by the river,* he thought as the afternoon waned and he had not come upon a stream of any kind to water his horse. At last, just as he was thinking he was going to have to settle for a dry camp, he spotted a line of trees beyond a low ridge in the prairie. There was water ahead, and a good supply, judging by the size of the trees. The buckskin had just started up the ridge when he heard shots.

Pulling the gelding to a stop, he quickly dismounted, pulled his rifle from the saddle sling, and dropped the reins on the ground. Then he scrambled up to the crest of the ridge to take a look. Below him, at the base of the ridge, a party of four Indians was spread in a half circle before a camp in the trees. Before deciding what he should do, he took a quick moment to look the situation over. Only two of the Indians had guns and they were firing as fast as they could reload their single-shot rifles. Their shots were being answered by one person, but he was armed with a repeating rifle, a Winchester by the sound of it. Ben could not see the man. He could see what looked to be two horses tethered in the trees, but little else. He assumed the person under siege was a white man, and he made up his mind to even the sides in the fight.

Pulling his rifle up beside him, he cocked it and laid the front sight on one of the Indians with a rifle. Squeezing the trigger slowly as he steadied the rifle, he was almost surprised when it fired and knocked the warrior facedown in the grass. The victim's friends reacted in alarm, but did not realize he had been shot from behind until Ben's rifle accounted for another fatality. Aware then that they were possibly surrounded, the remaining two fled to their horses and galloped away in the gathering dusk. When Ben was sure they weren't coming back, he slid back down the slope to his horse. After replacing the two spent cartridges, he climbed aboard and rode over the top of the ridge and halfway down the other side before stopping and calling out, "Hello the camp. Are you all right?" He could see what appeared to be a squat man approaching the edge of the cottonwoods on short, bowed legs. "Can I come in?" Ben yelled.

"Come on in and welcome!" the man answered as he left the shadow of the trees and walked toward the fallen warriors. "Can't be too sure," he said, and pulling his pistol, pumped one shot into each corpse. "Now I'm sure," he concluded, and stood waiting, eyeballing his surprise rescuer as Ben slow-walked the buckskin up to him. The grin on the man's face froze when Ben was close enough for him to get a good look at his visitor, but it was only for a moment before he recovered. "I was in a bad way there till you come along. Those sneakin' buzzards surprised me, and I caught a bullet in the shoulder before I even knew they were out there. It's not a serious wound, but it's in my blame right shoulder, so I had to shoot my rifle left-handed, and I ain't much of a shot left-handed."

Ben hadn't noticed the wound until he stepped down from the saddle, but there was a round circle of blood on the man's shoulder and it was about where he would rest the stock of his rifle when firing. Fully aware that the man could not help staring at his disfigured face, even though he was making an obvious effort not to, Ben tried to look as pleasant as he could. "Want me to take a look at that?"

Judging strictly by appearances, Cleve Goganis was not sure that he had not fallen from the frying pan into the fire. For that reason, he still held his pistol in his hand. "I reckon," he replied, uncertain. "Wouldn't hurt to take a quick look."

Ben followed him over to the fire and directed him to sit down. "You can go ahead and holster that weapon," he remarked as he pulled Cleve's shirt aside. "If I was thinkin' on shootin' you, I'da done it when I first rode up."

Cleve smiled sheepishly and returned the .44 to his holster. "I plumb forgot I still had it in my hand," he lied. "I appreciate your help," he said then, thinking that he had misjudged the man. "My name's Clever Goganis, but I go by Cleve."

"Ben Cutler," Ben answered as he examined Cleve's wound. "You're right. It doesn't look too bad. I could see a little better if I had somethin' to clean some of that blood outta there." Cleve supplied a cloth from one of his packs, and Ben wet it in the stream. After cleaning away some of the blood, he saw that the bullet had not gone very deep into the muscle and had lodged there before it hit the bone. "You're lucky. I can get that out. There wasn't much of a charge behind that rifle slug." After heating his skinning knife in the coals to make sure it was clean enough, he probed for the slug. When it was out, he reheated the knife and cauterized the wound.

Cleve sat quietly and expressionless through the entire procedure. When it was over, he nodded thoughtfully and said, "Much obliged." Taking another look at the menacing face, he hesitated before finally making up his mind. "You're welcome to camp here with me," he decided. "The least I can do is offer some coffee and grub for fixin' my shoulder, not to mention them two Injuns you killed."

"I'll take you up on that," Ben said, "but I was wonderin' if it might be a good idea to move the camp a mile or so up the stream in case your friends come back to get their dead."

"Well, now, you're probably right," Cleve replied. "I doubt there was ever more than the four of 'em, but you can't never tell." So Cleve packed up while Ben put out the fire. Then they rode north along the stream for a mile and a half until they found a spot they both agreed upon. "This'll do," Cleve said. "If they decide to come back for more, they'll play hell gettin' across that open flat before we see 'em." They unsaddled the horses and built a fire, and in short order there was a pot of coffee working away in the coals and Cleve had a frying pan filled with bacon sizzling over the fire.

Sensing the peaceful disposition of the man with the grotesque scar across his face, Cleve soon ceased to feel intimidated by the solidly built stranger—enough so that he boldly asked, "That's a right nasty-lookin' scar across your face. How in hell did that happen?"

"I ran into a fellow with a big knife," Ben answered, reluctant to go into details.

Cleve was studying him carefully now. "That scar

ain't been there very long," he said. "It's still a little pinkish lookin'."

"A few weeks," Ben replied, anxious to change the subject. "You said your name was Clever. That's a pretty unusual name."

"Yeah," Cleve drawled, demonstrating boredom with the question, having been asked about the name so often. "My mama named me Clever. I reckon she was hopin' I would be the smart one in the family, maybe grow into the name, but I never did." He grunted a chuckle as he recalled, "My pa used to call me Stupid—said I lived up to that name. He was killed in a gunfight when I was fourteen."

"Is that a fact?" Ben remarked. "Who with?"

"Me," Cleve replied.

Now it was Ben's turn to lift an eyebrow in surprise and wonder if he had reason to keep a sharp eye. He took a longer look at Cleve Goganis. A more harmless-looking man he could not imagine. "You killed your pa in a gunfight?" he had to question.

"I did," Cleve replied succinctly. "He beat my mother up one too many times. But he was my pa, so I called him out fair and square, although he was a little drunk at the time. Course he was most always drunk, so it was more like natural to him." Cleve's eyes seemed to mist a bit as he called to mind that fateful day in his young life. "Me and my squirrel rifle, him and that old Colt Navy revolver he was so proud of. He wanted Mama to count to three, but she wouldn't do it, said we was both crazy and went in the house. Pa said it had to be fair, so he pulled a squash outta the garden and said when it hit the ground we'd fire. Well, he threw it up, and when it came down, that old pistol of his misfired.

I didn't even pull the trigger—just stood there watching him trying to get that old revolver to fire. When he threw it down and took off running around to the back of the house, I reckon I finally woke up. So I took off after him, wantin' to take my shot. He was turnin' the corner of the house, headin' for the kitchen door, when I pulled the trigger—shot him in the back of the head." Cleve smiled to himself and slowly shook his head. "That was down in the Nations in Osage country. The Injun police didn't know what to do about it, but I figured I'd take off before they figured somethin' out. I been movin' ever since, and that was thirty years ago."

Ben was speechless for a few moments following Cleve's story. "Damn," was all he could mutter when at last he could comment. After a moment more, he asked, "Where are you headed now?"

"I'm goin' up into the Black Hills," Cleve answered. "I've been too late for every gold strike in the country, and I reckon I'm too late for this one, too. But I ain't got nothin' else to do."

Ben shared Cleve's opinion on that. It was much too late to cash in on the rich untapped veins of gold of the early days, by a half dozen years. But there were some individuals, like Cleve, who thought it worthwhile to pan the streams running through the Black Hills in hopes of striking the next big payoff. He shrugged. "Maybe this time you'll strike it rich."

"Never can tell," Cleve commented. "You never said where you're headin'."

"Nowhere in particular," Ben replied. "Just west, I reckon. Thought I'd go to Dodge City."

Cleve studied Ben for a long moment before he asked, "I couldn't help noticin' that ever'thin' you've got is new—new saddle, new boots, new clothes. You're on the run, ain'tcha?" Ben didn't answer, but Cleve could see that he had struck a sensitive chord. "The law? You rob a bank or somethin'? Or is it the feller that laid that scar across your face?"

Ben's hand automatically went up to feel the scar. "The man who did this is dead," he replied soberly. "And I ain't never stole anythin' in my life, if that's worryin' you."

"Now, don't get riled up." Cleve was quick in seeking to calm him. "I didn't go to get you mad. Your word's good enough for me." It was obvious to a man of Cleve's years and experience, however, that the young man was running from something, and he kept at it until Ben finally confided that he wasn't sure if he was being hunted or not. But the odds were good that the U.S. Marshal Service might be on the watch for him. Before the coffee was all gone, he told him what his crime had been.

"Sweet Jesus," Cleve uttered when Ben told him of the murder of his wife and son by a deputy sheriff. "I'da done the same thing you did. A man ought not be sent to prison for fightin' for his family, and that's a fact." He said nothing for a few moments while he absorbed the story he had just heard. "Makes it kind of hard to lie low, since that son of a bitch left his mark on you," he said, gazing openly at the jagged scar across Ben's face. "Why don't you come on to the Black Hills with me? There's enough outlaws and rough-lookin' fellers up in those hills that one more won't hardly be noticed."

Ben laughed. "That may be so, but I don't know anythin' more about minin' for gold than I did about farmin'. I know a little about cattle and horses, but nothin' about pannin' for gold. I doubt I'd be much good to you."

"There ain't much to learn about it," Cleve said. "Either you find it or you don't. I know enough to tell when there's color or not, so you might as well come on and go with me. I've got the tools and we'll split fifty-fifty on anythin' we find—which I doubt will be much—but what the hell?"

Ben had to laugh again. He couldn't help admiring the attitude of the gnomelike little man, in light of the fact that Cleve knew practically nothing about the man he invited to be a partner. He had to confess that the notion of joining Cleve held some attraction for him, especially since he knew the odds of hiring on with a cattle outfit at this end of the trail were very slim. "Are you sure you want me to be your partner?" he asked. "All you really know about me is that I killed a deputy sheriff, and I'm wanted by the U.S. Marshals."

"I know you're pretty damn handy with that new Winchester you're totin', and I can sure as hell use that. I know you jumped right in when you saw them Injuns comin' after me. There's a lot of folks that'da just gone the other way. Besides," he said with a chuckle, "I ain't got nothin' worth killin' me for right now. I won't have to worry about you shootin' me till we strike some color somewhere."

"Well, I guess we're goin' to the Black Hills," Ben said, and extended his hand. Cleve shook it and the partnership was formed.

Chapter 5

"Can I help you, gentlemen?" Harvey Green asked when he glanced up to see the two strangers in his doorway. He didn't see a lot of new customers in his little store on the south edge of Wichita, and these two weren't typical of the folks who traded with him for seed, flour, tools, and the like. Taking a closer look, he decided they were either outlaws or lawmen, hard-looking men, one of them big, and the other one bigger.

Barrett pulled his coat aside to show his badge, causing a sigh of relief from Harvey. "We're lookin' for a man who mighta come this way," Barrett said. "Maybe you've seen him—young fellow with a scar across his face."

Harvey's eyes answered the question before he opened his mouth to speak. "Couple of days ago," he blurted excitedly. "He came in my store and bought some coffee beans. What did he do?"

"Murdered a deputy sheriff over in Crooked Fork," Ike replied.

"Is that a fact?" Harvey responded. "I told my wife that man had a downright mean look about him. He talked nice enough, though. Didn't cause no trouble. Just bought his coffee and left." He paused to shake his head as he thought about it. "Murdered a deputy . . . Well, I'll be . . ."

"Did he say where he was headed?" Barrett asked.

"No, but he said he was lookin' to hire on with a trail outfit. I told him there wasn't much goin' on in Wichita no more, told him most of the herds were goin' to Dodge City. He didn't say he was goin' to head for Dodge, but I think he was thinkin' on it."

"'Preciate your help," Barrett said. "Was he still ridin' that buckskin horse?"

"Yessir, he was ridin' a buckskin."

"When he left your place, which way did he go?"

"West, he headed west," Harvey replied. "Like I said, probably goin' to Dodge."

"Step outside and show me exactly where he went," Barrett said.

Eager to help, Harvey led them out the door to the front yard. "Yonder," he said, pointing toward a gully that led down to a creek. "He crossed the creek between them willows, climbed up the bank, and followed the sun toward that line of ridges."

"Much obliged, Mr. Green," Barrett said, and started toward his horse.

"Glad to help," Harvey replied. "Anythin' you fellers need? Short on any supplies? I've got a pretty good stock of necessities."

Barrett shook his head as he climbed up in the saddle. Ike lingered, however. "I need somethin'," he told Harvey. He reached in a pocket of his saddlebag and produced a couple of coins. "Lemme have two of them peppermint sticks on the counter back there." Harvey hurried to fetch the penny candy, and with one in his saddlebags for later, and the other jammed in his mouth like a cigar, Ike followed Barrett to the creek.

When he caught up to him, Barrett was already out of the saddle, squatting on his heels while he studied the creek bank for hoofprints. "Take a look at this, Ike," he said without looking around, his finger tracing the outline of a print. "I'll bet you a month's pay that wide hoof is that buckskin he's ridin'."

"Maybe so," Ike allowed, already thinking it was probably Cutler's horse because of the simple fact that they were the only set of prints leading down between the two willow trees that the store owner indicated. Both men got back on their horses then, crossed the creek, and followed the tracks up the other bank, stopping at the top to gaze out in the direction the hoofprints were leading. "I'd say he drew a bead on that notch in that ridge yonder," Ike said. With Barrett in agreement, they set their course for the same notch.

At least two days old, the tracks were faint, but still in evidence, as the two marshals arrived at the notch, although they were forced to search in a wide circle at the top of the ridge before Barrett's sharp eye found a partial print in the grassy plain. "I say we oughta stay on the same line we've been ridin' on," Barrett said. "He ain't geed or hawed from this line since we left that store back yonder." Ike agreed, so they picked a spot to guide on atop another low ridge in the distance and continued on.

It was late in the day when they crossed over the ridge and surprised a flock of buzzards dining upon two carcasses. Squawking and screeching, the greedy birds protested the intrusion of the two law officers, refusing to leave their banquet until Ike took out his rifle and shot one of them. Only then did the defiant diners back away long enough for Barrett and Ike to identify the main course as the remains of two Indians. "Wonder if our boy had anythin' to do with this," Ike said. "Judging by what's left of them bodies, I'd say they were probably killed about the time Cutler would have been this far." Leaving the buzzards to return to their task of tidying up the prairie, they rode on up to the bank of a stream some fifty yards farther, where they found the remains of a campfire. "Looks like this is where he camped. I reckon the Injuns tried to jump him and he picked them two off."

"He's hooked up with somebody," Barrett called from the line of cottonwoods by the stream. "There were a couple of horses tied here in the trees, judging by these turds. Maybe it was some other feller's camp and Cutler just happened on it." This new finding served to complicate their job, for now it was necessary to determine if Cutler actually joined whoever was in the camp, or if they went their separate ways. Which was Cutler and which was the other? Theirs was no choice but to scout the camp carefully, working in a big circle around the camp. Tracks of more than one horse were soon found leading off on a more northerly course. Barrett was inclined to follow that trail, but could not until they were absolutely certain there was not another trail left by the horse they had been following since Wichita. Darkness set in before he could confirm his suspicions, forcing them to wait until morning to continue the search.

"We'll find his tracks in the mornin'," Ike said, free of the frustration that plagued his partner. He busied himself with the building of a fire, preparing to settle in for the night.

"He joined up with whoever was here," Barrett fumed. "I know damn well he did."

"How do you know that?" Ike asked, not really caring, but merely amusing himself by watching his intense partner stew over the fact that they had not yet run Ben Cutler to ground. Personally, Ike didn't care how long it took and, unlike Barrett, could live with it if Cutler escaped them altogether. He'd still draw his pay, win or lose. With Barrett, however, it was twisting his soul into a knot every day that Cutler remained free. Ike stirred his coffee with the remaining peppermint stick, a contented smile upon his face as he gazed at Barrett, who sat silently staring into the fire.

After a moment, Barrett answered Ike's question. "I just know it," he said. "I can feel it. I know how the man thinks."

"Well, hell, then," Ike joked, "why don't we just go on ahead to wherever he's goin' and wait for him, instead of followin' him all over hell and back?" Barrett's expression told him that he was not amused. But then, Ike thought, Barrett never was.

As soon as it was light enough to scout the area carefully, they were back working the circle around the camp. There was no evidence of any other trails out of the camp save the one that led to the north. Certain then that there was no single trail continuing west, they followed the larger trail along the bank of the stream as it led through the stand of cottonwoods. They had gone no farther than a mile and a half when they came upon the ashes of a second campfire and evidence of another camp. Another party? There was no increase in the number of tracks, so they finally concluded that they had simply decided to move their camp for whatever reason. After considering all they had found the night before and the present morning, they agreed on a situation as it had probably happened. Cutler had joined another traveler, helped him kill the Indians they had found, then moved the camp before they were attacked again.

"Well, that don't help us catch up with Cutler," Ike commented. "So what if he did join up with somebody?"

"One thing we know now," Barrett told him, "is Cutler ain't headin' to Dodge City no more since the only trail outta here is headin' north, and I was hopin' he was. It's gonna be a helluva lot harder to find him if he's wanderin' off to God knows where." He had been quite confident that they would find their man hanging around a saloon in Dodge. "Damn the luck," he cursed, already hating the unknown partner Cutler had just taken on. "Let's go," he hurled impatiently in Ike's direction. "I want this son of a bitch."

With a feeling of confidence that any marshals who might have been chasing him had by now given up, Ben rolled comfortably with the steady gait of the buckskin gelding. They were no more than a day's ride from Ogallala, a town that prompted memories of his life as a drover. With Cleve leading the way ahead of him, he let his mind wander back to the days before his life was violently tossed away. A Texan by birth, he had either been a hired hand or a partner on half a dozen cattle drives of Texas longhorn cattle to cow towns of Abilene, Wichita, and Dodge until he promised Mary Ellen he would stay put in one place. He had also committed to try his hand at raising crops, but in the back of his mind there had always been a plan to start a herd of cattle. Maybe small at first, but with plenty of good grazing land, he could eventually increase the herd to a profitable business.

All the herds he had driven up from Texas had been sold in towns like Wichita, but the big cattle barons who bought them more often than not moved them to Ogallala, where the Union Pacific Railroad had built holding pens. The little town between the forks of the Platte River had become a favorite place to hold cattle. The older ones were shipped out to the markets in the East, while the younger ones were held to winter range on the abundant grass there, even though it was covered with snow for much of the winter. If his plans had not been brutally shattered, he had envisioned raising his cattle a short drive from Ogallala, the town he was about to see for the first time.

"We'll hit Ogallala before noon tomorrow," Cleve commented when they stopped to make camp. "I'll buy some flour. I've got a cravin' for some biscuits, and I've been out of flour for three or four weeks now."

"We could use a few things," Ben replied, "some dried beans and some more bacon." The opportunity for wild game had failed to present itself, so a side of pork had been the primary source of meat.

Soon after breaking camp the following morning, they began to pass through vast numbers of cattle long before sighting the outline of stores that would be Ogallala. It seemed to Ben that there were cattle everywhere as he and Cleve moved slowly through the sea of bellowing critters. Approaching the town, he was surprised to see the unimpressive size of it. The main street was no more than a block or two in length, boasting a few stores, two saloons, and a hotel. It was hard to imagine that there were such huge sums of money exchanged there. When he commented on it to Cleve, the wizened little man replied, "I don't know about that, but I know a man can buy a drink of whiskey at the Cowboy's Rest, and that's what I'm thinkin' 'bout now. It's a right lively town this time of year, but if you was to ride through here in January, you'd think the whole town had died."

Ben had been to a few cow towns before and he knew them all to be wild and lawless when the cowboys hit town after months on the trail. He expected this one to be the same. Cleve told him that was not the case with Ogallala. "Oh, I wasn't foolin' when I said it was lively. You can get everythin' you want here, but Ogallala's got law and order. It ain't like Dodge City if Martin DePriest is still sheriff. He'll let the drovers have their fun. Hell, he came up here from Texas himself, but if the fun starts to get outta hand, he'll come down hard on you—him and his deputy, Joe Hughes. The last time I was here, two years ago June, ol' DePriest run some cowboys outta town for takin' target practice at the lamps on the undertaker's rig. They decided they was gonna *hoorah* the town then to show him who was boss. When they showed up in front of the Ogallala House, DePriest was waitin' for 'em. He ain't a tall man, short and stocky, but he's hell in a free-for-all. He waded right in the middle of them cowboys, and it didn't take long before those fellers from Texas decided they'd had all they wanted of Sheriff DePriest." Cleve paused to laugh at the memory of it.

Ben wasn't sure if that was good news for him or not. He couldn't be certain that his description hadn't been telegraphed all over the territory, so he would have preferred a lawless town at this particular point in his life. "Maybe I'd better lie low outside of town, in case they're lookin' for me up here."

"Hell, ain't no need for that," Cleve insisted. "There's so many cowboys in town, and a good many of 'em probably has scars on their faces, ain't nobody gonna pay you no mind. Besides, we're in Nebraska Territory now. They're most likely just lookin' for you in Kansas."

"Maybe so," Ben replied, still not convinced, but anxious to find out if Cleve was right, and possibly he was not sentenced to avoid all civilization for the rest of his life.

They continued on into town and Cleve led the way to the Cowboy's Rest Saloon, where they tied the horses out front at the rail. "I'd be proud to buy you a drink," Cleve said, "but I'm a little short on cash right now."

Grinning, for he knew Cleve had no money, Ben said, "Why, that's right sportin' of you, partner, but I insist on springin' for the drinks myself." He knew that Cleve figured he had some money, but he wasn't sure how much. Ben was afraid that if he told him, he might try to buy the saloon. He tilted the brim of his hat down low on his forehead and followed Cleve inside. Although it was still early in the day, the saloon was crowded from front to back with the trail hands and the soiled doves who were eager to entertain them. Those not crowded around the gaming tables were either sitting at the other tables or standing at the bar. With so much to occupy their minds, Ben began to think Cleve was right. No one was going to take the time to notice him. That was not to be the case, however.

"Damn, feller . . . ," the bartender exclaimed when they found an empty space at the bar. He caught himself before continuing, because of the sinister appearance Ben's scar gave him. "What'll you have?" He quickly recovered, although still staring at Ben.

"Whiskey," Cleve replied gleefully. "Whiskey for me and my partner." Ben immediately wondered if he had made a mistake in coming in, but he stood silently waiting while the bartender poured. "Here's to good times and a good partnership," Cleve said, and tossed it back. Returning the empty glass to the bar with a flourish, he asked, "Does Bill Tucker still own this place?" When the bartender said that he did, Cleve said, "Bill told me whenever I got back in town to come in the Cowboy's Rest and have a drink on the house." He then looked at the bartender expectantly.

"Is that a fact?" the bartender replied, his eyes reflecting boredom with Cleve's obvious attempt to get a free drink. "He's over there at the poker table. We can call him over so you can say hello."

"No, no," Cleve quickly insisted. "I wouldn't call a man from a poker game. Might give him bad luck."

Ben couldn't help laughing. "Pour another round," he said. "I'm buyin'."

Taking a little more time to enjoy his second drink, Cleve looked around him at the noisy barroom. The riotous celebration of trail's end obviously pleased him, judging by the wide grin on his face. At the far end of the room, a fiddler was doing his best to offer some musical entertainment, his efforts all but unnoticed in the steady clamor of boisterous laughter and the voices of the patrons, yelling to be heard above the din. To Cleve, it was the ultimate celebration of life. He looked back at Ben and smacked his hand on the bar. "Let's have one more for the road," he suggested gleefully. Ben nodded to the bartender.

The cowboy standing next to Cleve left the bar and a fragile-looking, gray-haired man slid in to take his place. He immediately ordered a drink, gazing at the bottle in eager anticipation as the bartender poured. Placing his money on the bar, he picked up the glass and took a moment to look at the amber liquid before bringing it to his lips. Then as he brought it up to his mouth, a rowdy young cowhand jostled him roughly, causing the whiskey to spill on the bar. The cowhand turned to see the consequences of his roughhousing and laughed when he saw the drink splashed across the counter. Looking back at his friend who had shoved him, he said, "Damn it, Travis, look what you made me do." His complaint brought more laughter from his friends.

With no particular interest in the incident, Ben watched the reaction of the victim of the horseplay. It struck him that the willowy little man was as out of place there as any man could be, and was obviously not one of the drunken trail hands who had caused him to lose his whiskey. The accident seemed to be of no concern to the two whose rough play had caused it. The man said nothing as he stared at his empty glass, and when he turned to look at the bartender, the bartender merely shrugged his shoulders. Still the man said nothing.

Witness also to the incident, Cleve was a step ahead of Ben in interceding. He tapped the young cowboy on the shoulder. It took a couple of times before the cowboy turned to face him. "Your horsin' around caused this feller to lose his drink." His statement was met with a look of indifference. "You owe him a drink," Cleve said.

"Hellfire," the young man responded. "It ain't my fault. He shoved me," he said, nodding toward his friend, who was watching the confrontation with a foolish grin still in place.

"Don't make no difference," Cleve replied. "The right thing to do is for you to buy him another one."

The young man's friends were suddenly silent, interested now in what he was going to do, and obviously amused by the situation. "Yeah," one of them said, "you owe the gentleman a drink, Tom." The injured party had still not uttered a word, and it was obvious to Ben that he never would.

The man called Tom turned back to sneer at the puddle on the counter, concerned now that his friends were waiting to see what he was going to do. "Well, hell," he said, pointing at it, "you ain't lost it. You just gotta lap it up off the bar." Again, his comments brought a wave of laughter from his friends.

The little gray-haired man turned to leave, wanting no further humiliation at the hands of the cowboys. He didn't get far before being caught by the arm and stopped in his tracks. Ben had seen enough of the senseless bullying. He pulled the man aside to stand next to Cleve, then roughly spun Tom around to face him. Having paid no attention to the silent man on the other side of Cleve, the cowboy was not prepared to confront the angry visage suddenly before him. The anger in the searing eyes seemed to set the long ugly scar ablaze, causing Tom to think that he had seen the devil in that instant. "You owe the gentleman a drink," Ben said softly, his tone deadly calm.

His vocal cords paralyzed by a shock of cold fear that raced down his spine, young Tom was unable to speak for a few moments. His voice returned simultaneously with his common sense. "Why, I was gonna buy him a drink all along," he stammered while digging into his pocket for his money. "We wasn't lookin' to cause no trouble."

Cleve took over then. "Course you wasn't. Just cowboys havin' fun, and no harm come of it. I knowed you wanted to do the right thing." He glanced at Ben, having seen for the first time that violent display of anger, and he wondered what his new partner was capable of if really enraged.

A helpless witness to the altercation to this point, the victim finally spoke. "I don't want to cause any more trouble," he said. "I'll just leave now."

"You ain't had your drink yet," Cleve told him, and slid the now full shot glass before him. Looking as if he had no choice, the man quickly drank it down, turned, and headed for the door. Tom and his friends moved farther down the bar, talking quietly among themselves. "I reckon we're done here, too," Cleve said. "We'll walk out with you."

Outside, the meek little man turned and waited for them. "I want to thank you for what you did in there," he said, extending his hand. "My name's Jonah Marple and I guess I had no business in that saloon. I was just gonna slip in and get a drink of whiskey real quick before I went back to the wagon. My wife will be getting worried. She's afraid to come into town as long as it's overrun with these wild drovers from Texas."

"So you don't live around here?" Cleve asked.

Marple shook his head and replied, "No, we were just passing through, but we've been stranded here for over a week."

"How come?" Cleve asked.

Jonah went on to explain the circumstances that brought him to be camping outside Ogallala. "We left Omaha a little over a month ago, my wife, our daughter, her son, and me, on a journey to join my son-in-law in Deadwood. My son-in-law, Garth Beaudry, went to the Black Hills to prospect for gold last spring. The last word we had from him was from Deadwood, and he said that he was seeing some success, and is working for the largest mine in the area. My daughter was determined to go out to join him, and we didn't want to see her make that journey on her own. So I sold my farm, lock, stock, and barrel and went with her. We hired a man named Seth Barnhill to take us out there."

"And he run off and left you," Cleve finished for him.

Jonah bit his lip and nodded. "Yes, that he did."

"He took his total payment, too," Cleve said. Again, Jonah nodded, looking quite embarrassed to admit it. "Well," Cleve continued, "you ain't the first that's been took by a low-down scoundrel that preys on innocent folks. He's most likely headed to Dodge with your money, if you're thinkin' about lookin' for him."

Jonah's facial expression told them that he was not likely to consider such action. "I don't want to see the man again," he said.

"So, now what are you gonna do?" Cleve asked.

"Well, I've been talking it over with my wife and daughter. We certainly can't stay here, but I don't know if I could find Deadwood if I just started out over this endless prairie country. So we decided the safest thing for us is to follow the river to Fort Laramie. I've heard that the government cleared a road from Cheyenne to Fort Laramie, and on to Deadwood. They say it's a stage road, and there's a lot of traffic of all kinds on it, so I think I can follow it to Deadwood without fear of getting lost."

"That's one way to get there," Cleve conceded, "and a smart way for someone who don't know the country." He studied the timid little man for a few moments more before asking, "How do you make your livin', Jonah—farmin'?"

"I'm a teacher," he replied, and reading Cleve's expression, quickly added, "I had a small farm near Omaha, though."

Taking no pains to hide his skepticism, Cleve pressed. "And you're gonna go up in the Black Hills and prospect for gold?"

Jonah shifted his gaze back and forth between the stumpy Cleve and his ominous-looking partner, who stood silently by. "Well, I don't know. Primarily, I guess I'm going up there to try to find my son-in-law, Garth Beaudry."

"Well, Mr. Marple," Cleve said, intending to end the conversation, "I wish you good luck in finding your daughter's husband. I hope you have a safe journey." Turning to go to his horse, he paused when Jonah asked one more question.

"I get the feeling that you two gentlemen are not with one of the cattle outfits in town. Is that right?"

"That's right," Cleve said. "We're just passin' through."

"Where are you heading?"

"The Black Hills," Cleve answered reluctantly, guessing what Jonah's next question would be.

"What are the possibilities that we might go with you?" Jonah asked, quick to see an opportunity. When Cleve hesitated to answer, he pressed. "I don't have much money left, but I can pay you and your friend to guide us, and we wouldn't have to lose the time it would take to go to Fort Laramie before heading back north again."

Cleve looked at Ben. It was plain to see that Ben was no more enthusiastic about such an arrangement than he. Looking back to meet the hopeful gaze of Jonah's, he hesitated before answering, "I don't know, Jonah. A wagon would slow us down an awful lot, and there'd be a chance we'll run into some of them renegade Injuns that have been causin' trouble between here and the hills. You might be a helluva lot safer goin' the way you was plannin' on."

Ben could see right away that Jonah was not going to be discouraged. Like Cleve, Ben had no interest in acting as a guide to a family from Omaha. He listened as Cleve tried to point out every reason he could think of to dissuade the frail schoolteacher, but also like Cleve, Ben did not have the heart to just come out and tell the man no. He felt sympathetic toward Jonah's predicament, and frankly felt sorry for the two women and the child who had to depend upon Jonah in the event of trouble. When Cleve turned to give Ben a helpless look, Ben simply nodded his okay.

"I swear," Cleve told Jonah, "you're as stubborn as a

mule. We'll take you to Deadwood, but we ain't gonna do it for nothin'."

The worried look they had seen earlier returned to Jonah's face. "I'll pay you what I can. How much are you thinking?"

"You said you was a teacher. I'll guide you to Deadwood if you'll teach me how to read and write my name. That's my price." An expression of pure joy captured Jonah's countenance. "You'll have to talk to Ben about his price," Cleve said then, and Jonah looked at once toward the solemn man with the horrendous scar.

"I reckon a cup of coffee would do it for me," Ben said.

"It's a deal!" Jonah exclaimed happily. "You fellows won't be sorry. My Mary's a wonderful cook. So is my daughter, Victoria."

Cleve couldn't prevent a chuckle. "I reckon we oughta introduce ourselves. My name's Cleve Goganis. My partner here is Ben Cutler." Jonah shook hands with each of them, and the deal was struck.

Jonah scrambled up on the back of the one horse at the rail with no saddle and led Ben and Cleve past the stables and out the north end of town. About a half mile outside Ogallala, they came to a small creek that emptied into the Platte. On the east bank sat a four-foot-by-ten-foot farm wagon with canvas covers. A horse, the other half of Jonah's team, was tethered nearby, and around the wagon in every direction cattle grazed on the rich prairie grass. "Maybe you oughta go on ahead and talk it over with your wife," Cleve suggested. "She might not want to head straight across the prairie with the likes of me and Ben." He was thinking that there still might be a chance that the deal just struck could be rejected by the little woman—at least, he could hope for it. He and Ben reined their horses back and let Jonah continue.

They watched from a few yards away as Mary Marple appeared from the other side of the wagon to greet her husband. She was joined in a few moments by her daughter and grandson. They all looked inquisitively at the two strangers idly watering their horses at the stream while Jonah explained their presence. A look of alarm flashed across Mary's face when she was told of the arrangement Jonah had made with the two ominous-looking riders. "Jonah!" she exclaimed, keeping her voice down so as not to be heard by Ben and Cleve. "What on earth were you thinking?" She turned to take a longer look at the two, which only caused her more concern. The scruffy-looking older man looked to have just come from a saloon, but the younger one with the scarred face was downright scary. "Seth Barnhill was a lying no-good drunk and a thief, but those two look like they might murder us in our sleep."

"They're all right, Mary," Jonah persisted. "They just look rough. And they can lead us straight to Deadwood from here. The best part of it is they don't want any money for doin' it."

This did little to convince Mary. "Of course they don't need to be paid," she retorted. "They're probably planning to kill us all and take everything we've got."

"What is it, Mama?" Victoria stepped closer to hear the hushed conversation between her parents. "Who are those men?"

"Your father has contracted with them to take us to Deadwood," Mary answered.

Seeing Victoria's look of astonishment, Jonah again tried to defend his decision. "They're perfectly all right, honey. They just don't have a lot of polish, but they sure saved my bacon in the saloon a little while ago."

"What were you doing in a saloon?" Mary immediately responded. "You went to town to buy salt."

"One little drink. I haven't had one since we left Omaha. Anyway, it's lucky I did, 'cause I ran into these two fellows, and they can save us a lot of time on the trail."

"In a saloon?" Mary retorted, not ready to let that matter pass without comment, then turned to give Victoria a bewildered look before chastising Jonah once more. "If you were looking for someone more dependable than the last scoundrel we hired, you sure picked an odd place to do it." She paused to take another look at Ben and Cleve, who were beginning to realize that Jonah's sales job was not going well. "Besides," Mary said, turning back to her husband, "that big one scares me. How did he get that awful scar across his face?"

"I don't know," Jonah replied, growing weary of the conversation. "I didn't think it polite to ask him. You can ask him." He threw up his hand then and beckoned. "Come on in and meet the family," he called, ignoring the daggers from Mary's eyes.

Like her mother, Victoria experienced a feeling of cold dread as the two strange men crossed the stream and rode up to the wagon. She unconsciously reached down and placed her hand on her son's shoulder when she felt him press against her leg. Upon closer inspection of their visitors, she and her mother both instinctively took a few steps closer to the wagon and the shotgun Jonah kept by the seat.

They stepped down from their saddles, and as had become the usual procedure, Cleve did the talking. "Howdy, ladies," he said. "We're pleased to make your acquaintance."

Jonah stepped in to do the introductions then. "This is my wife, Mary, and my daughter, Victoria. Girls, this is Ben Cutler and Cleve . . ." He paused then. "I declare, I forgot your last name."

"Goganis," Cleve said. "I have trouble rememberin' it myself. Cleve is good enough."

Standing a few steps behind Cleve, Ben sought to appraise the family he would be traveling with. Mary Marple was a short, stout woman with plain features and a ruddy complexion, no doubt the result of the many days spent traveling in a wagon. Her daughter looked very much like her, an unremarkable young woman in appearance, though unlike her mother, slender as a reed. At the moment, she exhibited a frown of apprehension, but he imagined hers a pleasant face in lighter circumstances. In an effort to ease some of her concern, Ben asked, "And who's this young man hidin' behind his mama's skirt?"

"This is Caleb," Victoria replied, and pulled the boy away from her leg. "Caleb, say hello to Mr. . . ."

"Cutler," Ben supplied. Being more sensitive to the air of uneasiness than his partner, he sought to further alleviate their fears. "Jonah here talked to us about travelin' to Deadwood together. You women might not feel comfortable with that, and I wouldn't blame you. Cleve and I are a pretty scruffy-lookin' pair. Like we told Jonah, it might be safer for you folks to follow the river to Fort Laramie and take the road from there to Deadwood. It's all the same to Cleve and me. We were on our way to the Black Hills, anyway. If you want to go along with us, that's all right with us, too."

There was a short silence that followed. His remarks had surprised both women, for they had prejudged the man because of his threatening appearance, and had obviously not expected anything from his mouth resembling intelligent conversation. Mary was the first to respond. "Well, Mr. Cutler, I'm sorry if we seemed a bit concerned. You have to understand that we had not discussed the possibility of hiring any more guides after our experience with Mr. Barnhill."

"We're not for hire," Ben gently reminded her. "We'll just be travelin' together." He paused, then added, "If that's all right with you."

She glanced at her daughter, searching for her leaning, and discovered a noncommittal expression. Looking back at Jonah, she was met with a wide smile. Ben's soft tone had somewhat disarmed her. "Well, I suppose it makes sense." She allowed herself to smile then. "I guess we'll have company for supper, Victoria."

Chapter 6

Pushing their way through the evening crowd at the Cowboy's Rest Saloon, the two deputy marshals scanned the busy room as they approached the bar. When the bartender got to them, they ordered a drink; then Barrett showed his badge and asked, "Have you seen a man with a long scar across his face in here lately? Maybe in the last couple of days?"

"Sure have," the bartender replied without hesitation. "Bad-lookin' feller, he almost got into a tussle with some cowboys over a spilled drink."

Barrett smiled at Ike Gibbs. "That's got to be our boy." Turning back to the bartender, he asked, "Is he still hangin' around town?"

"I don't know. If he is, he ain't been back in here."

"Much obliged," Barrett said. He tossed his drink back and turned to leave. "We'll take a look around town." He stopped then, just remembering. "You remember if this feller was with somebody?" When the bartender said that he was, Barrett asked him to describe the man.

"I don't know," the bartender started, trying to recall. "Kinda short feller, older than the jasper with the scar—rough and tumble lookin', though. That's about all I can tell you, except he's got a full crop of whiskers."

"Much obliged," Barrett repeated, although the information was of questionable value. The bartender had described probably half the men in Ogallala.

There were not that many business establishments in the town, so it was not a major task for the two lawmen to cover them all, hoping to find some clue that would tell them where Ben Cutler was heading when, and if, he had left Ogallala. "I reckon Martin DePriest is still the sheriff here," Ike said when they made their way through a gathering of cowboys in front of the hotel. "You think we oughta let him know we're in town?"

"To hell with him," Barrett replied. "He don't need to know we're here. He would just get in our way. We'll leave him and his deputy to worry about the drunk cowhands and the whores."

Their search of the town came up empty, and Barrett's frustration was growing by the hour, for there was no possible way to track Cutler out of town. He could have gone in any direction. Just when they were about to decide they had been beaten, they got the break that set them on Ben's trail again. It came from a boy who worked in the stables. "Yes, sir," he said. "I saw that man you're talkin' about. I couldn't rightly say where he was goin', but I saw him and his friend ride out of town with a feller by the name of Marple that's been campin' down by the river for about a week. Mr. Marple was ridin' a horse bareback."

Barrett's pulse began to quicken. "This Marple," he pressed, "where's his camp?"

" 'Bout a half mile up the North Platte," the boy replied. "It's him and his wife, and his daughter, I think. They're in a wagon on their way to the Black Hills. He brought the wagon in here to get a wheel fixed."

Barrett and Gibbs lost little time in putting Ogallala behind them. With detailed directions from the stable boy, they were able to find Jonah Marple's campsite. The wagon was gone, but there was no doubt that it was the right camp and there was a trail to follow. The sandy strand near the river was covered with hundreds of tracks. Most of them were left by cows, but there were the distinct tracks of a wagon pointing the way. Barrett stood looking north in the direction the wagon had been heading. "I told you this jasper would most likely head to Deadwood, where the easy money is. Damn it, I know how he thinks! And I'm gonna haul his ass back to prison."

"You know," Ike felt it his duty to remind his partner, "we're already one helluva long ways outta our jurisdiction." Barrett seemed not to even hear him. "Might be time to forget about this feller."

Barrett heard that. "Forget about him?" he demanded. "Like hell I will. I don't give a damn about jurisdiction. I'm takin' him back to Lansing, either settin' in the saddle, or lyin' across it. I don't care which."

Ike studied his partner for a long moment, wondering just how much deeper this fugitive was going to get under his skin. Barrett had the same attitude about any criminal he was sent after, but this particular man seemed to present a personal challenge to his record of arrests. It was especially puzzling to Ike because this man, Ben Cutler, seemed to have the best wishes of most of the folks in Crooked Fork. Ike himself could understand the man's need to avenge the murders of his wife and son, but he left the right and wrong of it to the judges and juries. In his opinion, however, he and Barrett had gone far enough in pursuit of Cutler. It was time to hand the job off to Dakota Territory marshals and go on home. After a few moments more, he decided to express his thoughts. "I'm gonna tell you the truth, Graham. I think you've let this feller get into your head. It's time we was headin' back to Topeka and passin' this on to the marshals in Dakota Territory."

"What's the matter, Ike?" Barrett scoffed. "You startin' to miss home cookin' and a soft bed? I ain't about to stop now. I'm gonna follow these wagon tracks right up Ben Cutler's ass. Hell, we've got him now. We oughta catch him before he gets to the Black Hills if he's ridin' along with this wagon." Seeing the lack of enthusiasm in Ike's face, he was moved to say, "If you've lost your stomach for it, you might as well turn back, and I'll go after Cutler alone." He was surprised by Ike's response.

"Maybe I will," he said. "I figure one of us oughta be workin' in the territory we're assigned to. The more I think about it, the more I'm thinkin' that feller ain't done no more than what you or I woulda done if it was our folks who got killed."

"Damn!" Barrett swore. "You, too? You're startin' to sound like those people in Crooked Fork. Go on back to Topeka. I ain't sure you'd be much good to me with that attitude. That's the same reason I don't aim to turn this over to the marshal's office in Dakota Territory. That sorry crowd up there don't wanna ride more'n a mile or two outta Sioux City."

"I expect you know me better'n that," Ike replied softly. "I think you're too damn stubborn to let go because of your reputation, but I think we've followed this feller long enough. I'm goin' back to headquarters. I'll see you when you get back." He climbed back in the saddle and turned his horse back toward Ogallala.

"Never figured you for a quitter," Barrett chastised, making no attempt to hide his disgust for his longtime partner. "You go on back, and I'll finish the job we were sent to do." Ike responded with no more than a sigh of exasperation before touching his horse with his heels. Fully angry then, Barrett pulled his pistol from the holster and aimed it at Ike's back. He held it there for a few moments before gradually lowering it and replacing it in his holster. With new determination, he climbed aboard the black Morgan he rode and set off to follow the wagon tracks.

"What happened to your face?"

Ben had wondered how long it was going to be before the young son of Victoria Beaudry asked that question. The boy had stared at him all day long whenever Ben happened to ride close to the wagon. He picked up another limb from the little pile he had gathered and threw it on the fire. "I fell on a crosscut saw," he answered, seeing no reason to tell the youngster how he really happened to be scarred.

"I bet it hurt like the dickens," Caleb said, his eyes wide as he openly stared at Ben.

"Yeah, I reckon it did," Ben said, although when he

thought back about it, he couldn't recall the pain when he was struck—only the severe pain afterward when he came to. "So you'd best remember to be careful if you're usin' a crosscut when you get a little older." Seeking to change the subject then, he asked, "How old are you?"

Caleb held up four fingers and said, "Four."

"So you'll fill up that hand on your next birthday," he said. It brought a smile to Caleb's face. Ben thought about his late son. Danny would have been seven on his birthday. These were things Ben had striven to ban from his thoughts, but talking to Caleb now made it impossible.

The boy was about to ask another question, when mercifully, his mother called from the cook fire near the wagon. "Caleb, come and eat your supper!"

The boy did not respond immediately. Ben could see that he was formulating another question. "Better run eat your supper, boy. Don't wanna rile your ma." It wasn't enough to prevent the question.

"Why are you staying way over here by yourself?" he asked. "Mr. Cleve comes to our fire all the time, but you never do."

The comment caused a chuckle from Ben. "Mr. Cleve does a lot of things I don't do. It's just better if I stay outta your ma's and your grandma's way." *That and the fact that they always look like they're afraid I'm gonna cut their throats*, he thought to himself. Caleb got to his feet and started back toward the wagon. The distinct aroma of pan-baked biscuits triggered some interest on Ben's part, and he gazed after the boy.

As she waited at the rear corner of the wagon for her son to come to supper, Victoria's gaze met that of their puzzling traveling companion. He immediately averted his eyes and turned his head away. She was not certain yet what to make of him, but she suspected that there must be an unhappy past that caused him to seem so withdrawn and melancholy. She also had a feeling that it was firmly connected to the silver chain that she had seen him holding when he thought no one noticed. She found a sadness in the way he held it close to his chest before returning it to his pocket. It was obvious that he made an effort to have as little contact as possible with his traveling companions—in sharp contrast to his partner. There had been only a few stops for meals since they had joined up, and Cleve had been the one to pick up two plates of food and bring them back to their separate fire. Her thoughts on the subject were interrupted by the arrival of her son by her side. "Come on," she said. "Time to eat your supper."

As he was staring at the wagon again, since the woman had returned to the fire, it appeared to Ben that Cleve had sat down with Jonah's family to eat, instead of bringing two plates as usual. *Damn*, he thought, *am I gonna have to go get my plate?* He preferred not to, but he didn't intend to skip supper, so he struggled to his feet. He didn't take a step toward the wagon because, at that moment, he saw Victoria heading toward him, carrying a plate of food.

"You don't have to do that, ma'am," Ben said as he hurried toward her to get the plate. "I thought Cleve was gonna bring our plates over here."

"It's no trouble at all," Victoria assured him. "Why don't you just eat with us at mealtime? We won't bite." She tried to make an effort not to stare at his face, although she found it equally insulting to him if she appeared to be looking away when she spoke to him. She knew her mother was frightened by the man, and she would be alarmed to know Victoria had invited him to their fire. But it just did not seem right to treat him like a leper.

"Thank you, ma'am," he said, taking the plate of food from her. "I just thought I'd try to stay outta your way. I know I make your mother nervous."

"Nonsense," Victoria replied, at once feeling remorse that it had been so obvious. "I put an extra biscuit on there, since Cleve said you both had been wishing you had some flour to bake some. I made these. I hope they're as good as you would have made."

"Ha!" Ben blurted. "They're bound to be a sight better'n any I could make, and I don't know if I'd risk eatin' any Cleve made." He shifted his gaze to his boots when he realized she was looking into his eyes.

Suddenly she was visited by a feeling of sympathy for this horribly scarred man, for she sensed that he was a decent person, respectful, even soft-spoken, and not at all what his appearance indicated. In spite of his discomfort, she studied his face closely while he continued to stare down at his boots. She decided that he had been a rather nice-looking man before his accident with the saw. Her precocious son had told her the cause of Ben's disfigurement. It didn't seem right that a man should be branded by the appearance of his face. "I must apologize for my inquisitive son," she said. "I hope he hasn't been too much of a bother."

"No, ma'am," Ben replied, "not at all. He's a right spunky little rascal. I expect you're pretty proud of him."

She laughed. "Sometimes, I guess," she said, then

paused before speaking again. "Come on," she decided, "you're going to have to get used to putting up with my family." She took the plate out of his hands and started back toward the wagon. He was left with no choice unless he wanted to break out some of his bacon and dried beans, and wait until they cooked.

Almost skulking, he followed her to the fire and quickly seated himself on the far side of Cleve, who was grinning openly at him. When he was settled, Victoria gave him his plate again, then poured him a cup of coffee. Noticing her mother's worried expression, she decided to expose it and speak boldly on Ben's behalf. "Look, everybody. Ben's joining us for supper. Everybody look at Ben's face. Isn't that a nasty-looking scar left by his fall on that crosscut saw?"

Ben immediately flushed scarlet. Jonah and Mary Marple both recoiled in astonishment at their daughter's insensitive remark. Cleve couldn't help laughing upon seeing the collective reaction. "Crosscut saw, huh? Is that what done your face like that?" He smiled at Victoria then and said, "I never thought to ask." As blunt and rude as it had seemed, it was successful in destroying the violent image they had created in their minds about the man accompanying them to Deadwood.

Mary was the first to offer words of sympathy for one she now judged to be acceptable company, since his injury had not been the result of a barroom brawl, or some such lawless activity. "Why, it's not that bad," she said. "When it's had more time to heal, it probably won't be that noticeable at all. Did Victoria put enough bacon on that plate for you?"

Victoria smiled to herself, pleased with the success

of her questionable approach to solve the problem. After that evening, meals were taken together. Victoria's efforts served to eliminate an awkward relationship between the family from Omaha and the two rough-appearing prospectors, for they would be bound together for a trip of a month or more. Because of the slow pace of the wagon, they would be lucky to average ten miles a day. Jonah and his family learned to appreciate the sacrifice their escorts were making, especially when realizing that Ben and Cleve could have made the journey in a week and a half or so on horseback. After a couple of days, the two were already Uncle Ben and Uncle Cleve to young Caleb Beaudry, and the boy would certainly have adopted them both if it had been left up to him. Victoria became completely at ease with Caleb's attraction to the rugged pair, never worrying about the time her son spent tagging along behind them. In fact, she worried more about the aggravation Caleb might cause them.

The first week found them approaching the Niobrara River. Ben, scouting far ahead of the wagon, came upon a herd of antelope sweeping across the prairie before him. Following the fleet-footed beasts at a safe distance, he was finally able to get close enough for a shot with his rifle when the antelope crossed over a low ridge and filed down into the river bottom to drink. He was able to bring down two of them before the rest scurried out of rifle range. By the time Cleve and the wagon caught up to him, he figured he would likely have already skinned and quartered one of the animals.

Beyond the low grassy ridge about a half mile to

the east of the creek, six mounted Sioux hunters halted
their ponies to speculate on the origin of the two rifle
shots they had heard only minutes before. "I think
someone has beaten us to the antelope," Wolf Kill said.
He and his friends had been trailing the herd since
early morning, but the animals seemed to know they
were being stalked. Consequently, they had continued
moving, never stopping to graze for more than a few
minutes at a time.

"There was only one rifle, I think," Dead Man, the
leader of the small band of warriors, said. It was pure
speculation, for there was really no way to tell if it was
one rifle firing twice, or two rifles firing once. It had
not sounded like the carbines the cavalry soldiers carried. But they could not be too cautious, being one of
many bands of warriors who had refused to go to the
reservation. They were constantly being hunted by the
cavalry patrols. Dead Man turned to the others and
said, "Wolf Kill and I will climb up to the top of this
ridge and see if we can get a look at who's doing the
shooting."

Lying on their stomachs at the top of the ridge, they
scanned the trees along the banks of the narrow creek,
at first finding no sign of the hunter. "There!" Wolf Kill
suddenly exclaimed, and pointed to a horse grazing
beyond a screen of willows near the water's edge. They
both concentrated their gaze upon the stand of trees.
After a few moments, Dead Man said, "There is only
one man, a white man."

They were able to determine that the white man
was in the process of skinning and quartering an antelope carcass. "One man," Wolf Kill repeated. "We can
kill him and take the meat for ourselves if we ride up

the river some distance and work our way back down to his camp."

"This is true," Dead Man replied. "He is only one man, and not a soldier, but maybe it would be a wise thing if we wait a little while to see if he really is alone. He might be a scout for an army patrol. Maybe they are not far behind him." Dead Man knew they were in no shape to battle a patrol. He and Wolf Kill had seven-shot carbines just like those carried by some of the soldiers, but the other four in their party had old surplus single-shot weapons from the war between the white men.

"You are right," Wolf Kill quickly conceded. "It would be best to watch this lone white man for a while." He turned his head to smile at Dead Man. "It's best to wait to kill him after he finishes butchering the antelope, anyway."

Dead Man moved back halfway down the ridge and signaled for the others. Leaving their ponies at the bottom, they joined Dead Man and Wolf Kill at the top of the ridge where they waited and watched to see if a detachment of soldiers would arrive. In a short while, a wagon appeared, following the line of the ridge toward the river on the west side. A man on a horse rode beside the team of two horses. Other than the one driving the wagon, there appeared to be no other men. Beside him on the wagon seat, one woman sat, while another walked beside the wagon with a small boy. A ripple of excitement immediately ran through the line of Sioux warriors lying in the grass atop the ridge. Still, Dead Man cautioned his friends to be patient. "Let's make sure there are no others following." When it was obvious that there was no one else to come, Dead Man led his warriors along the east side of the ridge to a point where they could intercept the wagon before it reached the man butchering the meat.

"Heyo, Ben!" Cleve shouted when he caught sight of his partner waving his rifle back and forth to attract his attention. "What was the shootin' I heard a while ago?"

"Fresh meat!" Ben yelled back. That was all the time there was for conversation, for all hell broke loose in the next second in the form of six charging savages, firing wildly as they swept through a notch in the ridge, their blood-chilling war cries echoing off the slope behind them.

Both Cleve and Ben reacted instantly, Ben running to get in the best position to fire, while Cleve slid off his horse, drawing his Winchester in the process. Terrified, Jonah froze. His initial inclination was to try to run for it, but Cleve yelled for him and Mary to drop down in the wagon. It was too late to run. Next Cleve picked Victoria up and deposited her roughly in the back of the wagon. Not having to be told, Caleb scrambled up in the bed of the wagon by himself. "Jonah!" Cleve shouted. "Get that shotgun out and get busy!" He then positioned himself behind the wagon with his horse and prepared to defend. From the front of the wagon, he heard a blast from the shotgun. "Jonah!" he cried again. "Wait till they're in range of that damn shotgun."

While Cleve was preparing the wagon for defense, Ben was running to gain a low mound in the valley floor in an effort to intercept the charging Indians before they reached the wagon. With bullets thumping the grass-covered hump, he made it just as the raiders came into a comfortable range for his rifle. He wasted no time in flattening himself behind the mound and selecting his first target. A squeeze of the trigger, and the warrior disappeared from the racing pony's back. Another second and the Indians were parallel with him now. He knocked another rider from his horse as they swept by him at a distance of forty yards. Now they were in Cleve's range, and he unleashed a blistering volley of fire, shooting as fast as he could pull the trigger and cock his rifle again.

Dead Man realized too late that he had made a fatal error in judgment. Behind him galloped three Indian ponies with empty saddles, and all around him he heard the whine of rifle slugs singing their deadly song. "Run!" he yelled to the others, and pulled his horse sharply toward the ridge. His cry was unnecessary, as the two remaining warriors had already scattered to escape the blistering volley. Ben was on his feet again, running toward the wagon as one last shotgun blast caused one of the riderless horses to kick his hind legs in the air when it caught a load of buckshot in its rump.

"Everybody all right?" he asked as he ran up to them.

"We're okay," a shaken Mary Marple managed to utter. She looked at her husband, who was still holding his shotgun at the ready in case the Indians returned. Then she looked back in the wagon at her daughter. "Are you all right, Victoria?"

"Yes, but I was scared to death for a while there." She smiled at her son then. "We were scared for a little while, weren't we, Caleb?" Caleb immediately insisted that he was not. Then she said what her mother and father were thinking as well. "Thank God you and Cleve were with us."

Cleve walked over to confer with Ben. "I think we mighta gave them Injuns more'n they wanted. I doubt if they'll try it again, now that they know what kinda firepower we're totin'. And we cut their number in half. They'd be crazy to try us again. Whaddaya think?"

"You're probably right," Ben said. "But I think we'd best move on up the river a ways before we think about makin' camp tonight. They might wanna come back for the ones we killed, and there's a couple of horses roamin' around out there somewhere. I didn't see but one of 'em followin' the Indians over the ridge." Cleve nodded in agreement and Ben said, "I'll go get my horse and we'll get started." He turned to leave, then stopped abruptly. In all the excitement, he had forgotten. "I've got fresh antelope meat over by the river. I don't know why I killed two of 'em. I guess I figured we'd rest a day and we'd have time to smoke it, but we can take the best parts and have a big feast tonight." He looked up at Mary, who was settling herself in the wagon seat again. "It'll save a little of that salt pork."

"It'll be a welcome change," she replied.

Graham Barrett sat somberly in the saddle, his eyes focused on the northern horizon, as he held the big Morgan gelding to a gentle lope, following the faint wagon tracks in the grass. As much as he wanted to maintain a brisk pace, he knew he was going to have to rein the horse back to a walk pretty soon. He had been struck with a little bad luck after Ike Gibbs turned back at Ogallala. His horse had thrown a shoe and he had to turn back himself to find a blacksmith. The delay had worsened his already frustrating pursuit of Ben Cutler. *It can't be much farther before I catch up with that wagon,* he thought. His determination to run Cutler to ground increased with each mile he traveled until he sought restitution from the fugitive for every bit of bad luck he encountered. He even blamed Ben for the thrown horseshoe. These thoughts were swirling around in his mind when he was abruptly jerked back to reality by the sudden sound of gunshots.

His initial reaction was to check to be sure his rifle was fully loaded and riding easy in the saddle scabbard. The shots had come from beyond a line of low ridges directly on his path, and from the sound of them, he could identify several different rifles. He immediately thought of the wagon he followed. *They must have been jumped by a Sioux war party*, he thought, for he felt certain that he had almost caught up to them. By his reckoning, he figured he could not be too far from the Niobrara. Maybe they had stopped there for the night. Foremost in his mind now was the thought that the Indians might have killed the entire party, depriving him of the satisfaction he needed in apprehending Ben Cutler. There was no concern for the fate of the other members of the party. Further thoughts along those lines were interrupted then by the sudden appearance of three Indians galloping over the crest of the ridge.

Barrett hauled back sharply on the reins and guided his horse into a gully, the only protection handy at the moment. He was lucky because the Indians were preoccupied with making their escape from the withering rifle fire on the far side of the ridge. Barrett slid off his horse with his rifle ready, but the warriors veered off toward the west, never even looking his way. The gully wasn't deep enough to completely hide his horse, and before they changed directions, the Indians had passed within a hundred yards of him. He also realized then that because he had not been forced to defend himself, there were no rifle shots to alert the folks with the wagon. It was easy to speculate that the people with the wagon had successfully repelled the Indian attack, considering the state of flight he had seen in the war party. He felt his pulse quicken with the thought that he had caught up with his quarry.

Telling himself to be patient, he climbed in the saddle and started for the ridge the Indians had crossed. He needed to see what the situation was on the other side, mindful of the possibility that Cutler and the people he was with would be wary of another attack by the hostiles. *I'll just bide my time,* he thought, *and see what kind of hand I've been dealt.* He really had no way of knowing how much opposition he would face.

Chapter 7

A campsite was selected about three miles upriver from the site of the attack by Dead Man and his warriors. Off to the west, Cleve pointed to two large hills in the otherwise gently rolling prairie. Like two dark monuments, they jutted up from the ground, standing alone in harsh contrast to the prairie around them. "Them hills are big medicine to the Lakota Sioux," Cleve told them. "They say there's bones of their ancient ancestors buried in 'em. I've heard tell that you can see bones in some of the cliffs if you get close enough."

"You ever seen any?" Ben asked.

"Nah, I ain't never had no cravin' to fool around with any kind of spirits. I'd just as soon let 'em be and maybe they'll let me be."

It was beginning to get dark by the time Jonah had started a fire while Ben and Cleve cut some willow limbs to serve as spits for the fresh meat. There still remained a slight feeling of uneasiness on the part of Jonah and the women. It was, after all, their first encounter with hostile Indians and it was difficult to dispense with the feeling that the prairie was crawling with countless parties of savages—this in spite of Cleve's attempt to assure them that most of the Indians were on the reservations, and parties like the one that attacked them were not that prevalent. "A good many of the wild ones have gone north to join up with some of the Sioux that Sittin' Bull took to Canada," Cleve told them. "This bunch that hit us today most likely will have to go back to the reservation, or join their friends up north if they run into anybody else that gives 'em what they got today."

Once the fire was right, Cleve took over the preparation of the meat. Soon the aroma of roasting antelope filled the circle around the fire until most of the fear of another hostile attack was all but forgotten. Everyone ate their fill of the freshly roasted meat, and then some. There was no bother with anything else; no biscuits, no beans, no dried apples, nothing but coffee to wash it down. By the time Mary and Victoria were ready to retire for the night, all parties had backed away from the last pieces of antelope. With eyelids weighed down by full stomachs, sleep would not be difficult to come by.

Primarily to give the women peace of mind, Cleve and Ben decided it best to post a guard, even though both men thought it unnecessary. "I'll stand the first couple of hours," Ben volunteered.

Feeling a much greater part in the protection of the party, Jonah at once piped up. "I'll stand a watch." His ego was inflated with a newfound pride for having helped repel the hostiles with his shotgun. He had not hit anything except the hind end of an Indian pony, but he had gained a great deal of confidence, knowing that he had stood firm and fired his shotgun.

"All right," Cleve said. "In that case, why don't you take the first watch? Two hours—then I'll take the next two, and Ben can finish up." He glanced at Ben for his okay, and Ben nodded. Cleve figured that, if the Indians had any notion of trying again, it would be later on, in the early morning. So it was best that Jonah take the first watch, and Ben, whose eyes were sharper than his, could take the watch just before dawn. The watch settled, Jonah got his shotgun from the wagon and positioned himself beside the fire until Ben advised him that he would be better situated outside the fire's glow where he could see better. Within a few minutes, the camp was quiet except for the steady drone of Cleve's snoring and the occasional whinny of one of the horses.

It had been a long day, climaxing at the frightening attack by the hostiles. It was a day like no other Jonah had ever experienced. He had often wondered if he would respond heroically if put to the test. While he had been terrified at first, and thinking only of flight, he had answered the call to defend honorably, and in his mind, accounted well for himself. Peering out into the darkness of the prairie beyond the opening in the cottonwoods, he thought that he would remember this day as one of his finest. And what better way to celebrate it than with a feast of fresh-killed meat? These thoughts danced around in his mind until there were gradually no conscious thoughts at all, and aided by his full belly, he drifted into peaceful sleep.

Even though Barrett had left his horse to stand with reins on the ground some forty or fifty yards behind him, the Morgan's presence was sniffed out of the evening air by the horses in the camp and announced by inquisitive whinnies. The communication between the horses went unnoticed by those sleeping near the fire. Pausing for a few moments to listen, Barrett knelt on one knee while he scanned the unsuspecting camp. Satisfied there was no one alert to his presence there, he got up and walked into the circle, stopping only briefly to look down at Jonah, dead to the world at his guard post. He carefully took the shotgun from the sleeping man's hand, then continued toward the two bodies on the other side of the fire. Peering down at Cleve, he paused for only a moment, long enough to take the handgun from the holster beside him and draw the Winchester from the saddle sling behind Cleve's head.

A thin smile of satisfaction formed upon his face as he moved several yards farther to stare at the face of the man he hunted. There was no doubt that this was the right man, for the tragic scar shone in the firelight like a jagged flame. Collecting Ben's weapons, as he had done from Jonah and Cleve, he stood silently over the sleeping man, savoring the moment, almost reluctant to wake the camp in order to enjoy his triumph longer. With an unconcerned glance at the wagon, for he anticipated no trouble from the women, he broke the breech on Jonah's shotgun to make sure it was loaded. When he clicked it shut again, Ben sat upright, alert. Barrett slammed him in back of the head, swinging Jonah's shotgun like a club. Ben went facedown in the dirt, knocked senseless. When there was no response from the rest of the camp, Barrett held the shotgun up and fired a load of buckshot into the night sky. Then he stood unmoving while he watched the wild scramble of confusion that resulted. Cleve's frantic fumbling for his missing weapons and the dazed reaction of Jonah reaching for his shotgun served to amuse the big lawman as they soon discovered they were helpless before him.

He stood there, with their weapons piled at his feet, while the camp woke up to what had just taken place. Three heads appeared under the canvas sheets of the wagon as the women and boy peered out at their grim visitor. "You ladies best stay right where you are," Barrett ordered. "This is police business." Returning his attention to Cleve and Jonah, he cautioned them, "I'm a United States deputy marshal, so I advise you not to interfere with this arrest unless you wanna go back in chains with the prisoner."

His mind still reeling, Ben struggled up to his hands and knees, trying to make sense of what had just happened. Barrett watched his efforts dispassionately for a few moments before suddenly swinging the shotgun, knocking Ben to the ground again. The act caused a scream of alarm from the horrified women in the wagon. "I'm arrestin' this man, Ben Cutler, for the murder of a deputy sheriff in Crooked Fork, Kansas," Barrett stated.

Mary Marple was the first to protest. She scrambled down from the wagon, disregarding Barrett's orders to stay put. "You're making a mistake, Marshal," she said. "You've got the wrong man. If it wasn't for him and his friend, we might have all been killed by savage Indians!"

A wry smile parted Barrett's lips. "Oh, I've got the right man, all right. There ain't too many runnin' around loose with a scar like that on their faces."

"Even if he is the right man," Victoria said as she climbed down to join her mother, "you've no reason to treat him like that." She found it almost impossible to believe Ben could be a cold-blooded murderer. The man had a gentle nature. She thought of the way he had been since joining them, and the way he was with her son. Surely there must be some mistake.

"That's the way I treat all murderers," Barrett replied, then swept all of them with a warning gaze before adding, "and anybody that tries to help 'em." He then pursed his lips and whistled two sharp notes. In a few seconds, the dark Morgan gelding trotted into the camp, its reins dragging on the ground. Victoria started to run to offer some aid to Ben, who was struggling to get to his hands and knees again. Barrett stopped her with a warning shot from his revolver, kicking up dirt a few feet in front of her. "Leave him be!" he roared, pointing the pistol directly at her. Her mother grabbed her arm and held her back, terrified that the marshal might come closer with the next shot.

When his horse came up to him and stopped, Barrett untied a coil of rope from the saddle. "Get up from there," he ordered. Still woozy from the blows to his head, Ben staggered to his feet to stand swaying while a trickle of blood ran down the back of his neck. "Stick out your hands," Barrett commanded. Knowing he had little choice, Ben did as he was told and stood there on shaky legs while the marshal bound his wrists.

Watching helplessly to this point, and getting madder by the second, Cleve took a step closer to the pile of weapons at Barrett's feet. Barrett immediately responded. "Try it! Goddamn it, I wish you would!"

"Don't try anythin', Cleve," Ben managed to say. "No sense in gettin' yourself killed. This son of a bitch will shoot you."

"Now, that's a fact," Barrett crowed, "and damn good advice." He cocked an eye at Cleve and asked, "What's your name? I might have paper on you."

"None of your damn business, that's my name," Cleve responded. "You ain't got no paper on me, and you ought not have none on him. He shot that low-down deputy in Crooked Fork in self-defense after the deputy killed his wife and child and left him for dead."

Barrett gave Cleve a dismissive glance and said, "I expect that's his story, but it was hardly self-defense. Cutler walked right up to the deputy while he was havin' his supper, and shot him down without no warnin'. We don't call that self-defense in Kansas."

"You ain't even in Kansas," Cleve retorted. "You ain't got no jurisdiction here."

"I'm a U.S. marshal. I've got jurisdiction wherever the hell I happen to be. Now, you'd do yourself a favor if you'd just back down and keep your nose outta official business."

Somewhat recovered from the blows that had knocked him senseless, Ben said, "Back down, Cleve. There's no sense for you to get mixed up in this. Looks like he's got all the cards."

"That's right," Barrett said with a sarcastic smile. "I've got all the cards. Now, we'll get the prisoner on his horse and we'll leave you good people to enjoy the rest of your evenin'." Guessing that it would be too much trouble to spar with Cleve, he locked his gaze on Jonah, who was still in a state of shock from the startling episode. "You!" Barrett ordered. "Fetch his horse over here. From what I've been told, it'll be that buckskin yonder."

With no notion to defy the formidable lawman, Jonah did as he was told and brought Ben's horse into the small clearing. Upon Barrett's instructions, he saddled the horse, then helped Ben up in the saddle. "I'm sorry, Ben," he muttered before he stepped back out of the way, laden with the guilt that if he had not fallen asleep, things might not have turned out this badly.

"Don't fret over it, Jonah," Ben said. "Cleve will get you to Deadwood. I hope you find your son-in-law all right."

"Well, folks," Barrett announced grandly, "it's been a real pleasure meetin' you, but I've got a long ride ahead of me, so I reckon we'd better get started." He pulled a length of rope from the coil and ran it through the lever of Cleve's Winchester, then through the buckled gun belts holding his pistol. He took the end of the rope and looped it around his saddle horn. Next he ejected all the cartridges from Ben's rifle and put it back in the scabbard—the pistol and belt he hung on his saddle horn along with Cleve's weapons.

"You can't leave us out here with no weapons," Cleve complained.

"I ought to," Barrett replied, "for harborin' an escaped prisoner." He let that sink in before continuing. "I'll drop 'em off yonder, by those three tallest cottonwoods. You oughta be able to find 'em when it gets light enough in the mornin'." Having completed what he came to do, he rode out of the camp, leaving them to stare in shocked silence until he disappeared into the darkness.

"I can't believe we were traveling with a murderer," Mary said, still finding it hard to think of Ben as a criminal.

Cleve immediately spoke up in Ben's defense. "He ain't no murderer. He killed a deputy, but he ain't no murderer." He then told them how the incident occurred, as Ben had told him, and which he believed was the truth. "That deputy sheriff had left Ben for dead," he concluded, "along with his wife and kid, burned his home to the ground. When Ben got back on his feet, he went after the deputy—anybody would have. And it ain't right to send a man to prison for that."

There was a long silence after Cleve had finished talking, as Jonah and his family absorbed the tragic story of the man they had so recently embraced as a friend. Victoria's thoughts immediately went back to the times she had seen Ben holding the silver chain. Young Caleb was the first to breach the void. "Then he didn't really fall on a crosscut saw, did he?"

"No," Cleve replied. "That deputy hit him with a sawed-off sword." There followed another long period when no one could say what to do now. "I reckon I could try to trail 'em, but there ain't much I can do to help Ben. I doubt that marshal will make it very easy to find my guns in them trees. I'll probably have to wait till daylight to find 'em." He was in a quandary when it came to making the right decision. He had heard Ben tell Jonah that he would see them through to Deadwood, and Cleve felt that responsibility. He didn't like Jonah's chances if he left them alone and went back to try to help Ben. Then, too, he had to consider the fact that Barrett was a U.S. deputy marshal, doing his job, even if he was wrong as could be, and a son of a bitch to boot. Right or wrong, Cleve didn't like the idea of going after a marshal.

To enforce that concern, Jonah spoke up. "What can you do, even if you trail them? You can't help Ben unless you shoot the deputy marshal—and you can't do that."

"I know it," Cleve said, obviously distraught, "but it don't make me feel no better."

Caleb was the only member of the party who finally fell asleep that night. The others stayed awake, discussing possibilities for Ben's salvation over and over, finding none that would solve the problem. In the end, as daylight approached, the only conclusion that could be reached was that life was not fair, and Ben was the unfortunate victim of one of fate's unkindest plots. "Well," Jonah finally declared, "I guess we should break camp and get started again."

"What about this meat we've got all cut in strips and ready to dry and smoke?" Mary asked. The antelope had been forgotten in all the chaos of the night before.

"Yeah," Cleve mused as he looked over the racks he and Ben had devised, "we're gonna wish we had some of this meat if the bacon starts to run out."

"I say we should stay here and dry it," Victoria declared. "After last night, we could all use a little more rest, anyway." She had to admit to herself that she was a bit reluctant to move on without Ben. Maybe staying over an extra day or two, until the meat was ready, would make the departure easier. Cleve shrugged his indifference and her father and mother nodded their agreement with the suggestion. That settled, Victoria put more coffee on to boil and Cleve went to look for his firearms.

Ben rolled with the buckskin's even gait, his wrists tied together and bound to his saddle horn, staring monotonously at the broad back of the deputy marshal. His head ached as a result of the blows he had received, but he felt pretty sure now that nothing was broken. They had ridden late into the night, and Ben knew that Barrett was going to have to stop soon or he would tire the horses to exhaustion. Ben's buckskin was still pacing smartly, but the Morgan Barrett rode was beginning to droop. He had plenty to think about during the long hours of the night. Without question, escape was the only option he would consider, but he was not sure if he would be given much opportunity. Barrett had far too much experience in the transport of prisoners, and he had already demonstrated his ability to control a potentially dangerous situation when he took over their entire camp with little trouble at all.

Finally, when they came to a tiny stream that seemed to materialize from nowhere, Barrett announced that they would stop there to rest the horses. A man not accustomed to carelessness, he untied Ben's wrists from the saddle horn and checked the knot tying his hands together. Satisfied, he backed away a couple of steps and ordered Ben to dismount. Ben grabbed the saddle horn, swung his leg over, and dropped to the ground, staggering a step because of the lack of circulation in his legs. Barrett watched him closely as he ordered him to find kindling for a fire. Now that he had his man in custody, and headed to prison,

Barrett's attitude toward him was no longer so bit-
terly antagonistic, seemingly replaced by one of bored
indifference. There was no evidence of concern, however, for the injuries he had caused to Ben's skull, and
no effort to clean away the blood already drying on
the back of his neck. When Barrett decided to catch a
couple of hours of sleep to make up for riding all night,
he bound Ben hand and foot, then tied him to a tree.
Satisfied that his prisoner was helpless to escape, Barrett drifted off to sleep right away. With Ben, however,
trussed up like a lamb for the slaughter, sleep would
not come, no matter how hard he tried. It was of no
concern to his captor. In fact, he had a notion that this
was part of Barrett's strategy, to keep him in a state of
exhaustion to diminish thoughts of escape.

With thoughts of Jonah, Mary, Victoria, Caleb, even
Cleve, far behind him, Ben's only concern was the
opportunity to escape before reaching Lansing and
the iron bars that would lock him away. Reverting to
the indifferent frame of mind he had possessed before
crossing paths with Cleve, when he had no dread of
death, he was prepared to risk even the smallest opportunity, no matter the odds. With his family gone, death
was better than prison. So far, however, there had been
no possible break in Barrett's routine for handling a
prisoner.

After the first night and the next morning with vir-
tually no words from the somber lawman, other than
direct commands, Ben was surprised when Barrett
decided to make conversation when they stopped again
to rest the horses. The spot Barrett picked was a shallow valley with a free-flowing stream down the middle. The thing that made it unusual was the mature

cottonwood tree standing by the bank, the only tree in sight in any direction. "I'm damn glad you've got some provisions," Barrett suddenly blurted as he searched through Ben's saddlebags. Holding a bag of coffee beans he had just found, he turned and pointed a finger at Ben. "That's the reason you're gonna have somethin' to eat on this trip. I'll fix food for you as long as you supply it. Hell, most of the murderin' scum I escort back ain't got shit. Hell, I ain't gonna feed 'em." He cracked that thin smile Ben had already been accustomed to when Barrett was about to say something sarcastic. "But you're gonna be fat and sassy when I get you back where you can get you some of that good prison food."

Thinking that the big lawman might be letting up on his intensity of purpose, Ben decided to make an attempt to engage him in further conversation. *Maybe,* he thought, *if I get him to think I'm resigned to serve my time, he may get a little lax in his rigid routine.* "Whaddaya think my chances are they'll make me serve the full ten years?" he asked.

"Ten years?" Barrett responded. "Is that all Judge Blake gave you for killin' a deputy sheriff? If you had any sense, you'da just gone ahead and served the time. You stepped in a big cow pie when you ran. Hell, boy, I'll bet they'll double your sentence now—might even hang you."

"What would you have done if somebody killed your wife and child, and left you for dead—burned your house down, your barn, too?" Ben asked, intent upon searching for any sign of empathy in the big man's heart.

"Why, I'da gutted the son of a bitch and strung his entrails on the fence," Barrett replied, his eyes gleaming with the thought of it. He looked at Ben then and smiled as he walked over to stand close over him. Suddenly, he lashed out, planting one huge fist flat against Ben's jaw. Caught completely by surprise, Ben was not set to take the blow and ended up on his side, his face in the dirt. "And just so you know, I don't give a damn whether you had reason to shoot that bastard or not—all the same to me. My job is to take you in and that's what I'm gonna do, so it ain't no use in you tryin' to get friendly with me."

Lying there, stunned for a few moments, with his face still flat against the dirt, Ben tried to shake it off, wondering how much abuse his head could take from this brute before his brains were completely rattled. In another moment, his eyes cleared and he sat up, unprepared for what happened next. Towering over him, his malicious grin still in place, then gone in the next second, Barrett uttered a surprised grunt as the shaft of an arrow suddenly appeared in his chest. Staggering backward, he instinctively grabbed the arrow and tried to pull it out as the snap of a bullet passed over Ben's head to make a small black hole in Barrett's belly. The big lawman dropped to his knees and remained there, his eyes wide as if staring into the great unknown until two more arrows tore into his body, causing him to finally keel slowly over.

It all happened in the span of a few dozen seconds. Ben knew the only reason he was not dead was that he was flat on the ground when the attack came. Aware that he probably had moments only to make a desperate effort to keep from joining Barrett, he crawled over to the dying man. Barrett's eyes stared lifelessly as Ben rolled him on his side to get to the bowie knife the lawman wore on his belt. With no idea how long he had before the Indians would be upon him, he pulled the knife and struggled furiously to cut the rope binding his hands together. More shots passed over his head as he worked away at the stubborn rope, at this point with no choice but to ignore the bullets.

He heard the pounding of their horses' hooves bearing down on him as the knife finally cut through his bonds. His heart racing now, he drew Barrett's .44 from the holster and, without taking the time to aim, rolled over on his back and emptied the gun at the charging ponies. In his haste, his accuracy suffered, but although he didn't hit one of the three warriors galloping toward him, his sudden barrage caused them to veer from their intended path. With time only to scramble over Barrett's body, Ben lunged toward the lawman's saddle and the Winchester rifle in the scabbard. Looking around him frantically, he spotted the three warriors as they pulled up beyond the stream and prepared to charge again. In the small clearing Barrett had selected to make his camp, there was no natural cover, so he used the only protection available. Keeping as flat to the ground as he could, he pulled himself up behind the massive body of the late deputy marshal and laid the Winchester across Barrett's shoulder. From this macabre redoubt, he sent five quick shots at the three warriors just as they crossed the stream, killing one and wounding another.

Wolf Kill cried out in pain, "I'm hit!" He jerked his horse's head around and buried his heels in the animal's sides. "Get out of his range!"

Dead Man pulled his horse around to follow, but hesitated to look back at the rifleman in anger. *"Nah-zay,"* he exclaimed. It was the scar-faced white man who had been his nemesis at the wagon. Infuriated to have been beaten back twice by the white devil, he held his pony back long enough to scream his defiance before wisely galloping after Wolf Kill.

Finding it hard to believe that he was still alive, Ben got to his feet and watched the two departing warriors until they disappeared from his sight. He looked down then at the body of the deputy marshal at his feet, the arrows buried half the length of their shafts in his chest, and thought, *I didn't kill him, but they'll probably say I did*. He wouldn't think of the irony of it until sometime later. The marshal had saved his life the first time when he had suddenly knocked him down on the ground. Judging by the number of bullet holes in the corpse, he'd likely saved him again by shielding him with his body. The foremost thought in his mind at the moment, however, was to get his saddle on his horse and get out of there before the Indians returned. He had been given his life back by the three warriors. Too bad he had been forced to thank them by killing one and wounding another. A lot of things in life didn't make sense. This was just another one of them.

He was thankful that Barrett had tied the horses close to the camp, so the shooting didn't cause them to scatter. He quickly saddled the buckskin, and remembering that the marshal had emptied his rifle, he loaded the magazine again and slid it into the scabbard. He paused then to take a long look at the lawman's Morgan gelding. It was too fine a horse to set free on the prairie, but he wondered about the wisdom of being in possession of a dead marshal's horse and saddle. *I'll decide later*, he thought, and saddled the horse. It made it easier to carry the extra weapons and cartridges, all of which would certainly come in handy. He had an uneasy feeling about searching the marshal's body for anything else of value, but he reasoned that it made no sense at all to leave anything useful to any scavenger that happened upon the body. His search resulted in the gain of a pocketknife and a small amount of money. When he was finished, he stood up and gazed down at the man who had run him to ground. "I suppose the decent thing to do would be to bury you," he said. "That's the least I could do since you saved my bacon." He lingered a moment more before deciding. "I ain't got the time," he said, and turned to leave, only to pause again. As an afterthought, he reached down to pull one of the arrows out of the corpse. The head had managed to attach itself firmly to something inside Barrett's chest, causing Ben to have to break it off. He examined the arrow briefly before pushing it into his saddle sling with his rifle. In the saddle again, he turned back to retrace the trail they had traveled to this fateful point in the prairie. *I hope to hell those damn Indians have finally had enough of me*, he thought as he gave the buckskin his heels.

Leaving Jonah and the women to finish packing up the dried venison, Cleve rode out around the camp on a wide circle, just to see if there was any trouble that might be coming their way. They had stayed at that campsite for two days to take care of the meat that Ben had supplied. Cleve knew that it might not be the smartest thing to do, in view of the fact that they had already been attacked once by Sioux warriors. Still bothered by the circumstances that prevented him from helping Ben escape from the law, he realized how much he missed having Ben's solid presence in the face of danger. He was about to tell himself to get his mind back on scouting the perimeter of his camp when his eye caught movement to the southeast. He immediately focused on the low ridge where he was sure he had seen something. After a few moments, he found it. At that great distance, it was hard to determine exactly what it was, but as it gradually moved closer, he was sure that it was a rider leading a horse. Indian or white man? He was still too far away to tell. At least it appeared to be only one man, and one man, friend or foe, he felt certain he could handle. *Besides,* he thought, *I ain't sure he's heading toward our camp yet.* That question was answered within the next few seconds, when the rider swung to a more westerly direction, which would lead him directly to their camp. "Well, hell," he complained. "Looks like we're gonna have company." Figuring he had better return to the wagon to alert Jonah and the women, he remained for one long, last look. "Well, I'll be go to hell," he uttered then, scarcely able to believe his eyes. He at once found himself in a quandary of confusing thoughts. While overjoyed at the sight of his partner, he was also concerned with the circumstances of Ben's freedom. If Cleve wasn't mistaken, that looked like the deputy marshal's horse that Ben was leading, and Cleve could think of but one way the horse could find itself in Ben's possession. "That might be a helluva mistake," he muttered.

He waited until Ben had approached within a hundred yards of the trees, from which he had watched him, before riding out in the open and waving his arm back and forth. Ben pulled up abruptly as soon as he caught sight of him, then recognizing Cleve, started toward him at a gallop. "I swear," Cleve called out to him as he pulled up beside him, "I never figured I'd see you again." He didn't ask what happened right away, not really sure he wanted to know.

Ben answered his question without being asked. "I didn't kill him," he said. "Indians got him—some of the same ones that attacked the wagon, I think." He went on then to explain what had happened, and how he was able to escape.

"Thank goodness for that," Cleve remarked, greatly relieved. "I sure am glad to see you, but I was afraid you'd got to killin' lawmen as a habit. Don't a lot of folks care about that deputy you shot in Crooked Fork, but a federal marshal, that's somethin' else. They wouldn't never stop huntin' you for that."

Ben reached for the arrow he had jammed in his rifle sling and handed it to Cleve. "I brought you a souvenir in case you were thinkin' what you're thinkin'."

"Ah, hell, Ben," Cleve protested, "you know your word's good enough for me." He wouldn't admit it, but the arrow went a long way to enforce his confidence in his partner. He turned the arrow over several times, scrutinizing the markings on the shaft. "Lakota Sioux, I reckon. I've seen 'em with these markin's on 'em before and they were Sioux, but I don't know one tribe from the other. They're all Injuns. Some are friendly and some ain't." He handed the arrow back to Ben. "Come on, you got here just in time. We're fixin' to move outta here and get on our way again. There's gonna be some surprised folks when they see you."

"I'm surprised myself," Ben said. "I didn't expect you'd still be here. I thought you'd be long gone."

Cleve laughed. "I reckon we woulda been if you hadn't left us with so much meat to cure."

"Surprise" was a mild term for the reaction felt by Jonah's family when the two partners came riding back into their camp. But what was initially a welcome sight was followed by a feeling of foreboding when they saw the empty saddle on the marshal's horse, just as Cleve had experienced earlier. As Ben stepped down from his saddle, he was met with questioning faces, with the exception of the expression of joy on Caleb's face. The boy ran up to greet the ominous-looking man. "I knew you'd be back to take care of us," he said.

Ben reached down and playfully tousled Caleb's hair. "You did?" he responded. "Well, you knew more than I did." He looked around at the cautious faces confronting him, and guessed what they were thinking. "I didn't kill him," he declared softly.

"It was Injuns!" Cleve blurted, then went on to relate the incident as Ben had told it to him. "Ben's got one of the arrows he pulled outta the marshal's body. Show 'em, Ben."

He retrieved the headless arrow from his saddle scabbard and handed it to Caleb, who examined it in awe until Victoria told him to bring it to his grandpa. Jonah made a show of looking the arrow over, although he had no idea if it was Sioux or not. Both Victoria and her mother continued to study Ben's face as Jonah held the arrow. There was a strong desire on the part of both mother and daughter to believe Ben had no part in the marshal's death. But there were emotions much like their initial feelings when Jonah had first brought the two guides to their wagon in Ogallala. The man just looked capable of violence, even more so with a new swelling on the side of his eye, the result of Barrett's fist. Had it occurred during a fight that ended with the marshal's death? It was difficult not to think of such possibilities.

There was no time for discussion now, since the wagon was packed, the horses hitched, and the fire extinguished, so they pulled out of camp to continue the trek to Deadwood. With Ben and Cleve out front, they rolled into Dakota Territory during the afternoon, and both scouts turned their attention to finding the next campsite. Cleve came upon a small stream some seventy-five yards west of the trail they had ridden. He called Ben over to see.

"Looks okay to me," Ben said. "You got water and enough trees to hide in. It beats everythin' I've found east of the trail." That settled, they rode back to meet the wagon and led it to the campsite. The women immediately set to gathering firewood and setting up the camp while Jonah, with Caleb's help, unhitched the team and took them to water. Everyone was so accustomed to the routine that there was little need for oversight on anyone's part. In less than an hour's time, they sat down to supper. Sitting a little more apart from the others, in comparison with nights passed, Ben ate his meal in absolute quiet. There was none of the normal light conversation that had become a regular part of the day's end. Ben was certain he knew the reason why, so he finished his supper and got up from the circle around the fire. "I'm gonna take a little ride around this valley and just take a look at where we'll be goin' in the mornin'," he announced. When Cleve started to get up to join him, Ben told him to stay put and help Jonah finish the pot of coffee. Cleve needed no more encouragement than that. He settled back in his place.

"Can I go, Uncle Ben?" Caleb asked, jumping to his feet.

"I don't care," Ben said, "if your mama says it's all right." Seeing the look of indecision on Victoria's face, he said, "I won't be out long. We'll be back before his bedtime."

"I don't see any harm," Victoria said after a moment's hesitation.

He placed Caleb behind the saddle, then climbed on board himself and they started out of camp at a gentle walk. Ben had an idea that there needed to be some discussion among the others in regard to the circumstances of his return. He had sensed a difference in their attitude toward him all during the day's travel and he figured this would give them the opportunity to decide if they were better off without him. He couldn't say that he blamed them if they were a bit concerned about it.

Ben's notions about a definite coolness toward him were not a creation of his imagination, with the exception, of course, of Cleve Goganis. In the short time since they had become partners, Cleve was secure in the knowledge that he could count on Ben Cutler one hundred percent in word and deed. Jonah and the two ladies were not as certain. Their concern was not that he would do them any harm. They were more troubled about their association with someone who might have killed a federal law officer. Mary turned to Cleve and asked point-blank, "Do you think Indians really killed that deputy marshal? Ben may have had that arrow all along."

Cleve didn't hesitate to confirm that he believed Ben's story without doubt. "As for that arrow," he said, "I been livin' with him night and day ever since Wichita, and I can tell you he ain't never had no arrow. I'da seen it."

Victoria spoke up then. "I'm sure Ben would never do anything intentionally to harm us. I think what we're concerned about is what the law might do when they find out their deputy is dead, and whether or not we would wind up in trouble because we're with him. They might think we had something to do with it."

"Or even punish us for harboring a criminal," Mary interjected.

Cleve was astonished to learn of their concerns, considering the fact that without Ben and him, these folks would be lying out there on the prairie without their scalps. *Well*, he thought, *I suppose it's up to women to worry about everything.* A glance in Jonah's direction, however, told him that the frail little man had much the same worried expression that adorned his ladies' faces. "In the first place," he explained patiently, "it's gonna be one helluva long time before the marshal in Topeka knows that somethin' happened to one of his deputies. By the time he figures out his man ain't comin' back, there won't be nothin' left of that deputy to find—even if he knew where to look for him. If we run into any more marshals between here and Deadwood, they'd have to come from the moon. So I think you're wastin' your time worryin' about associatin' with an outlaw." He paused to spit in the fire. "And I'm damn glad he showed up again, 'cause we'll likely meet up with a helluva lot more Sioux between here and Deadwood than we do deputy marshals."

No one commented for a couple of minutes while they rethought the situation. Then Jonah spoke. "Cleve's right. We've got no call to question Ben's word. He's been nothing but a friend to us. I don't think he's guilty of anything but having bad luck." He turned to look accusingly at his wife and daughter. "What was he supposed to do when the Indians killed that marshal? Ride all the way back to Kansas and turn himself in?"

"Of course not," Mary responded. "Don't talk foolishness. Of course we're glad to have Ben back with us."

Victoria smiled to hear her mother's complete reversal. She was genuinely thankful to have his strong presence with them again. They had a long way to go yet before reaching the Black Hills and Deadwood, traveling over country that the Sioux still believed rightfully theirs, guaranteed to them forever through treaties broken by white men. She felt a lot safer with Ben along with them. When Ben and Caleb returned from their scout, she met them at the campfire. "I saved you a cup of coffee," she said to Ben. "And you, young man," she told her son, "can get yourself ready for bed."

Ben glanced at Cleve, sitting comfortably with his back against a young cottonwood, a smug smile upon his grizzled face. He took the coffee cup from Victoria, then shifted his gaze to glance at Jonah and Mary standing near the wagon, each wearing compassionate smiles. At that moment, he felt that the jury had come in and he had been acquitted of his crimes. It was a feeling of mixed emotions, for he wasn't aware that he was guilty of any crimes. He welcomed the change, however, for he had developed a genuine fondness for these people, and he had regretted the uneasiness they had recently felt over his unexpected return. He sat down next to Cleve to drink his coffee, leaving his horse to wait before being unsaddled.

Victoria picked up the blanket she had been seated upon and carried it over to sit down with them. "Well, did Caleb talk your ears off?" she asked Ben.

Surprised by her overture, Ben replied, "Oh no. He's already learned that you gotta be quiet when you're scoutin' someplace." They both laughed then. "That boy of yours . . ." He paused, searching for words. "He's a pistol. I bet his daddy is proud of him."

"I suppose so," Victoria replied, a smile of pride gracing her plain face.

"How long's it been since your husband's seen Caleb?" Cleve asked.

"Over a year," Victoria answered. "He won't believe his eyes when he sees how much he's grown." She was curious to know about Ben's little boy, but thought it better not to ask, especially since Cleve had told her how Ben's wife and son had died. So she directed her question to Cleve. "Do you ever think about a family, Cleve?"

Her question brought a chuckle. "Oh, gracious no, miss. I ain't never felt no urge to strap myself down with wife and young'uns—beggin' your pardon. That's somethin' that's right for some men, but don't fit at all to fellers like me."

She laughed at his response. "Why, I bet you'd be a wonderful father with a little baby to bounce on your knee," she teased.

He shook his shoulders as if a chill had run down his spine. "I'd just as soon you hung an anvil around my neck." He quickly recovered then to say, "Course, if they was all as spunky as Caleb, that'd be a little different."

Afraid that her next questions about family would be directed at him, Ben abruptly got to his feet. "Thank you for the coffee. I guess I'd best unsaddle my horse before he starts fussin'."

Chapter 8

They broke camp early the next morning with a new sense of urgency. Already enough time had been spent on delays at Ogallala as well as the past couple of days just taken. August was just about used up and they were still possibly two weeks away from Deadwood. It was difficult to predict their daily rate of travel because of the uncertainty of Indian attacks as well as the terrain ahead of them. Cleve had been to the Black Hills on an earlier occasion before the strike in Deadwood Gulch, but not with a wagon. While the memory of the route he took on that occasion had faded somewhat in his recollection, he still remembered the rugged, rocky trails he followed once he reached the hills. With that in mind, it increased the necessity to make as good time as possible while still on the prairie. They decided to start out an hour earlier in the mornings and stop for the night an hour later, depending upon the availability of water.

Cleve and Ben decided it best to ride out ahead and

to each side of the wagon, acting as scouts, because of the danger of hostile Indian parties. So each morning Cleve would indicate the line of travel for Jonah and he would guide on some point in the distance. As they had done ever since leaving Omaha, Victoria and Caleb, and sometimes Mary, would walk beside the wagon. The travel plan went without incident for the first couple of days, but their good fortune was not to last. Trouble was still in store for them in the form of one vengeful Lakota warrior.

Resting in a camp of twenty-four people, Dead Man cleaned the last scrap of meat from an antelope rib and tossed it in the fire before him. Looking across the fire at his friend, Wolf Kill, as he ate one-handed, the result of a bullet in his shoulder, Dead Man scowled, thinking of the pain he had suffered because of one white man. *Nah-zay*, he thought, the scar-faced white devil who had killed four of his friends. Man Above must have sent this white man to test him, for he was there with the wagon; then he was there with the lawman. He pulled out the badge he had taken from the lawman's body and stared at it. Its medicine was not strong enough to protect the large white man. Even now his scalp was drying on Dead Man's lance. He squeezed the badge hard as he thought about the scalp he wanted so badly, until he felt the edges of the badge cutting into his palm. He did not relieve the pressure, but stared defiantly at the trickle of blood that dripped from the pad of his hand.

His anger was born with the breaking of the treaty with the Lakota that said Paha Sapa—what the *wasicu* knew as the Black Hills—would belong to the Lakota

Sioux forever. It was a sacred place to the Sioux, and still the hated whites kept pouring into the hills, looking for the foolish yellow dirt they craved. Dead Man was angry that most of his people had gone to the reservation to live like camp dogs, awaiting the white man's scraps. His hatred for these people who invaded his lands was such that he desperately needed a face to put upon it—and now he had found that face—one appropriately wearing an ugly scar. He felt that if he could kill this demon, it would be a major defeat for the white men, so this is what he resolved to do.

"Your hand is bleeding," Wolf Kill said, when Dead Man seemed not to notice. "What are you thinking so hard about?"

"I am going to kill the scar-faced white man," Dead Man replied.

"How do you know where to find him?" Wolf Kill asked.

"He will find me," Dead Man answered. "I will find the wagon and he will be there. It is me he plagues, so if I find the wagon, he will come to drive me away. But this time, he won't drive me away because I will defy him and his medicine."

Wolf Kill was skeptical. "I think his medicine is his gun that shoots many times and it is too strong. I say it is best to leave him alone. Two times we have tested his medicine and there are four fewer of us, and I am wounded. We should go with Red Sky and his people. There are too many soldier patrols in this valley now." Dead Man frowned, displeased with his friend's comments. He had suffered too much because of the scar-face, and he was convinced that his death would change this war between the Sioux and the white man in the Indians' favor. "Have you talked with Red Sky about this man?" Wolf Kill asked. "Is he going to send warriors with you?"

"No," Dead Man replied, his tone reflecting his anger. "He wants to keep his warriors close to protect the women and children. He wants to leave this camp and move downriver."

"I'm sorry I can't go with you," Wolf Kill said. "With one arm, I would be no good to you, anyway. I am going with Red Sky."

"It's all right," Dead Man assured him. "This thing is for me to do. I alone am the one to be tested. I will find the wagon. It leaves a trail easy to follow, and he will be there waiting for me. Then I will kill him."

Ben counted eight Indians—four men, two women, and two children—two packhorses, one pulling a travois loaded with their belongings. They were crossing directly over the line Cleve had set out for the wagon, traveling from east to west. Lying on his stomach in the high grass that covered the top of a slight ridge, he watched them until they had disappeared off to his left, probably passing before Cleve by then. It was the second small group they had seen during the past two days' travel. Cleve seemed to think it was a sign that there was a big gathering of bands somewhere, maybe Wyoming Territory. At any rate, they had not spotted the two scouts or the wagon behind them. He crawled back down the ridge to his horse and climbed in the saddle again. He had thought that it was time to look for a good spot to camp, but upon seeing the Indians, he figured it would be better to push on a little farther before stopping for the night. When he examined the

Sioux party's tracks, he discovered a great many more, older ones, which told him that it was a commonly used east-to-west trail they traveled, and therefore a definite reason to move on to find a better place.

There had been many streams in the last few miles, so he wasn't worried about passing up the one he was now crossing. In less than a quarter of an hour, he saw Cleve cutting across the prairie to intercept him. He seemed to be in no hurry, so Ben continued on the course he was riding and let Cleve catch up to him. "You see that last little party of Injuns?" Cleve asked when he pulled up alongside him.

"Yeah. Looks like there's a meetin' somewhere yonder way," Ben answered, pointing toward the west. "I'm thinkin' it's gettin' on about quittin' time for the day."

"Me, too," Ben said. "Let's stop at the next likely stream and wait for Jonah to catch up."

They found a good campsite before going another mile and a half, so they dismounted and let the horses drink while Ben walked back to the edge of the trees that bordered the stream and looked for the wagon. "Jonah's draggin'," he said when there was no sign of the wagon. "Horses must be gettin' tired."

"I didn't think we'd got that far ahead of him," Cleve said, walking up to stand beside Ben. They both stared back over the way they had just come. After another twenty minutes had passed, he said, "Maybe we oughta go on back and look for 'em."

They both climbed on their horses again and started back. In a short while they spotted the wagon standing in a wide treeless draw, the horses idly grazing on the prairie grass while Jonah and the others stood around the back of the wagon. "Uh-oh," Cleve said. "Looks like trouble." They urged their horses into a lope and pulled them to a stop beside the wagon. "What's the trouble?" Cleve asked.

"Wheel," Jonah replied, "same one I had fixed in Ogallala. It doesn't look like they did a very good job." He then showed them how the spokes had dried out enough to pull away from the iron tire. "If I go much farther on it, it's gonna collapse."

"Can you fix it?" Cleve asked.

"Yes, I can shore it up like I did last time—enough to hold it together until we get to Deadwood, I guess. It'll take a little time, though. I'll have to take the wheel off."

"Well, let's get you out of the open," Ben said. "Can you drive it another half mile till we get to a stream up ahead?"

"I think so," Jonah replied.

He climbed back up on the seat and started the horses. The two women and Caleb walked along behind him until the boy ran up beside the buckskin and Ben reached down and picked him up. Perched behind the saddle, he grinned at his mother as he wrapped his arms around Ben's waist. "I declare," Mary Marple said, "I believe you could lose that boy."

"I think you're right," Victoria replied with a chuckle. "He wouldn't keep him long before he'd drop him back on my doorstep, though."

Jonah pulled the wagon into the cottonwoods lining the wide stream and unhitched the horses. When the best place to build the fire was decided upon, the men gathered firewood. Soon the women had supper cooking, while Cleve watered his and Jonah's horses and hobbled the team so they could graze. As was his custom, Ben, with Caleb behind the saddle, rode out to scout the terrain around their camp. When everything looked peaceful to his satisfaction, he returned to the camp and unsaddled the buckskin while Caleb told his mother about the antelope they had seen on the other side of the stream. It would have been easy enough to bring down some fresh meat for supper, Ben explained to Mary. But he didn't think it wise to fire his rifle when they had seen so many stray parties of Indians during the last couple of days of travel. "Well, we've certainly got enough put away from the last two you shot," Mary said as she went about helping her daughter prepare some of the smoked venison. Ben went over to give Jonah a hand. He had already started bracing the wagon up in preparation for removing the right rear wheel. Cleve was standing by in a supervising capacity, generously offering advice.

Taking a close look at the wheel, after Jonah got it off the axle, Ben suggested that he could probably shape a couple of replacement spokes from a cottonwood limb with his hatchet and Graham Barrett's bowie knife. Cottonwood was not especially the ideal wood for spokes, but it should do just fine until they reached Deadwood. So he worked on the limbs until breaking for supper, then finished them after they had eaten. When the job was finally finished, the wheel appeared to be solid enough, so they were set to start out again in the morning with no delay in their travel.

The camp was almost ready to start out. Cleve was helping Jonah pack up some of the luggage and supplies that had been removed to make working on the wheel easier, while the women packed away the cooking utensils for travel. Ben rode out about a mile ahead to see what might lie in their path. This time, he was able to get away from the camp without his frequent companion, Caleb, the boy having walked into the woods downstream to answer nature's call.

Crouching low behind a thicket of bullberry bushes, a lone figure drew his knife as the boy approached. There could be no sound to alert the people at the wagon. Dead Man prepared to grab the youngster and muffle his screams while he slit his throat. Nearing the bushes that hid the vicious warrior, Caleb abruptly decided to pick a better spot than the berry bushes, and selected a willow thicket instead. Dead Man relaxed the tension in his legs and dropped to one knee. There was still the matter of silencing the boy. He would have to be dealt with, for Dead Man could not afford to have the camp alerted to his presence. Being careful not to move a branch, lest the rustle of leaves might cause the child to run, he slowly rose to a crouch again, and carefully placing one foot in front of the other, he moved toward the unsuspecting boy in the willow trees.

His attention captured by a frog sitting in the edge of the stream, Caleb amused himself by throwing tiny pieces of willow twigs at the amphibian to see if he could make him jump. His distraction was sufficient to cause him to be unaware of the savage and the razor-sharp knife blade in his hand. Suddenly, the frog jumped, and Caleb, having done all nature's business he was going to do, lunged in an effort to catch it. It was no contest. The frog hopped successfully away from the boy with his trousers around his ankles.

"Caleb," his mother's call came from the camp.

"Yessum, I'm coming," Caleb answered as the dark

shadow hovering over him sank quickly back in the willows. The boy gave his bottom a quick swipe with the cloth intended for the purpose and ran back toward the wagon without once looking behind him.

Following the boy's path, moving cautiously from one spot of cover to the next, Dead Man made his way to a double-trunked cottonwood from which he could see into the camp. He knelt to watch the activity of the family preparing to move. He saw the two women, the boy, and two men, but the *nah-zay* was not there. The Lakota warrior had been so sure that the scar-faced one would be there that he was beside himself with frustration. He lifted his rifle. At this close range, he could easily shoot the two men before they had time to defend themselves. The women would be no trouble to kill after that. He raised the carbine and laid the front sight on the middle of Cleve's back, remembering the short stocky man as one of the two with repeating rifles. With his finger on the trigger, he hesitated when a thought occurred. What if Scar was scouting ahead of them and might be with the wagon after all? Dead Man slowly lowered the rifle. He decided he could not afford the risk of alerting the man with the scarred face. Once again, he sank back to wait and watch. Within a few minutes' time, his decision proved to be a wise one, for he caught sight of a buckskin horse with the hated white man in the saddle approaching the camp from the north.

As the rider came closer, Dead Man's hands tightened on his rifle and his heart beat wildly in his anger and excitement, for he could see the grotesque scar across his enemy's face. He thought of his Lakota brothers who had fallen victims of the white man's rifle,

and the anxiety to avenge them was overwhelming—
to the point where he could restrain his hatred no longer. Releasing a war cry that shattered the stillness of
the morning calm, he rose and fired at the scar-faced
demon.

In immediate panic, the camp erupted into a state
of frenzied confusion as everyone scrambled to find
cover. Taken completely by surprise, Cleve only had
time to grab Caleb and pull the boy behind the wagon
with him while yelling to the others to find protection
anywhere they could. Victoria and her mother had no
choice but to get under the wagon while Jonah dived
into the wagon bed.

The sharp snap of a rifle slug passing within inches
of his ear caused an instant reaction from Ben. With
no time to think about it, he immediately slid over to
hang on the side of his saddle, using his horse as cover.
He was not sure where the shot had come from, other
than somewhere on the south side of the camp. Two
more shots were fired in his direction as he guided
the buckskin into the trees above the camp, where he
was able to draw his rifle and dismount. His concern
now was for those in the camp. He heard several more
shots, but without any sound of lead flying around
him, so whoever their attacker was had shifted his firing toward the wagon. Ben listened, but he could hear
no return fire from Cleve or Jonah. He could not know
that Cleve's rifle was in his saddle sling, and his horse
had bolted with the first rifle shots fired, and his grizzled old partner was huddled under the wagon, trying
to protect the women with his body.

With no knowledge of who or how many, Ben
started making his way closer to the standing wagon

as Dead Man cut loose with a series of five shots that tore holes in the wagon sheets and ricocheted off the metal tires. Ben could not determine if anyone had been hit or not, but he was able to pinpoint where the shots had come from. Scurrying to a better position from which to fire, he dropped to one knee behind a tree trunk large enough to give him protection, drew a bead on the cottonwood with the double trunk, and waited for the shooter to show himself. "Cleve, you all right?" he yelled.

"We're all right so far, but I can't get to my rifle," Cleve yelled back. "I think it's just one man, near as I can tell."

"Keep your head down," Ben replied. Just then, he saw the barrel of a rifle sliding into the V where the two trunks separated. He didn't wait for their assailant to fire. Four shots in rapid succession tore large chunks of bark from the trunks and knocked the rifle from the notch. As soon as he saw the rifle fall, he left the cover of his tree and ran to the wagon. By the time Dead Man recovered and was able to fire his weapon again, he was too late to catch Ben in the open. Furious, he emptied the magazine of his carbine, sending seven bullets whining through the wagon's rigging. Amid their deadly song, a sharp cry of pain was heard from beneath the wagon. "Mama!" Victoria cried when she saw her mother recoil with the impact of a bullet in her shoulder.

Enraged by the sight of the woman falling back into her daughter's arms, Ben left the cover of the wagon and headed straight for the forked tree. It was a foolish gamble, but he was sure the bushwhacker's carbine was empty. Seeing his hated enemy advancing boldly toward him, Dead Man accepted what he perceived to be a challenge from the *wasicu*. He threw the rifle aside that he had been frantically trying to load, drew his long scalp knife, and leaped up from behind the tree. Emitting another bloodcurdling war cry, he charged to meet the scar-face in hand-to-hand battle. Ben saw then, as the fearsome warrior ran to meet him, that it was one of the Indians who had attacked them before. Not being a foolish man, Ben cocked the Winchester in preparation to let the Indian do battle with a .44 slug. Before he could raise his rifle to fire, the canvas sheet on the side of the wagon rose a few inches, enough to allow the blast of both barrels of Jonah's shotgun to discharge. The impact at such close range knocked the savage over backward as his feet ran out from under him, and he landed flat on his back no more than a few yards from a startled Ben.

He walked over to stare down at the warrior, whose chest was torn apart by the double load of buckshot. There was no question concerning whether or not he was dead. Ben figured he was dead while he was still sailing through the air. Astonished, he looked back to see Jonah scrambling out of the wagon box. "Damn!" he exclaimed—all he could think of to say at that moment. Jonah paid no attention to the dead Indian at Ben's feet, instead crawling under the wagon to go to his wife's side. Concerned as well, Ben followed immediately after him.

Afraid to move her mother at first, Victoria was still holding her tightly as a red stain began to spread, from a small spot, until it became the size of a dinner plate. "Mary!" Jonah sobbed when he saw her, calling her name over and over until Mary quieted him.

"Stop blubbering, Jonah," she said. "I'm not hurt that bad." Her statement caused both husband and daughter to blubber then. "Help me out from under this wagon if the shooting is over."

Ben and Cleve exchanged glances, then jumped to help the lady out so Ben could pick her up and place her on the tailgate of the wagon. Recovered from her first fright at seeing her mother bloodied, Victoria was quick to take charge then. "We need to see how bad you're wounded. It may be worse than you think."

"You might oughta get that bullet outta there," Cleve said as Victoria started unbuttoning the bloody blouse. "I've took out a right smart number of slugs in my time."

"Well, you're not taking this one out," Mary informed him, and grabbed Victoria's hand to stop her. "You men get away from here. I'm not exposing myself for you to stand around and gawk at me. Shoo! Victoria can do the doctoring for me." Her expression told them that she meant what she said. "And take Jonah with you. He gets faint when he sees the sight of blood."

Ben and Cleve looked at each other again and had to laugh. "All right," Cleve said. "You can holler if you need us, Victoria. Come on, Jonah, we got to get ready to roll before another crazy Injun decides to pay us a visit. I'll help you hitch up the horses; then I'll see if I can find my horse. First, I reckon we'd best drag this carcass outta sight of the women." Cleve and Ben each grabbed an ankle and pulled Dead Man over behind some berry bushes. "You sure made a mess of him," Cleve said to Jonah as he winked at Ben. "Both barrels—I reckon you're a sure 'nough Injun fighter now."

Jonah did not reply to Cleve's japing. He was

thinking that he had just killed a man. Even if it was an Indian, it was still a man. And he wasn't feeling well because of it, but he had just gotten mad when he heard Mary cry out in pain, and his instinctive reaction was to punish the man who had hurt her. Later on, when he would think back on this incident, it would serve to give him a greater understanding of Ben's blatant execution of the Crooked Fork deputy.

Victoria performed the surgery on her mother's shoulder, extracting the bullet without a great deal of difficulty. The slug had not gone very deep into the muscle, probably as Cleve speculated, because the shot had evidently ricocheted on the wagon side boards before striking Mary. As patiently brave as any soldier, she lay quietly during the entire procedure while Victoria probed the wound with a knitting needle. When the innocuous-looking piece of metal was finally extracted, Mary insisted that Victoria should cauterize the wound, but her daughter didn't want to do it. It seemed so merciless to sear her mother with a red-hot knife blade. "If you don't, I'll do it myself," Mary threatened.

"Maybe Papa should do it, or Cleve. He says he has done it many times," Victoria pleaded.

"Certainly not," Mary replied in a huff. "I'm lying here with my shoulder bared almost to my breast—a little more than I care to show Cleve—and your father would be worse than you. So heat a knife in the fire and bring it to me. Hurry, now, we've got to get started sometime today."

Although reluctant, Victoria performed the cauterization, just as she had done the surgery, and Mary was back on her feet, her shoulder freshly bandaged.

One of the first things she did was to thank Ben and Cleve for protecting her family once again. "The one you need to thank is Jonah," Ben told her. "He's the one who came stormin' up outta the wagon to blow that Indian into kingdom come. He probably saved my bacon, too."

Surprised, Mary turned to cast an inquisitive look upon her husband. "Did you do that?" she asked.

"I did," he answered simply with a slight hint of embarrassment.

With a proud smile upon her face, she walked over to him and planted a modest kiss on his cheek. "You're my hero," she said, "just like always," deepening his embarrassment to the point of producing a blush.

"Let's get going," he commanded. "We're wasting daylight."

"Yes, sir," Cleve replied smartly, a wide grin on his face as he strode past Ben and headed for his horse. "We'd best get movin', Ben."

Chapter 9

Jonah pulled his team to a stop beside his two scouts as they sat waiting for him at the top of a road that led down into the lower end of Deadwood Gulch. Both of the women climbed down to gaze at the long-awaited end of their desperate journey, and Caleb wedged his way between them to see for himself. "Well, there she is," Cleve announced. "Deadwood. It took us a sight longer than I figured, but we made it."

"It's bigger than I expected," Jonah declared, "a regular city."

They paused there for a few minutes more, most of them finding it hard to believe they had actually found the town. Looking down upon the main street that appeared to be about a mile long, they were surprised to see the line of wooden stores, shops, saloons, even a couple of hotels, that ran the length of the street. It was not a serene town, for even seen from their lofty perspective, it resembled a beehive of activity. There appeared to be people everywhere, filling the streets with all manner of conveyance: horses, mules, bull wagons, even carriages. The canyon was obviously too narrow to accommodate more than one street, but that had not prohibited the building of houses on the north hill on streets cut into the slope, like steps that ran parallel to the gulch. The south slope, being too steep, had no buildings except for a few shanty-type dwellings, each one seeming to clutch the side of the hill in desperation, threatening to go bouncing down upon the people below at any minute.

"How will I ever find Garth in this place? It looks like an anthill."

Ben glanced down when he heard her speak, unaware that she had moved over to stand by his horse. "We'll help you look for your husband," he said. "Did he give you any idea where to find him—or where he was stayin'?"

"Well, no, not really," she said, a note of hesitation in her voice. "The last I heard from him was that he had joined a large mining company. He doesn't really know I'm coming, but it's been so long since I've received word of any kind that I'm worried that something might have happened to him." The sight she was gazing upon at the bottom of the gulch was not the picture of Deadwood she had formed in her mind. She had not thought that there would be so many people concentrated in the narrow canyon, instead expecting a town like the small cow towns they had come through in Kansas and Nebraska. The scene that confronted her now was discouraging to the point of despair.

"We'll look till we find him," Ben said, trying to encourage her.

Cleve interrupted their conversation bluntly. "We

ain't doin' no good standin' here gawkin'," he said. "We'll help you find a spot to park your wagon and make camp." He paused to look around for a few moments more when he realized that it was not going to be a simple task. It appeared that every foot of ground in the gulch had a building on it. "You might have to camp up here on the hill," he said, "but, hell, we'll find someplace." He was of a mind that the arrangement made with Jonah was completed. He and Ben had escorted them to Deadwood. That was all they had agreed to do. Jonah and his family were on their own from this point forward, as far as he was concerned. The extra time it had taken to travel at the wagon's slow pace and the approaching winter were cause for anxious thoughts regarding his and Ben's camp. When they had decided to go to the Black Hills, it had never been with Deadwood in mind. They were too late to mine for gold there where every inch of land had already been turned over and run through a sluice. He remembered how hard winters were in the Black Hills, with heavy frosts coming in September and heavy snows sometimes falling well into June—too much of the year when a man couldn't do any mining. So if he and Ben were going to go deeper into the mountains to set up a camp, there wasn't any time to spare. It was already late August.

"We'll help you find your husband," Ben repeated to Victoria, whose frown lines were etched deeply into her forehead. "First, let's find a place to set up camp before it starts to get dark."

Finding a place to camp proved to be easier than they had anticipated, for they found several abandoned shacks on the hillside above the Bella Union

Saloon. There was only one such house with space enough behind it to park the wagon, however. It sat on the second street up the slope from the main thoroughfare. As could be expected, the former occupants had not been especially keen on keeping a clean house, so Victoria and Mary, with her arm out of the sling now, set about making the place livable while the three men went down to walk the main street in search of information.

"We don't know much about this son-in-law of yours," Cleve told Jonah. "Do we look for him in the church or in the saloon?"

"It's hard for me to say," Jonah replied. "We never got much of a chance to know Garth very well. He and Victoria lived with his folks for the first three years they were married. His folks have a good-sized farm about fifty miles from Omaha, so Mary and I didn't get to see them very often. Then Garth took off to look for gold and Victoria came back home."

It seemed that almost every other building was a saloon, but there were also stores and shops of all kinds, even a newspaper office. "We might as well start askin' around," Cleve said. "We can start with this saloon here. Probably wouldn't hurt to have a little drink while we're at it. It's been a long time since Ogallala." The suggestion caused a wry smile to appear on Ben's face, because he knew Cleve still didn't have the price of a drink. To his surprise, however, Jonah thought it was a good idea also and insisted that he certainly owed them a drink.

The saloon was doing a lively business for this early hour of the evening, and when Cleve commented on it to the bartender, he replied, "I reckon you fellers are new in town. Hell, we don't ever close. It's busy as hell all the time." He was about to ask them their pleasure when he looked into Ben's face. The sudden look of surprise in the bartender's eyes reminded Ben of the stigma he carried. Over the past weeks, he had forgotten the impact caused by his appearance and the guarded expressions it caused.

"Whiskey," Jonah called out boldly. "My friends and I will have a drink of whiskey."

"Yes, sir," the bartender responded, and placed three glasses on the bar.

Cleve looked at Ben and winked. Ben nodded in response. They were both thinking of the last time they had been in a bar with Jonah, and how meek he had been when facing the cowboy who spilled his drink. *I guess killing a man changes your attitude a little,* Ben thought.

"I reckon you boys are here for the same reason everybody else is," the bartender commented as he filled the glasses. "If you are, you're a little late to find much gold. Placer mining is still turning up a little money—that and quartz mining—about enough for grub, but nobody's getting rich, except maybe the big outfits. They own most of the gulch now."

"That a fact?" Cleve said, not really interested because he and Ben were intending to forge deeper into the mountains to find their fortune. He raised his glass and proposed a toast. "Here's to us gettin' our asses safely to Deadwood."

"I'll certainly drink to that," Jonah replied. After he downed the whiskey, he turned to the bartender again. "Actually, we're here to find someone, my son-in-law.

By any chance do you know him? Garth Beaudry's his name."

The bartender shook his head. "Mister, there's thousands of people come through this town. I mighta seen him. I couldn't say. I don't ask any of 'em their names." He glanced briefly at Ben before adding, "A lot of 'em ain't using their real names, anyway."

"The last we heard he was working for a large mining company," Jonah said.

The bartender shrugged. There were several companies operating in the gulch, some modest that employed ten to twenty men, others truly larger in scale and payroll. "Maybe he's working at the Homestake Mine, about three miles over the hill in Lead," he suggested. "That's the biggest one."

"We'll check on it," Cleve said.

After leaving the saloon they stopped in a few other stores that were still open in the early evening, but no one they asked knew Garth Beaudry. "I expect we'd better get back up the hill," Jonah said when they were leaving the Gem Saloon, where they indulged in one more drink. "The ladies might be getting worried about us. I'll go find the Homestake Mine in the morning. That's probably the place Garth was talking about, and we won't take up any more of you fellows' time. You've already done more for us than is reasonable for a person to ask."

Cleve glanced at Ben, already knowing that his partner had a great deal of concern for Jonah and his little family. With that in mind, he also knew that Ben was not going to leave them until they had found Victoria's husband, and they were settled in safely. *If he was as mean as he looks,* he thought, *we'd already be on our way into the mountains.* Since he wasn't, Cleve decided to extend their help a little further. "Why, hell, Jonah, we'll go to Lead with you. Me and Ben ain't in that big a hurry to leave."

Ben smiled when he saw the look of relief in Jonah's face.

With their generous supply of antelope meat, and the provisions they had carried in the wagon, the party had all the food they would need for a while, until some permanent arrangements could be made. They were counting heavily upon Victoria's husband to lighten the burden of subsistence. When they returned to the shanty they had claimed, supper was ready, and Victoria met them at the door, searching their faces anxiously. "We didn't talk to anybody who knew Garth," Jonah said, "but we got the name of a big mining company we'll go see in the morning."

There was little trouble in finding the Homestake Mining Company, the operation founded by Fred and Mose Manuel and their partner, Hank Harney, recently bought out by George Hearst. When directed to the engineering office, they were met by Arnold Freeman. "Oh, you can't talk to Mr. Hearst," Freeman told them when asked to speak to the owner. "He don't hang around here. What is it you want? Lookin' for a job?"

Jonah spoke up. "No, sir, we're looking for my son-in-law and wondering if he works here. His name is Garth Beaudry."

The mention of the name brought an immediate reaction from Freeman, although he quickly tried to disguise it. He cocked a wary eye, foremost in Ben's direction, before a cautious reply. "Your son-in-law," he repeated, while he paused to choose his words carefully. "Garth Beaudry did work here at one time." He hesitated again. "And still does some work for Mr. Hearst from time to time."

Ben was not comfortable with the man's obvious reluctance to talk about Victoria's husband. There was more to the story than Freeman seemed willing to discuss. "Do you know where we can find him?" he asked.

"Well," Freeman responded, still hesitant, "I don't know if he's in town or not."

Growing more impatient by the moment, Ben said, "That ain't what I asked you. Where's he live? Has he got a house? His wife and son have come all the way from Omaha to find him, and you're actin' like you don't want to tell us where the hell he is."

Seeing the anger building up in the menacing face, Freeman sensed that he might be dealing with a powder keg with a very short fuse. Two other men at the other side of the office, upon catching the irritation in Ben's voice, began to shift around nervously. Just as a precaution, Cleve sidled over toward them and smiled. "How you fellers doin'?" It was enough to discourage any action they might have been considering.

"I'm sorry," Freeman said. "I can't tell you where Mr. Beaudry lives."

"Can't, or won't?" Ben pressed.

"I mean I don't know for sure," Freeman quickly replied. "He was livin' in the hotel for a while, but I don't know if he's still there or not."

Ben was rapidly losing his patience with Arnold Freeman. He had a feeling that Freeman knew exactly

where to find Garth Beaudry, and for some reason, he
didn't want to tell them. He glanced briefly at Jonah,
who stood motionless, astonished by Freeman's lack
of cooperation. It only made him madder. He shifted
his gaze back to fix on Freeman again. "I'm gonna
ask you one more time, and this time I expect an honest answer outta you. If you wanted to talk to Garth
Beaudry, where would you go to find him?"

The look of the scar-faced man was terrifying to a
man of mild nature like Arnold Freeman. Thinking it
in his best interest, he answered at once. "He's got a
little office next to the Bella Union in Deadwood."

"Much obliged," Ben said, and turned to leave.
Without a word from either, Cleve and Jonah followed
him out the door. Once outside, Ben confided to Cleve,
"I don't know what that was all about. Did it strike
you the same way, that that feller didn't want to tell us
where to look for Victoria's husband?"

"He was mighty peculiar about it," Cleve agreed.
"We'll get to the bottom of it," he added for Jonah's
benefit.

Inside the mining office, one of the two clerks who
had overheard the entire conversation walked over to
the window where Freeman was standing and watching the departing threesome. "Beaudry's wife and
boy," he said. "Angel's gonna be plumb tickled to hear
that."

"I doubt Garth's gonna be too pleased, himself,"
Freeman replied. "Maybe you better ride on back to
Deadwood and let him know they're comin'." When
the clerk started for the door, he added, "You better
hurry. They might be goin' straight to Beaudry's place.
Take that buckboard. It's still hitched up out front."

Startled by the sudden burst of the young clerk out the door behind them, the three paused to wonder what had caused his hurry. They stood there for a few moments, about to climb on their horses, astounded by the young man's seemingly frantic leap onto a buckboard tied at the front rail. Lashing the horse as if he were going to a fire, he took off up the road. "I got a feelin' if we follow that feller, he'll take us right to your son-in-law," Cleve commented.

"I agree," Ben said.

They followed along behind the man in the buckboard, holding to a pace that kept him in sight, but not close enough to crowd him. Ben and Cleve riding easy in their saddles, Jonah bouncing along on Graham Barrett's Morgan. Right from the start, there was little mystery as to where the clerk was going, for he retraced the trail they had used when they came to Lead. He did not spare the horse for the entire distance of the three-odd miles back to Deadwood, where he drove the buckboard around behind the Bella Union Saloon.

Garth Beaudry looked up in surprise to see Toby Wilson, a clerk at the Homestake, burst into his cabin. In the midst of packing his saddlebags in preparation to leave town, he didn't have time to talk. "What the hell are you doing here?" he asked rather harshly.

"Mr. Freeman sent me to warn you that some fellows came to the mine looking for you. He wasn't sure if you'd wanna see 'em or not."

"I already knew that," Beaudry replied impatiently. The bartender in the Bella Union had told him that three fellows had been in the saloon earlier, asking about him. One of them had claimed to be his father-in-law. "Pete told me, and Freeman's right. I sure as hell don't wanna see them." There had been a lot of changes in his life since he had left the farm near Omaha. He was a different man, with a different life—one he had no desire to share with the plain little woman he had married before he came west and got a taste of the life he craved.

He was proud of what he had accomplished. He had status with the operators of the Homestake Mining Company, status you didn't get if you worried about the right and wrong of things. George Hearst had expanded the properties of the mine by fair means whenever possible, buying out the claims that would sell. Other claims were acquired through the courts, awarded by judges who were not averse to under-the-table persuasion. Although Beaudry never received orders directly from Hearst, he was noticed early in his employment by his boss, Arnold Freeman, as a man willing to do most anything to get ahead. His opportunity to gain the status he enjoyed came when a stubborn claim owner, whose property was a key piece in the Homestake's future plans, refused to sell. Garth volunteered to convince the owner to reconsider. The man was found dead at his sluice box the next morning, and by that afternoon, Homestake took over his claim.

Garth Beaudry had been Freeman's bully boy ever since. It was a position Garth enjoyed, and one he was well paid for. In the wide-open, lawless town of Deadwood, it was easy enough to hire ruthless men to do his bidding, so it was no longer necessary to soil his hands taking care of the dirty details of the mine's

business. His responsibility was to facilitate the acqui-
sition of difficult land parcels, and Arnold Freeman
preferred not to know how it was accomplished. People were killed, or simply left their claims every week
in Lead and Deadwood. Those remaining cared very
little about the reason. The only thing that could spoil
Beaudry's world had fallen upon him now, like a bad
dream that had come to fruition, and it could not have
come at a worse time for him. Freeman had recently
informed Garth that the company's plan was to run
him for sheriff. With him in the sheriff's office, it would
make a lot of things that much easier. Of particular concern to Freeman was to get the backing of the mayor
and council, and the support of the merchants and
working people of the town. That might be difficult
with a wife and child showing up to sully his reputation when there had already been concern by the mayor
about the fact that Garth lived with an ex-prostitute.

Thoughts of the plain, almost homely girl he had
married only because she was pregnant were enough to
give him a sick feeling inside. Had it not been for his
father's threats to castrate him if he didn't do the proper
thing by the naive young lady, he would never have considered marriage. Three years he endured the simple,
hardworking life on his father's farm, mainly because
of the novelty of having a woman to submit to his car-
nal pleasures whenever he desired. But familiarity soon
wore the shine off that pastime and he became more
and more aware of Victoria's dull, listless hair and plain,
simple face—and he felt he deserved something better.

It had taken a lot of convincing on his part to get his
father to finance his trek to the Black Hills, supposedly

to capture a portion of the wealth being taken out of the ground and use it to establish a solid life for his young family. On the day he set out from Nebraska, however, Garth had no intention of ever seeing his father or his wife and child again. Not long after he had arrived in Deadwood, he sent his father a wire, telling him that he was doing well. The only reason had been to keep the family ties a little longer in case he might be in need of more money. But things had moved rapidly for him, and he had no further need of his father's help. And now this. He thought of the plain, innocent face of his lawful wife and compared it to the sensual, full-lipped visage of Angel Lopez, the saucy senorita who had retired from her position in Madame Dora DuFran's brothel to practice her art of seduction exclusively for him.

The thought of his mistress prompted him to say to Toby, "Here's fifty dollars, paper. Go up to my rooms in the hotel and give it to Angel. Tell her I've got to go out of town for a few days. That oughta hold her till I get back." Toby turned toward the door, but Beaudry grabbed his arm. "And damn it, when I get back, I'm gonna ask her if you gave her fifty dollars."

"I wouldn't cheat you, Garth," Toby replied. "I've got better sense." He took the money and started again for the door, just in time to hear horses' hooves outside in the alley behind the saloon.

With one accusing look at Toby, Garth stepped quickly to the window and peered out at the three riders pulling up before his cabin. "Damn you!" he spat at Toby. "You've led them straight to my office." Standing to the side of the dingy window, he peeked out at the insignificant little man who was his father-in-law.

"Damn!" he swore again. "That little worm." He stared then at the two men with him. They looked like hired gunmen, he thought, and two he had never seen around Deadwood before. "All right," he blurted, trying to decide the best thing to do. "You go on out there and tell them I'm not here. Tell 'em you don't know where I am."

Toby walked out the door just as the three riders were dismounting. He walked over to the buckboard, stopped there, and turned around to face them. "If you gentlemen are lookin' for Mr. Beaudry, he ain't here."

Jonah's face reflected his disappointment, and he would have climbed back up on his horse, but Ben wasn't satisfied with the young clerk's assertion. There was a feeling about the reaction of everyone they had asked about Garth Beaudry that didn't seem right somehow. Like a worm in his mind, the thought continued to bother him until he began to wonder if something had happened to Victoria's husband, something that a lot of people were trying to cover up. "Is that Beaudry's house?" Ben asked.

"Ah, no, sir. That's his office—I reckon you would call it. But he ain't there."

"I notice the door ain't locked. Reckon when he might be back?" Ben asked.

"I don't know," Toby answered, visibly flustered. "Not for a long time, I s'pose."

"Well, I reckon we oughta go in, anyway," Ben said. "Leave him a note maybe. Let him know his wife and kid are here. I'm sure he'd appreciate it." The look of distress in the young clerk's face told him that there was definitely something that wasn't right about the whereabouts of Garth Beaudry, and he intended to satisfy himself that Victoria's husband was all right.

Picking up Ben's sense of suspicion, Cleve commented, "Yeah, that'd be the decent thing to do, leave him a note. His pappy-in-law here is a schoolteacher. He can write it."

When they started for the door, Toby wasn't sure what he should do. Garth had told him to get rid of them, but he didn't know what else he could say to dissuade them from going inside. And one look at the menacing face of the big one discouraged him from trying to insist that they not go inside. Being an otherwise fairly bright young man, he did the sensible thing. He got in the buckboard and went back to the mine.

Inside the cabin, peering out of the curtains Angel Lopez had hung on the windows, Beaudry scowled. "That little son of a bitch," he muttered when he saw Toby drive away. There was no back door to his cabin. He was going to have to deal with his visitors, so he moved quickly back to sit down at a table he used as a desk and waited. The first one through the door was Cleve, and Beaudry looked up, feigning surprise. "Can I help you?" he asked.

Before Cleve could reply, Jonah shoved past him to exclaim, "Garth! I didn't think we were going to find you! We're here, Mary and me, Victoria and Caleb. It took a long time, but we made it." He stood there, waiting for a response equal in enthusiasm to his own, puzzled when his son-in-law showed no sign of joyous surprise. "That fellow outside said you weren't here."

Beaudry rose to shake the hand Jonah extended, his focus fixed momentarily on the intimidating man standing beside him. "Toby," he said. "Don't pay any attention to him." Shifting his gaze back to Jonah, he said, "Mr. Marple, I'm glad to see you made it all right. If you'da let me know you were coming, I woulda been a little more prepared."

"Victoria and Caleb are both in good health," Jonah went on, "and anxious to see you."

"I was just gonna ask you about 'em," Beaudry said.

"You're not going to believe how much your son has grown since you've last seen him," Jonah continued, crediting Garth's lack of excitement to shock at having his family suddenly appear out of nowhere. "Caleb's looking more like you every day." Remembering then, he gestured toward his friends. "This is Cleve Goganis and Ben Cutler. They joined us at Ogallala and graciously volunteered to help me find you."

Beaudry nodded briefly. "I wish I had known you were in town." He gestured toward the saddlebags on the table. "I was just fixing to leave town on some business for the mine." Noting the look of astonishment on the faces of all three men, he hastened to add, "But I reckon I can postpone it long enough to visit my family." He glanced at Ben again, unable to get over the feeling that the eerie-looking individual was measuring him. "Where are Victoria and the others?"

Jonah gave him directions to the miner's shanty they had confiscated, and Beaudry suggested that he should take care of some urgent business, but would join them for supper later on. Then he walked them to the door, leaving Jonah in a state of confusion outside by their horses, perplexed by his son-in-law's cool reception. Jonah was no more mystified than Ben, however. The reunion left him wondering just what kind of cold, emotionless man Victoria's husband could be; after being away from his wife and child for over a year, a normal man would have rushed immediately to see them. Cleve defined the meeting succinctly for them when he commented, "He didn't exactly turn cartwheels when he found out his family was here, did he?"

Deep in thought, Jonah hesitated a moment before reflecting. "Garth always was a little bit reserved, I guess. Mary and I never got to know him really well." He looked up then and smiled hopefully. "I expect he's probably just in shock to find us here."

"Yeah, that's probably it," Ben said, while thinking their arrival seemed more like bad news to Beaudry.

Totally astonished, Victoria could scarcely believe that Garth had not come back immediately with her father when told that she and Caleb were here to join him. Surely there had to be some miscommunication, but there was no reasonable explanation for it. She could not help feeling embarrassed, even shamed, by his blasé reaction. He had not seen them for a year! It was difficult to explain to Caleb why his father was too busy to come to see him right away. She could not escape a feeling of despair while she busied herself by helping her mother prepare supper. It was hard not to compare the sensation she felt now to that of the evening when Garth came over to her father's house in Omaha to stand by her when they announced her pregnancy. "What?" she asked, just then realizing that her mother had spoken to her.

"I said Garth was probably so shocked when your father walked into his office with those two rough-looking men, he didn't know what to think. I'm sure he'll be just as excited as you are to be together again."

She made the statement as much for her benefit as for her daughter's. In her heart, she had never forgiven Garth for taking advantage of her daughter. Victoria had been so young and innocent, and because of her lack of beauty, starved for affection. Mary did not deny her failing in preparing Victoria for rutty young boys like Garth Beaudry. Instead, she tried to keep Victoria from growing out of her little girl stage. *Well, no harm done in the long run*, she thought, *as long as they build a solid marriage.* "I suppose we should go ahead and feed the men," she said. "No use letting the food get cold. Maybe Garth will show up pretty soon." She went to the back door of the shanty and called to Cleve and Ben.

"He's missin' some mighty fine eatin'," Cleve commented as he reached for another biscuit. He was going to miss Mary's and Victoria's cooking, since he and Ben planned to leave in the morning and head back into the mountains. They had already stayed longer than planned, primarily because Ben wanted to see that Victoria and her husband were all right. "Speak of the devil," Cleve commented as they heard the sound of horse's hooves outside the shack.

With a quick look at herself in a hand mirror, Victoria brushed her hair back with her hand, smoothed her apron, and ran to the front door to meet her husband. Eager to greet him after so many months apart, she didn't wait for him to come in, but ran to him in the small front yard. He turned from his horse in time to catch her rather stiffly in his arms, as she pressed tightly against his chest. At once aware of his awkwardness, she released him and stepped back to look up into his face.

He frowned and asked, "How've you been, Victoria?"

"What's the matter?" she asked, confused by his apparent constraint. "Aren't you glad to see me? Don't you want to see your son? What's wrong, Garth?" She searched for the excitement in his eyes that she had felt until this very moment when he seemed unresponsive to her greeting. There was no tenderness in his gaze.

"You shouldn't have come out here, Victoria," he told her in a voice calm, but cold. "This is no place for a woman like you." He glanced through the open door behind her at the people seated around a small table. "And it's certainly no place for a man like your pa. This place will eat him up and spit him out." He nodded his head toward the door. "Who are those two men with your pa?"

"They're friends who helped us get out here to see you," she replied. "I'm not sure we would have made it without them." She quickly returned to his comment that had just sent her reeling. "I had not heard from you in so long, I was afraid something had happened to you. I missed you. We all missed you. Don't you want to see your son?" She turned her head briefly to call Caleb, then returned to gaze beseechingly at her husband.

"He has grown a lot," he said when Caleb ran out and pressed against his mother's skirt, shy before this stranger. He wished then that he had told Jonah the straight of things earlier at his cabin, so he quickly returned his attention to Victoria. "Look, Victoria, I came up here to tell you things have changed. Go on back east. It's the best thing for you to do. Our marriage is over. I never wanted it in the first place. This is where I'm gonna stay, and I don't want you around. Is that clear enough for you?"

Afraid she was going to fall, she backed up until she felt the edge of the low porch against her calves. Then she sank heavily down on the porch, feeling as if her entire nervous system was going to fail her. Unable to understand what was happening to his mother, Caleb tried to pull her up again, until she quieted him. "Go back in the house," she said, in a voice drained of emotion. "Tell your grandma that your father won't be staying for supper."

"Damn it, Victoria," Garth exclaimed, "you've got nobody to blame but yourself. You had no business coming out here till I sent for you, anyway."

"And when was that going to be, Garth?" Her initial shock was giving way to anger now. When he didn't answer, she answered for him. "Never. Is that about right, Garth?"

"That's about it," he replied coldly, and prepared to put his foot in the stirrup. "I'm an important man in the Homestake Mining Company, so take my advice and tell your friends to stay outta my way. That's for their own good."

Her whole world seemingly turned upside down, Victoria continued to sit on the edge of the porch, finding it hard to believe her ears. She didn't get up when Jonah walked out on the little stoop and asked, "Garth, where are you going? Supper's getting cold." Confused, he looked from his son-in-law to his daughter for an explanation.

"He told me to go back to Omaha," Victoria said

softly. "He doesn't want me out here. He doesn't want to be married to me anymore."

"Why, you low-down cur!" Jonah cried, all his doubts about Garth crashing back at once. He had worried from the beginning that the no-good son of Sam Beaudry was going to break his little girl's heart, even though he had prayed to be mistaken about the boy's character. He marched up to face Garth, who stood fully a head taller than he. "I knew you were trash from the very start."

Garth took hold of the saddle horn, but did not step up right away. "You'd better watch your mouth, old man, or I might decide to close it for you."

"Papa!" Victoria cried. "Let him go, and good riddance."

"We'll see about that," Jonah exclaimed, his ire past the point of concern for the size difference. He reached for Garth's arm, trying to pull him away from his horse.

"Why, you little shit!" Garth exclaimed. He jammed his free hand in Jonah's face and shoved the smaller man sprawling to the ground. "I don't have to take any of your guff anymore."

"Maybe not, but you've gotta take mine."

Garth turned to take the full impact of Ben's right hand flush on his nose. Knocked off his feet, he landed under his horse, causing the animal to buck sideways, almost stomping him in the process. Those inside the shack had heard the argument heating up outside, bringing them running to investigate. Seeing Jonah manhandled so roughly by the sullen bully was the spark needed to ignite Ben's wrath. He had not liked what he had seen in Garth Beaudry from the first, and even then he thought it only a question of time before the two of them met on a collision course. He pushed Beaudry's horse to the side to get at him again. Beaudry pulled his .44 from his holster and raised it to shoot, but he was not quick enough to aim it before Ben kicked it out of his hand. Cleve immediately pounced on the weapon, taking possession of it. Desperately looking for room to get to his feet to defend himself, Garth started crawling on all fours as fast as he could manage. Right behind him, Ben placed his boot squarely in the seat of Garth's pants, and sent him skidding to fall flat on his face.

"Ben! Ben!" Victoria screamed. "That's enough! Let him go!" She had never seen Ben this angry before, and she was afraid he might kill Garth. She did not crave vengeance. She had been hurt deep in her very soul on this evening, but she just wanted him gone from them.

Ben stopped and stood over the fallen man, his face a livid mask of fury, causing the jagged scar to appear white hot against the flush of his skin. "I reckon he's about ready to end this little visit," Cleve said, a calm voice in the ministorm. Holding Garth's gun on him, he told him to get up and be on his way.

Keeping a wary eye on the scar-faced devil who had bloodied his nose, Garth got slowly to his feet. Once he was in the saddle, he recovered a portion of his bravado. "I'll have my pistol back," he demanded sullenly.

"Sure thing," Cleve replied, his tone accommodating. He opened the cylinder and emptied the cartridges on the ground, then tossed the weapon to him.

"This is a helluva long way from over," Garth snarled as he holstered the empty pistol. "You've messed with the wrong man, mister."

"I don't wanna hear about you, or anybody you know, causing any trouble for these folks," Ben told him. " 'Cause if I do, I'm comin' after you, and I ain't gonna stop at a bloody nose next time. See that you remember that. There won't be any second warnin'.'"

They stood there in the front yard, watching Garth's departure, until he disappeared in the growing darkness of the evening. Mary sat on the porch beside Victoria, her arm around her daughter's shoulders, doing her best to comfort her, at the same time feeling the burn of her contempt for her former son-in-law. After a few moments, Jonah walked over to the porch and sat down on the other side of Victoria, and the two of them rocked her slowly back and forth in their arms. Cleve grimaced, then smiled when he looked at Ben. "Damned if this ain't the liveliest family reunion I ever did see."

Ben's face suddenly lost the image of unbridled fury it had reflected moments before and a smile slowly replaced it. "I reckon," he replied. There were soon other concerns, however. Maybe Beaudry would be willing to let this confrontation be the end of it. Then, again, maybe he would be inclined to make more trouble as he had threatened. Ben was afraid he and Cleve might have to stay around a little longer to make sure Jonah and the women were all right. He assumed that they might consider going back to Omaha, or anywhere other than Deadwood, but it was too close to winter for them to start out now.

Chapter 10

"I think it might be broken," Angel Lopez said as she tenderly dabbed a wet cloth under Beaudry's nose in an attempt to clean the blood away. "I'm sorry, darlin'," she cooed when he flinched in pain. "A lot of it's dried up and it's hard to get it off."

"That son of a bitch is a dead man," Garth fumed. "He hit me when I wasn't looking. They all ganged up on me, and by God, they're gonna pay for it. I tried to tell 'em in a nice way, but they wouldn't have it that way," he went on, offering excuses for coming out on the losing end of the confrontation. "They came in here with a couple of hired guns. That one fellow, the scar-faced one, he's nothing but a back-shooting bushwhacker, but he's gonna get what's coming to him. I can promise you that."

"I hope you told that bitch you have another woman now," Angel said as she rinsed the cloth out in a pan of water, "one who takes care of you. Maybe she might understand better if I go up there and scratch her eyes out."

"Don't you worry about it," Garth assured her. "Nobody gets away with trying to mess with Garth Beaudry. If they know what's good for them, they'd better be on their way outta town right now."

In the shanty on the hill above the Bella Union Saloon, that very decision was being discussed in earnest by Ben, Cleve, and Jonah. There had been no alternative plan, simply because no one in Jonah's family had made provision for the possibility that Garth would react in any way other than joyful. Jonah had not been sure what he was going to do in Deadwood, but he had not been overly concerned about it because he thought he had Garth to rely upon. Now he was suddenly on his own, once again the sole provider for his wife and daughter and his grandson in a strange place, owning no property, and with no trade other than that as a schoolteacher. Prospects for the winter looked pretty bleak.

Cleve was the first to offer, although Ben was about to. "I reckon me and Ben could stay around awhile till you make up your mind what you're gonna do. Right, Ben?" He glanced at Ben to get his nod of approval, then went on. "We got to get outta this town, though, and build us a camp before the heavy weather shuts everythin' off. Me and Ben can feed all of us out in the mountains—there's game a'plenty—but there ain't nothin' we can do in this damn town."

"I guess we could go on back to Omaha," Jonah suggested, but without much enthusiasm.

"Too late," Cleve replied at once. "Hard winter will

most likely set in another month from now, and you'd probably get caught in the middle of the prairie with about eight or ten foot of snow—that is, if the Injuns let you get that far."

Jonah shook his head slowly, reluctant to make the only other suggestion he could think of. "There's lots of houses for sale around here, and they're cheap. I've still got money left from the sale of my old place in Omaha. I guess I could buy a place a little more decent than this shack, so the women wouldn't have to spend the winter here."

Ben spoke up then. "I don't think you'd wanna do that, Jonah. The reason houses are goin' cheap in Deadwood is there's a lot of folks leavin' this town. All the small claims have just about been worked out. I think it'd be a bad idea to spend your money on a good house, then this spring or later when you decide you wanna sell it, you won't be able to get your money back. Hang on to that money. Cleve's right. It's too late to go back home, but he and I can build a stout cabin back up over the hill somewhere that'll take you through the winter. Then, come spring, you can decide where you wanna go."

"Ben's right," Cleve said. "We can get you through the winter."

"You'd do that?" Jonah asked, looking at Ben; then turning to look at Cleve, he repeated, "You'd do that?"

"Hell, ain't nothin' to it," Cleve replied. "Me and Ben can go scout up a place tomorrow." He cocked a mischievous eye at Jonah. "If you and the women ain't tired of havin' us around." It was evident by the undisguised expression of relief on the frail little man's face that the answer to that was *not by a long shot.*

They went inside to inform Mary and Victoria of the decision to build a winter home outside Deadwood. Mary's initial reaction was to question the sensibility of leaving the safety of town to expose themselves to the danger of Indian attacks in the mountains around Deadwood. "We ain't talkin' about goin' deep in the mountains, like me and Ben was thinkin' about to pan for gold," Cleve assured her. "Just on the edge of the settlement where it'd be easy for us to hunt for food." Mary was still skeptical, but she decided that she could rely on their opinion. There was no comment one way or the other from Victoria. She was still foundering hopelessly amid the wreckage of all her hopes and dreams of the past year. "We'll see what we can find in the mornin'," Cleve said. "Whatever it is, it'll be better'n this shack." It was settled then. The discussion over, Ben and Cleve said good night and went outside to sleep in Jonah's wagon. As they walked out the door, Cleve bent down close to Victoria and whispered in her ear, "I know you're feelin' bad right now, but you're lucky you found out before you wasted your whole life on that sorry son of a bitch. You'll see." She looked up at him and smiled, knowing he was right.

Mary was up early the next morning. She wasn't sure when Ben and Cleve planned to leave, but she wanted to have breakfast ready for them before they did. Soon after her mother was up, Victoria joined her in the kitchen half of the shack to help with breakfast. When she came from behind the quilt hung up to divide the sleeping quarters, Mary turned to look at her closely. Aware of the reason for her mother's close scrutiny, Victoria said, "I'm all right, Mama. I'm over it already."

She was not, but she was determined she soon would be. Her life was far from over. She had been rejected, but it was not something she couldn't deal with. Being a plain, uninteresting girl and woman, she was used to it. At least she had not come away from the experience with nothing gained, for she had Caleb, and he was worth the pain of being discarded. It occurred to her that she was glad she had not named him Garth Jr.

Resolved to find work of some kind, so as not to squander the money he had set back for their future, Jonah announced that he was going to scour the town to see if there were opportunities for men of his situation. Mary did not think to discourage him; in fact, she was proud of his undefeated attitude, in spite of odds she did not feel favored his success. "Victoria and I will try to make some kind of home of this miserable shack while you're looking. Maybe I'll make something with the last of the salt pork in the barrel. We've had so much venison, I'm beginning to feel like an Indian." She turned to Victoria then. "You and I can go down the hill to town. We need some dried beans, and while we're at it, we'll look around to see what this busy town has to offer."

Unaware of the determination of Jonah and the women to make the most of their situation, Ben and Cleve rode up the gulch to see what they could find. There was no talk of the original plans they had had for their journey to the Black Hills, although both men realized they were now bound to Jonah's family for an indefinite period. Ben wasn't sure if Cleve resented the delay in their goals, but for himself, he really didn't care, and he had to admit that he had saddled himself with a feeling of responsibility in regard to their welfare. They weren't going to be able to do much placer mining in the winter, anyway. They might as well spend the time in Deadwood.

After riding up in the hills on either side of the gulch, which extended for a distance of about ten miles, they began to wonder if Cleve's boast about finding a place to build a cabin close to Deadwood was a bit naive, for every foot of ground had been claimed. There was plenty of pine with which to cut logs for a cabin, but no longer convenient to town. The logs would have to be hauled from a considerable distance, even if land close in was available. A little before sundown, they headed for home with no good news to report. When they arrived back at the shanty, they found that their day had been good compared to Mary and Victoria's.

"I'm proud of her," Mary told them. "We went down the main street, looking at the shops and stores, and I think we were both enjoying the opportunity to window-shop, even though we didn't buy anything except these beans you're having for supper. Do you know there are two newspapers in this town? There's a theater, the Gem Theater. All this in this unlikely spot for a town in the middle of Indian Territory. Anyway, we were walking past the saloon. The walkway was crowded with some of the roughest-looking men I have ever seen, but they were all very polite and quick to step out of our way. We had almost passed the saloon when this painted hussy burst out of the door and proceeded to accost us. 'You homely bitch,' she cursed at Victoria, 'go on back where you belong.' And she grabbed Victoria by her hair and almost pulled her off her feet. I was trying to get her off Victoria. 'He's through with you,' she yelled. 'He's got a real woman now.' 'A real whore!' I yelled. You should have seen the gaudy frock she was wearing, and her face all painted up. She was still holding Victoria by the hair, but she started cursing me after I called her a whore. I thought she was going to let Victoria go and come after me, but that's when Victoria took a swing at the hussy with her fist. And she hit her right in the eye." Mary had to pause for a moment while she chuckled over the incident. "Well, she let go of Victoria then and started holding her hand over her eye, and Victoria hit her again, on her pretty little nose. And it started bleeding! She got herself back in that saloon then, crying like a baby. I was so proud of Victoria."

Embarrassed, but unable to suppress a smile of satisfaction, Victoria said, "That's not a proper story to tell anyone, Mama, especially in front of children." She placed her hands over Caleb's ears and scolded, "What will Caleb think of his mother?"

"I expect he'd be pretty proud of her," Cleve answered, a wide smile on his face, matching the one Mary wore. Before long, they were all laughing, even Victoria. It was a much-needed respite from the somber overcast that had descended upon the party since arriving in the lawless mining town.

Having sat quietly, enjoying the telling of his daughter's vengeance upon her husband's lover, Jonah waited until there was a lull in the conversation to tell them his news. "I found myself a job today," he announced, capturing everyone's attention at once. "I guess I'll be teaching again. I talked to the folks who run the Congregational School, and they were fairly tickled to find that I was a teacher, because they've been needing one ever since the last one left to return to the East." His statement was met with a round of applause, and a proud hug from his wife and daughter. It brought forth a new issue, however.

"How far is that school?" Cleve asked.

"Not far from here," Jonah replied. "In fact, I could walk to the school."

"Then I reckon Ben and me have been lookin' in the wrong place to build a cabin," Cleve said. His remark caused a lull in the chatter for a few moments.

"Why don't we just build another room onto this place?" Ben suggested. "Looks to me like you folks would be better off in town for a spell, anyway. And I know Mary wasn't too comfortable with the idea of livin' outside the town."

"This shanty is going to need a lot more than an extra room," Mary announced emphatically.

"That'll be part of it," Jonah said, already seeing Ben's suggestion as one he favored. "We'll fix up this place like a regular mansion. New windows and a new door will help keep the cold out, and you can walk to town." Mary nodded her acceptance of the plan, and that was it as far as a place to live was concerned.

The next few days were spent planning the new construction of their house, and soon after the actual work began. With Jonah's wagon, lumber was hauled up from a sawmill on Sherman Street and the addition to the original cabin was well along the way to completion before the middle of September. The work was being done by Ben and Cleve, with Jonah helping out after school was over for the day. The women kept the workers fed properly, and Caleb made himself useful fetching nails and tools when needed. Their neighbor on the downhill side of them happened to be the proprietor of a hardware store, so he made it a point to introduce himself to the builders right away. His name was Malcolm Bryant, a widower, and his thirteen-year-old son, James, was happy to deliver supplies, even staying on sometimes to help with the construction, especially if it happened to be close to mealtime. Before long, James came to be a regular visitor, even when there was no delivery to be made. Everyone participated in the making of the home. The project, and the excitement generated, served as a gentle balm to ease Victoria's broken spirit. Her evolution was noticed by her mother most of all and was the primary reason for the constant smile on Mary's face.

"They ain't leavin'," Floyd Trask said. "They ain't thinkin' about leavin'. They're buildin' onto that shanty up above Bryant's house." Following Beaudry's instructions, the meek young man had been trying to keep an eye on Jonah and the women. He didn't like working for Garth, but it gave him an opportunity to be close to Angel Lopez, whom he had worshipped from afar ever since she first came to Deadwood on a wagon train with Charlie and Steve Utter and found employment in Madame Dora DuFran's brothel. It was a sorrowful day for Floyd when Angel retired from the business of prostitution and moved in with Garth.

"Damn!" Garth Beaudry swore, and slapped the table with the palm of his hand, almost upsetting the whiskey glass at his fingertips. "I warned that little snake to take his mouthy wife and his homely daughter the hell back east where they belong."

Standing beside the table at his elbow, Angel scrunched her painted lips into a pretty pout. "I want

her out of here, Garth. I don't want her in this town."
She reached up to feel her eye where the bruise had
finally disappeared. "That bitch attacked me. She coulda
marred my face," she whined, and rubbed up against
his arm, while enjoying the pitiful look of envy on
Floyd's face. "You would have protected me if you had
been there," she teased the young man. "Wouldn't you,
sweetie?"

"Yes, ma'am, I sure woulda," Floyd replied awk-
wardly, his face now crimson with embarrassment. He
would have given his life to save her honor if the occasion had called for it.

"You'd have probably gotten your ass kicked real
good," Garth commented sarcastically. He grew weary
of the love-struck boy's doting eyes on Angel. "I'll
take care of Jonah Marple and his friends. They won't
stay in this town very long." He might have taken
some action before this to show his in-laws just how
unwelcome they were, but he couldn't help thinking
about the two men Jonah had evidently employed.
According to Floyd, Cleve and Ben were building
Jonah's house. Maybe so, Garth thought, but one look
at the scar-faced gunman and anybody would know
he wasn't a carpenter. Still smarting from his earlier
confrontation with the ominous stranger, Garth's initial thought had been to have him killed. A day or
so after, however, his passion for revenge had cooled
somewhat, to the extent that he had come to consider
the wisdom in a killing that would automatically be
linked to him. So his intention was to wait until the
two strangers went on their way; then he planned to
make things so uncomfortable for Jonah that he would
pull up stakes and leave. Now the failure of the two to

move on called for Garth to revert to action of a more
serious nature. He decided the time to clear Jonah and
his daughter out of his life had come. *It's their own fault*,
he thought. *I warned them.* "Floyd," he ordered, "ride
down the gulch to Elizabeth Town and tell Cheney I
wanna see him."

"Yes, sir," Floyd said, and with one more long look
in Angel's direction, he went to do Garth's bidding. *A
selfish son of a bitch like Garth Beaudry does not deserve
the attention of a woman of Angel's beauty*, he thought. *He
should go back to that plain-looking wife of his.*

Later that afternoon, Sam Cheney walked into the
cabin behind the saloon that Garth called his office. He
didn't bother to knock before entering. He never did.
"That little snail that works for you said you wanted to
see me. You got another miner that don't know when
it's time to git?"

"I've got another job for you and your boys," Garth
replied. "This ain't got nothing to do with any mining claims, but it's somebody I wanna run outta town,
and it needs to be done so there's no chance they might
wanna come back. You could run into a little trouble,
'cause they've got a couple of men that look like hired
guns hanging around them, so you might need all
your men." He went on to tell Cheney what needed to
be done, and emphasized the fact that the people he
was targeting lived in town, so he would have to be a
little more careful than usual.

A wry smile creased Cheney's face. "This sounds
like somethin' kinda personal," he said. "Somebody
stick a burr under your saddle?"

"Never mind the reason. It just needs to be done,"

Beaudry said, "and make sure nobody sees you do it." Garth didn't like Cheney, but then again, he didn't need to. Cheney was a man to be bought. There was nothing the tall, lean viper wouldn't do if the pay was right. There was nothing imposing about his appearance, and nothing unusual except for one show of vanity. He wore his long sandy hair in a single ponytail that extended below his shoulder blades.

"Ain't nobody ever seen me doin' none of your work yet," Cheney boasted. "It won't be no different this time, but it might cost you a little bit more, this job being right here in town. Me and my boys are gonna have to be a whole lot more careful. Besides that, it sounds like we're gonna have a couple of gun hands to take care of."

Beaudry had anticipated as much. "All right, but this is the way it's gonna be. You'll get your usual pay right now. Then if you do the job nice and neat, and there ain't any mess left behind that points to me, I'll pay you half the usual price on top of what I give you today."

"All right," Cheney said. "When do you want it done?"

"Whenever you're ready," Garth replied. "The sooner, the better. I just don't want to know how you plan to do it, or nothing else about it. I just wanna know when it's done." He got to his feet, dismissing the smug bushwhacker, knowing the insolent smile was meant for him and all men Cheney deemed too gutless to perform the acts he was hired to do. "Floyd here will go with you now and show you the house you're gonna hit." He remained standing while he watched the assassin get on his horse and follow Floyd between the buildings back to the main street. Although he did not tell Cheney to kill the two men Jonah had hired, he knew full well that was bound to happen. *Then we'll see how long Jonah hangs around here without his protection,* he thought. He reached up and carefully felt his nose, still swollen as it slowly healed.

September 25, 1879. Jonah carved the date on the header over the back door, painstakingly writing out the whole thing. When it was finished to his satisfaction, he stepped back to admire it, then turned to Mary and beamed. "It's official. She's finished."

The small gathering assembled to celebrate the completion of the cabin applauded appropriately and Mary said, "Let's have some of this cake. I hope it's fit to eat. This oven bakes a little hotter than my oven back in Omaha."

Victoria smiled, because Mary said that every time she cooked anything at all in the oven. "I'm sure it'll be delicious," she said, and stepped up to help her mother serve. "First slice goes to Mr. Bryant," she said, and went around the table from there, handing a plate to each person. Mary began filling the coffee cups and gave Cleve a mock look of disapproval when he said they should be celebrating with something a little stronger. Malcolm and his son, James, had been invited over to celebrate with them as a gesture to express their appreciation for their neighborly support during the building period. It was a welcome night with spirits high after a monthlong push to complete the house before winter came to the narrow canyon.

"Ben will be sorry he missed out on the cake," Jonah said as he held out his cup so Mary could fill it.

"I'll save him a piece if there's any left," Mary replied. "It's his own fault if there's none left. He could have waited till tomorrow to go hunting."

Overhearing, Cleve commented, "You know Ben. Once he decides to do somethin', you might as well save your breath tryin' to talk him out of it."

In truth, had anyone suggested a celebration might be held, Ben would have delayed his hunting. But it had been a last-minute decision when Mary thought it appropriate to bake a cake. Ben had threatened to go up in the hills to hunt for several days after their supply of venison had been depleted, but he stayed until the last nail had been driven before leaving early that morning. Victoria thought about the tall, almost silent man, and how much her family owed him for his help and protection. *If there's none left, I'll make him a cake of his own.*

The modest celebration continued into the late evening hours, well past everyone's bedtime. Finally Malcolm Bryant stood up and announced that it was a wonderful party, but he had to get up early and open the hardware store. "It's gettin' along toward midnight," he said. "I can't remember the last time I was up this late. Come on, James, we've got to go." Good nights were exchanged all around, and Jonah and Cleve walked outside to see Bryant and his son off. When they had disappeared down the hill in the darkness, Cleve said, "I'm gonna sleep till noon tomorrow." He could not have been more mistaken.

After it was over and done, folks say the fire started in Mrs. Ellsnera's Bakery on Sherman Street at around two o'clock in the morning. How they figured that was hard to say, but there was no question that the flames immediately spread to the hardware store next door, where eight kegs of gunpowder sat waiting to send the flames ripping through the entire town of wooden structures. The blast that ensued woke everyone from their slumber, no matter how late they had gone to bed. The fire spread through the town so rapidly that there was nothing anyone could do but watch the flames as they devoured building after building.

Like thousands of other residents, all the folks at Jonah's house ran out to see what had happened. Walking down the hill as close as they dared, they stood horrified to see an entire town turned into a roaring furnace.

Equally stunned by the sudden blast that turned Deadwood into a flaming hell, four riders drew up abruptly on the street above Jonah Marple's house. "What the hell . . . ?" Sam Cheney blurted, while trying to hold his horse from bolting when the frightened horses of his three companions bumped nervously into each other.

"What in the name of hell was that?" Frank Worley yelled as he looked down at the fire spreading in the gulch below them. "And I'm settin' here holdin' on to a can of kerosene."

"It ain't likely to get up this high on the hill," Shorty Fagen retorted.

His mind back on what they had come to do, Cheney said, "It's gonna spread to one house on this hill. Let's get goin' while everybody is watching the fire down there." There was no reason for Cheney to care if Deadwood burned to the ground. His rented room was in Elizabeth Town, farther down the gulch. In fact, he looked upon Deadwood's tragedy as a real stroke of luck for him. With the whole town ablaze, no one would notice one more house burning to the ground in all the confusion.

They stood horrified by the chaotic scene below them, as they watched from two streets above the town, people running to save what they could from the rapidly spreading flames. The roar of the fire, as it fed on the wooden structures, was like that of a hungry dragon seeking to devour everything in its path as it leaped from building to building, belching smoke and sparks that rose into the cold night air.

One street below them two small children ran from a log cabin, frightened by the fiery eruption so close to their home. A moment later the terrified mother emerged from the cabin, holding on to a third child, frantically calling for the other two. "She needs help with those children," Mary said, and immediately started down the steep slope toward the street below them.

"I'll help you," Victoria called after her, and taking a firm grip on Caleb's hand, she followed her mother, leaving Cleve and her father to watch on the street above them.

"I ain't never seen nothin' like this in my whole life," Cleve said. When he glanced up toward the street above them, he was stopped in his tracks by what he saw. "Jonah!" he blurted, and pointed. Jonah turned to follow the direction he indicated. "Jonah!" Cleve exclaimed again. "Flames! They look like they're comin' from our place!"

"Oh God, no!" Jonah cried. "They can't be!"

Cleve didn't wait to make sure; he started running

up the hill. "The horses!" he yelled. Jonah followed right behind him. Forcing his stubby legs to the extent of their capability, Cleve gasped for air as he ran up the steep incline. The flames were already reaching up to engulf the new section of roof, causing him to strain even more in a desperate effort to save guns and ammunition inside and move the horses away from the burning house.

By the time he reached the edge of the street cut into the side of the hill, he could see several men on horses riding around the house. Thinking at first that they were trying to help, he hoped they had been able to get his rifle and cartridge belt out of the front room. "Come on, Jonah," he called behind him, wheezing with each breath, the result of the exertion in climbing the hill. Only then did he realize that the men he saw were not there to help. Instead, they were soaking the porch, not yet on fire, with kerosene. "Stop!" he roared, and reached for the handgun that was not there. He had left it beside his bedroll in the house. Still, he charged toward the four riders with no weapon but his wrath.

Sam Cheney jerked his head around to discover the two men running toward him. "Damn!" he cursed, seeing that he and his men had been caught in the act of burning the house. His concern was eliminated within a few seconds when he realized the two charging up from the road were not armed. They were obviously the two gunmen Beaudry had warned him about. "Well, now, ain't that handy?" he said to Bull Lacey, who just then pulled up beside him. "Just sit right here and let 'em get a little closer."

It occurred to Cleve that he had let his anger get in

the way of his brain, something he had always prided himself in never permitting. But it was too late now. With no weapon, he should have turned and run for cover as soon as he had realized what was happening. Already too late to correct his error, his concern now was to try to warn Jonah. "Go back!" He managed to get the two words out before the first bullet slammed into his chest. He was still trying to save Jonah when the next bullet tore into his back, dropping him to the ground. His last word spoken on earth was "Jonah!" His last conscious sight was that of the frail little man's body bucking from the impact of a volley of pistol slugs before he collapsed in death.

"Shorty!" Cheney barked. "Go down to the road and see if anybody else is comin'. Bull, you and Frank throw them bodies into the middle of that fire." He figured by the time anybody found them, they'd be burned so badly that no one could tell that they had bullet holes in them. "They'll just think they got trapped in the fire and couldn't get out," he said when Bull and Frank carried Jonah's corpse by him. "Hold on a minute," he said, looking down at the spindly body. "I thought these two mighta been the two gunmen Beaudry warned me about. He sure as hell don't look like no hired gun to me." He glanced over at Cleve's body, still lying where he had gone down. "Him, maybe, but not this one." He didn't particularly care who the victim was, but it told him that at least one of the men Garth had described was still alive. He was sure of it when it occurred to him that neither of the bodies had the scarred face he had been told about. As long as there were no witnesses to the shooting and arson done here on this night, however, there was nothing to worry about.

"Maybe this one is the feller that hired the two gun hands to protect him," Frank Worley suggested.

"Maybe so," Cheney replied, then laughed. "He'll most likely want his money back when they get to hell." When both bodies had been tossed into the growing flames, and Shorty signaled from the road that no one was coming, Cheney said, "Run them horses outta here. Might as well take 'em with us."

"Ain't you afraid somebody'll see us with them horses?" Bull asked.

"Hell, what if they do?" Cheney replied. "Can't nobody say we didn't happen to find 'em after they ran away from the fire."

"I reckon that's right," Bull responded happily. A huge bull of a man, hence the origin of his name, he was the possessor of an uncomplicated brain. His body had far outgrown his mind, leaving him mentally stranded in childhood. "After we're done here," he asked excitedly, "can we stay around and watch the fire?"

Chapter II

Making his way along a hogback that would lead him to the last of the higher mountains that stood between him and the lower hills and canyons, Ben looked up at the low clouds drifting past the peaks. Thin, dark clouds, he thought at first glance. Then he took a longer look and realized that it was smoke floating on the lofty winds. Smoke was always a sign to be cautious of in the mountains, and nearly always associated with Indians, so he began to take in his surroundings more carefully, lest he ride unsuspecting into a Sioux camp.

Once he worked around to the north side of the mountain, leading Graham Barrett's horse packed with meat, he was able to get a better look over the lower foothills. He could see at once that there was a heavier layer of smoke drifting over the hills and gulches. He could smell it now, and the wind was blowing it from the direction of Deadwood Gulch. *A forest fire?* he thought, for there was such a great volume of smoke, too much for even a large village of Indians. Without knowing if he should be concerned or not, he urged the buckskin to pick up a quicker pace.

After riding approximately five miles through the lower hills, he topped a low rise and reached the road that wound down the hill on the north side of the gulch. Below him, the smoking ashes of three hundred buildings lay smoldering, filling the gulch with blackened ruins. The entire city of Deadwood had been incinerated from one end to the other of its approximately one-mile length. Ben could barely believe his eyes. It was almost impossible to imagine that such a thing could happen. Thinking it might be the work of hostile Sioux tribes, he at once rejected that idea, for there were hundreds of people below, sifting through the charred timbers of what had been stores and saloons and homes. With some sense of relief, he looked to the sides of the hills where many houses were still intact. Eager to get home, he nudged his horse again and started down the road.

Long before he got to the street directly above the ruins of the Bella Union, he saw the dark smoky void where the house should have been. Passing Malcolm Bryant's house, he felt a sinking sensation in the pit of his stomach, for there was no question now that of all the houses on the hillside, Jonah's alone had burned down. He kicked the buckskin firmly. Up ahead he saw two people standing beside the charred remains of the house he and Cleve had rebuilt. It was Malcolm and Victoria. There was no sign of Cleve or Jonah, or Mary and Caleb.

Victoria turned to see Ben, and immediately ran to meet him. When she was close enough, he saw the tracks of tears down her soot-smeared face. He quickly jumped down from his horse to meet her and caught her in his arms. Pressing her head against his chest, she put her arms around his waist and, clinging tightly to him, began to sob. He held her close for several minutes until she regained control of her emotions; then at the same moment, they both became aware of the closeness and she stepped back. Looking up into his face, she told him. "Papa and Cleve," she said, catching a sob in her throat. "They're gone, Ben."

It struck him then that her multitude of tears was not for the loss of their house. "Gone?" he exclaimed. "What do you mean, gone?" When she just shook her head slowly, fighting back more tears, he repeated the question. "Gone? . . . Dead?" She nodded then. Almost stunned, he looked from her to Malcolm Bryant, who stood silently by, leaning on a shovel, while she told him. "How?" Ben pressed.

"Looks like they burnt up in the fire," Malcolm answered.

Ben went numb all over. Cleve could not die. Ben thought that Cleve would always be there. The funny little stump of a man had been the only reason Ben had managed to look life in the eye again after the death of his wife and child. The many saloon brawls and Indian attacks that Cleve had survived, and now he was to believe that he had perished because he could not escape a burning house? His attention was brought back to Victoria again, and he berated himself for forgetting her loss for a moment. "I don't know what to say," he said gently. "I'm sorry for the pain I know your father's loss brings you. I'm sorry I wasn't here. Maybe I mighta been able to do something."

"Her mama and the boy are down at my house,"

Malcolm said. "They can stay there as long as they need to."

"Why don't you go back with your mother?" Ben urged Victoria. "I'll be down there in a little bit, after I take care of the horses."

"I'm glad you're back," she said, and turned to leave. She felt safer when he was there.

Once again thinking clearly after absorbing the shock of what he had returned to find, he turned his attention to Malcolm. Looking to the right and left, he then said, "Out of all these houses on this hillside, this is the only house that caught fire. What are the odds of that happenin'?"

"As near as anybody can figure, it musta just been some bad luck—a spark carried up on the wind caught somewhere on the house—then the rest went up like tinder," Malcolm said.

"Even so, how did they get caught inside the house?"

"I don't know," Malcolm replied. He went on then to relate what the women had told him of the early morning hours when everybody was outside to look at the fire in the gulch below. "They said they were down the hill, trying to help some woman with her kids. They didn't even know the house was on fire. Cleve and Jonah musta run back to try to save it. By the time Mary and Victoria found out what was happening up above them, it was too late to save anything. And Jonah and Cleve were gone. They couldn't find 'em—and nobody knew what happened to 'em till daylight and the fire had died out."

"Well, that don't make a bit of sense to me," Ben said, his grief turning more toward anger. "Somethin' ain't right about this. Cleve's too smart to get caught in a trap like this." He paused and stewed over it for a moment more before asking, "Where's Cleve's body? Have you buried him?"

"Just fixin' to," Malcolm said. "James went to get another shovel and a pick. This ground's pretty hard. The bodies are lyin' over there by the back corner of the house. We wrapped 'em in some old sheets on account they looked pretty bad. I didn't want Mary and Victoria and Caleb to see 'em like that."

Ben walked directly to the back corner of the house and the two white bundles lying there. Intent upon seeing the remains for himself, he had to pause and give himself time to prepare when the numb feeling returned to his spine. He could not prevent his mind from taking him back to the fire that had consumed his wife and child. Once again, he found himself facing the loss of someone close to him killed in a fire. Taking a deep breath, he rolled the nearest body over, unwinding it from the sheet. Even though he had prepared for it, the sight that met his eyes was overwhelming. The charred, heat-deformed body did not resemble anything human. He was only able to identify it as Jonah's because it was smaller than the other one. He was devastated for a moment when he wondered if Mary Ellen's and Danny's bodies had looked like this, and he gave thanks that Jim White Feather had possessed the foresight to bury them before he had a chance to see them. Forcefully willing his thoughts to return to the present, he turned his head to inhale deeply before continuing. The odor of seared meat was sickening, but he made himself inspect the corpse closely, confirming what he already suspected. Backing away, and taking another deep breath, he turned to look at Malcolm. "Did you look at these bodies?"

"Well, yeah," Malcolm answered. "I had to look at 'em to drag 'em outta the house. I didn't look at 'em real close, though. Matter of fact, I tried not to look at 'em at all. It wasn't something I wanted to see real close. I'll be dreaming about 'em as it is." When Ben continued to fix him with a gaze made menacing by the ugly scar that always appeared to stand out when he became angry, Malcolm became nervous. "Why?" he asked.

"Because they were murdered," Ben said, his voice calm and deadly, "murdered, then thrown in the fire." He stood up and pointed at Jonah's remains. "There's a pattern of bullet holes in his chest." He didn't have to unroll Cleve's body to verify that similar holes would be there also. He didn't care to remember his partner in this state.

Horrified to hear what Ben declared, Malcolm had to see for himself, thinking that Ben must surely be mistaken. He walked over to Jonah's body and took his first close look. "My Lord in heaven," he gasped as he peered down to see the bullet holes in the puffy seared flesh. He quickly stood up again as James appeared, carrying a pick and shovel. "He doesn't need to see this," Malcolm said, and walked to intercept him.

Having seen all he needed to see to know what had taken place here, Ben rolled Jonah's body back in the sheet. "Where were you fixin' to bury him?" he asked. When Malcolm pointed to a flat spot where the wagon had been parked, Ben nodded. "Good a spot as any, I reckon." Speaking to the boy then, he said, "Hand me that pick, son." He desperately needed some form of release from his anger, and physical labor was the only thing available to him at that moment. He set in to his labor as if to tear the very earth apart, breaking the rock-hard ground into clumps as he swung away with the pick. When he finished with one grave, he immediately started another while Malcolm and his son went to work on the first grave with their shovels. Oblivious of everything but the pick in his hands, he hacked away at the stubborn dirt, unaware of the low, whispered conversation between father and son. When he finally worked the second grave to a point where the shovels could take over, he stepped out of the hole, breathing heavily from his labor, to find Malcolm and James standing there staring at him. Puzzled, he shifted his gaze directly at the boy, but James immediately dropped his chin to stare at the ground. "What is it, boy?" Ben demanded.

Malcolm answered for his son. "There's something we ain't told you," he said. "I didn't know myself till James told me this morning. It didn't seem to make much difference, 'cause it didn't change anything, and it might be better for Mary and Victoria not to know."

"Know what?" Ben demanded, impatiently.

"After we ran out to look at the fires below in the gulch, James here went back home to put the dog in the house, 'cause he wouldn't shut up his barking. When he started back to where we were watching, he saw this house on fire and it looked like some men riding their horses around it."

His interest captured immediately, Ben asked, "Did you know them?"

James nodded and began to speak at last. "Yes, sir, I knew them, all right. Everybody knows them, but I didn't know what they were doing. I thought they had seen the house burning and maybe they were trying to put it out."

Malcolm interrupted then. "I didn't know what they mighta been up to," he said. "Now I reckon I do, since I saw those bullet holes. I don't know what you might be aiming to do, but I don't want James mixed up in any of this. There were four of them. I'll give you their names if I have your word you won't tell anybody who gave 'em to you. Is that a deal?"

"You have my word," Ben replied, his voice deadly quiet.

"All right, then," Malcolm said, "tell him who you saw, James."

"Sam Cheney, Shorty Fagen, Bull Lacey, and Frank Worley," James said.

"Where can I find them?" Ben asked, still emotionless.

"They aren't usually hard to find," Malcolm replied. "They hang out around the Pair-A-Dice Saloon on the lower end of the gulch, near Elizabeth Town, almost to Montana City. I don't know what you're thinking, but I gotta warn you, there ain't a meaner bunch of scoundrels in this whole gulch."

"Are they miners?"

"Ha," Malcolm snorted. "Hell no, they're not miners. I don't imagine any one of the four has ever done a day's labor in their whole lives. No, they ain't got any occupation that anybody knows about, but they always seem to have plenty of money to gamble and buy whiskey with." He paused while watching Ben closely, trying to read the intent in the scarred face. "Ben," he said, "I know this is a terrible thing that's happened here, but I'm trying to warn you that Sam Cheney and his friends are a dangerous bunch to mess with. My advice would be to talk to the sheriff about this, if there is a sheriff after the fire." He paused again, this time to shake his head sadly before continuing. "If there is a town at all. But you need to think it over before you get yourself in a corner. There's been a few miners turned up missing all up and down this canyon, and most folks suspect it ain't Indians that done 'em in. You just be careful before you make too much noise about Jonah and Cleve. Cheney's boys are a pretty rough bunch."

"I 'preciate the advice," Ben said. He directed his next question to James. "You're sure all four of those men were here at the house?" When the boy confirmed that they were, Ben walked to his horse and fished around in his saddlebags to find a piece of cardboard that had once been the bottom of a box of .44 cartridges, and the stub of a pencil. "Tell me their names again," he said, and he wrote them on the piece of cardboard as James called them off. When he was finished, he put the list in his pocket and returned to the graves. "I expect we'd best get these bodies in the ground," he said, his tone still minus any hint of emotion. "I'm sure Mary and Victoria will wanna say somethin' over Jonah's grave." He paused then as if just remembering. "I'll have to do somethin' with that load of meat on that packhorse pretty quick. The weather's been cold enough to keep it from spoilin', but it won't be fit to eat if we don't do somethin' with it pretty soon."

Ben stood apart from the rest of the small group of mourners gathered to say a few prayers to send the

two departed on their way. Malcolm and his son were
in attendance to lend their support to Mary, Victoria,
and Caleb, even though they had known Jonah's family for only a brief time. Malcolm would ordinarily
have been tending his store, but like every other busi-
nessman in Deadwood, he had no store left to tend.
After the brief funeral, he would go down to talk to
some of the other members of the town's business dis-
trict to plan the rebuilding of the town. Ben watched
the grieving wife and daughter as they wept beside
the rough grave of the simple schoolteacher. Then he
thought of the free-spirited and ofttimes humorous
little gnome whose body lay in the grave beside that of
Jonah's, and he knew he would sorely miss his friend.
He had learned a lot of things from Clever Goganis,
most important of which was life goes on, and no matter what happens, you go on with it. He smiled when
he thought about the day he had first met Cleve. His
mother had been right, he had grown into his name.
He was a clever little man. *I'll see that they pay for what
they did to you, partner.*

He shifted his thoughts to what he might do after
he tracked down the four men who murdered Cleve
and Jonah, and he found that he had no plans beyond
that. With Cleve gone, he had no interest in panning
for gold. Looking again at the mourning women, he
told himself that he would stay around long enough to
see that they were safe and had some kind of plan to
survive after Jonah's death. Malcolm seemed sincere
in his invitation for the women to stay with James and
him. And, he pointed out, Caleb would be like a little
brother to James. It was not his problem, Ben told himself, but he confessed to feeling a caring concern for

them and the boy. At the same time, he knew there was no way he could remain with them, even if they wanted him to—not with the job he had sworn himself to do. Once the battle started with Cleve's four murderers, he could not bring it home to Victoria and Mary, and he had assured Malcolm that he would not connect him and his family with any action he took. *So,* he decided, *as soon as I think they're safely settled, I'll be saying good-bye.*

When all had been said over the graves, they left the ruins of the home that they had planned to be theirs through the winter, and walked the quarter mile down the road toward Bryant's house. Victoria moved up beside him, walking with him for a few moments before she made up her mind to speak. "You're thinking about going after the men who did this, aren't you?" He didn't reply, merely shrugged his shoulders. "Please think about what you're doing. We've already lost Papa and Cleve. There's no sense in you risking your life now. It won't bring them back."

"If they don't pay for what they did, then it's the same as sayin' Cleve and your father's lives weren't worth anythin'," he answered. "I owe Cleve more than that. He'd do the same if it was me lyin' back there in the ground."

"Please, Ben, go to the sheriff, and let him handle it," she pleaded.

"Maybe," he said, trying to pacify her concern. "We'll see if there is a sheriff in Deadwood. There's not a buildin' standin', so I don't know where to look for him." He hoped that would satisfy her that he wasn't going to do anything right away, although he had no real intention of going to the law with his problem.

Before the jail burned down, they might have received a telegram from the U.S. Marshal Service, describing a scar-faced fugitive wanted for murdering a deputy sheriff in Kansas. He was not willing to take that risk. As for Malcolm Bryant, Ben understood there would be no help from the hardware store proprietor on this matter. All that was necessary was for Malcolm to tell the sheriff the same thing he had told him, and let James testify as a witness. But Malcolm had made it pretty plain that he feared for his life and family if he fingered Cheney and his cronies as the guilty parties. It was just as well, he thought, for he didn't have faith in the sheriff's office to seek the punishment Cheney and his gang deserved. Remembering his own trial, and the verdict handed down by Judge Lon Blake, he didn't trust the judges to rule fairly as well. This was a crime that called for *an eye for an eye* punishment, and he was the only person capable of rendering it.

As he had promised himself, he stayed close to Victoria and Mary for a couple of days until satisfied that Malcolm was sincere in his invitation to them to remain there indefinitely. It was apparent soon enough that Malcolm was delighted to have two women in his house, especially when it was time to cook something to eat. Ben used much of that time to make sure his weapons and other gear were in good shape. Malcolm spent most of the two days meeting with the other business owners down in the gulch, planning to rebuild the town. This time, he told them, they would build it back with brick and stone, instead of the tinderbox of wood and canvas that it had been before. When all the damage was counted, the fire had destroyed over three hundred buildings, leaving two thousand people homeless. "But we don't aim to sit around sucking our thumbs and weeping about it," Malcolm told them. "We're gonna build Deadwood back better than ever."

"I expect you will," Ben told him. "I'll be leavin' for a spell now that the folks seem to be gettin' along all right. I've got a little bit of money I've been savin' for a long time. I'll leave you some of it to help out with the expenses. It's in greenbacks instead of gold dust, but as soon as you folks get your bank back in business, it'll spend as good as dust."

"Ah, hell no, Ben," Malcolm at once refused. "I won't take any money for keeping these folks. They're welcome here. I think it'll be good for James to have someone to talk to besides a grumpy old man, anyway."

Ben was sure that a major share of Malcolm's generosity was born out of guilt for shying away from pointing a finger at Cheney.

Ben tried to convince him to accept at least a small sum, but Malcolm was adamant in his refusal. "All right." Ben finally gave in. "At least I can drop you off some fresh meat once in a while. There's plenty of elk and deer and antelope back up in those mountains where I'll be."

"You'd best watch your scalp in those mountains," Malcolm warned. "Those damn Indians are looking for any white man that strays too far from Deadwood."

"I'll be careful," Ben said. He tightened the girth strap on the buckskin and gave his saddlebags a tug to make sure they were riding snug. He had decided to leave before the women got up to fix breakfast, so he wouldn't have to justify his reasons for going to everyone. He nodded toward the late deputy marshal Barrett's horse in Malcolm's corral. "I'll leave that Morgan here till I can come back for him. Tell Caleb and the women good-bye for me, will you? Tell 'em I'll be seein' 'em again."

"I will," Malcolm said, then stepped back to give Ben room to step up in the saddle. When Ben was settled, Malcolm shook his head and grimaced. "Boy, you be careful. You're going up against a bad crowd in that gang that runs with Sam Cheney." Ben touched his finger to the brim of his hat in salute and turned the buckskin toward the road.

Chapter 12

Marvin Thompson, owner of the Pair-A-Dice Saloon, glanced up when a customer walked into his establishment. What he saw caused him to take another, longer look. A stranger, the man commanded attention because of his powerful frame, but the cruel, scarred face was the reason for a startled second look from the bartender. Thompson's saloon had become a hangout for many men of suspect morals, so for his own good, he had adopted a policy of no questions asked. Outlaws and saddle tramps were going to get their whiskey somewhere, he rationalized, so he might as well be the one to take their money. On their part, his questionable clientele were content to gather peacefully in his saloon, adhering to an unspoken rule that any trouble between customers should be taken outside. If he was looking for men of his element, this stranger looked as if he had found the right place. So Marvin welcomed him cordially.

"Howdy, stranger. What'll it be?"

"A glass of beer," Ben said. "My throat's kinda dry. I think I musta breathed in too much of that damn smoke." He took a casual glance at the men sitting around a table in the back of the room, playing cards.

"You come down from Deadwood?" Marvin asked. "That smoke is still driftin' down the gulch."

"Looks like it'll be here for a while yet," Ben said, making casual conversation. "Those buildings are still smolderin'." He waited for Marvin to set his glass of beer on the bar, then took a long drink of it before continuing. "Feller up in Deadwood sent me with a message for somebody down here, said I'd find 'em in your place, but I don't know 'em by sight, never seen the fellers before. All I've got is their names."

"Well, maybe I can help you," Marvin offered. "Who you lookin' for?" Ben pulled the piece of cardboard from his pocket and recited the four names. "One of 'em's here right now," Marvin said. "Frank Worley, he's settin' back there at the poker table, little, short feller with his back to the corner."

"Much obliged," Ben said, casually pulled the pencil stub from his pocket, and struck a line through Worley's name. Then he took his time to finish his glass of beer before nodding to Marvin and ambling over to the back table.

All six of the cardplayers looked up to gape at the ominous-looking stranger approaching them, causing a pause in the card game. "You Frank Worley?" Ben asked, directing his question to the man Marvin had pointed out.

Surprised to be called by name, Worley responded. "Who wants to know?"

"I got a message for you," Ben replied.

"From who?"

"Cleve and Jonah," Ben said.

"Who?" Worley responded, baffled. "I don't know no Cleve and Jonah."

"Sure you do. They're the two men you and your friends shot full of holes before you burnt their bodies up in that house you set on fire the other night. You remember now?"

Startled, Worley dropped his cards and pushed his chair back, fumbling to draw the revolver he had stuck in his belt. By the time he got his hand on the handle, Ben's .44 was already in his hand and leveled at him. When the first shot smashed his breastbone, Worley's reflex tightened his trigger finger and sent a bullet through his hip. Toppling his chair, he landed on the floor, still struggling to get his pistol out of his belt. Ben moved deliberately around the table and placed another shot between Worley's eyes. Then he stood there for a few moments to make sure Worley was dead, taking only a quick glance toward the bar to make sure Marvin wasn't reaching for a weapon under the counter. With his pistol still in hand, and held high enough for everyone there to see that he still had it out, he said, "Go on with your game, gentlemen. Sorry to interrupt."

With no show of urgency, he walked back toward the door, his .44 held in a ready position, as he scanned the room quickly in case Worley had friends there who might gamble with thoughts of avenging him. As he had figured, no one there really gave a damn if Worley lived or died, and no one moved until he reached the door and went out. Outside, he moved much more quickly, holstering his weapon and jumping in the saddle, and was galloping away before anyone made a move to react.

That's one of them, Cleve, he thought as the buckskin carried him swiftly away from the Pair-A-Dice Saloon. The other three might be quite a bit more difficult to deal with, for now they would be alerted to expect the deadly messenger. He was also aware at this point that his task had become almost impossible, since he could not identify the remaining three murderers. He was counting heavily upon the probability that the other three would likely come after him. They would sure as hell have a description of him, since everyone in the saloon who witnessed Worley's execution could describe his scarred countenance. The question was, where would they search for him? He decided that he was going to have to give this some more thought. When he had come to the Pair-A-Dice this evening, he had hoped all four would be there. *I should have waited until they were*, he scolded himself in hindsight. He had been too impatient to administer justice when he saw Frank Worley casually playing cards. He vowed to be patient from now on, even if it took the rest of his life to track them all down. It was time to plan more carefully, so he tried to imagine what the other three men would do when they found out about Worley. *They'll most likely want to get me before I can get them*, he thought. *And they'll probably go back to the house they set fire to and look around. They won't know any place else to look. So I'll make sure they find something.* He couldn't say it was the best of plans, but it was a plan, so instead of heading toward the mountains, he rode back to Deadwood.

It was well past dark by the time he reached the road where Jonah's house had stood. He could see a lamp burning in the kitchen window of Malcolm Bryant's house as he rode silently by. Someone was still up, and it was tempting to stop in and get a couple of Mary's biscuits to go with some coffee, but he had no desire to let them know he was back at the house. When he arrived at the burned-out foundation of Jonah's house, he paused for a time to decide the best place to set up his camp. He decided upon the level spot beside the two new graves and walked over to stand and look around him. The hill rose steeply behind the house, leading up to another street cut into the slope. There were few trees of any type on the entire hillside except for a line of young pines, clumped close together about halfway up between the two streets. The thicket did not provide much cover in the daylight, but it would do to hide a horse and rider at night.

Collecting small pieces of wood left unconsumed by the house fire, he built a fire to boil his coffee and roast some strips of venison for his supper. When he was finished, he made sure there were enough scraps of evidence to indicate someone had camped there. It was doubtful that the men he expected would be nosing around there this soon after Worley's death, but to be safe, he took the buckskin to a stream several hundred yards away where he often watered the horse. Thinking it as safe a place as any, he spread his bedroll there for the night.

"Damn, Cheney," Shorty Fagen said when he walked in the door of the saloon. "Where have you been? Me and Bull have been lookin' for you all mornin'."

"I've been lookin' for that son of a bitch Beaudry," Cheney replied. "He owes me money, and I can't find the bastard. I figured he'da gone up to Lead City, since he's supposed to be workin' for the Homestake, but he wasn't up there." He was about to rant on, but he noticed the concerned looks on both their faces. "What the hell's eatin' at you two?" he asked.

"Worley's dead," Shorty said. "Somebody shot him last night when he was playin' cards right here in the saloon."

"Damn," Cheney responded, surprised, but not overly concerned. "I don't wonder. Somebody finally caught him cheatin', I reckon."

"No," Bull Lacey was quick to respond. "Frank weren't cheatin'; at least nobody caught him at it. It wasn't one of the fellers he was playin' cards with that done it. It was some stranger that just walked up to the table, asked him if he was Frank Worley, then pulled out a gun and shot him."

"It was that feller with the scar," Shorty said. This caught Cheney's attention.

"That's right," Bull exclaimed, and repeated, "Marvin said he just walked right up to the table and asked him if he was Frank Worley. Then he said he had a message for him from them two fellers we shot and threw in the fire." This served to capture Cheney's full attention. Wanting more details firsthand, he walked over to the bar where Marvin was wiping some shot glasses with a rag.

Always a bit nervous when Cheney and his friends were all in his saloon at the same time, he repeated the story he had told Bull and Shorty before. Seeing no sense in disclosing every detail, he didn't tell Cheney the part about Ben asking which one Worley was, and the fact that he had pointed him out. "He was a bad-lookin' jasper," Marvin went on. "Had a helluva scar across his face, like somebody had laid it open with an axe. Worley never had a chance. Before he pulled out his gun and shot him, he said you boys killed two fellers and burned a house down."

Marvin's last statement caused Cheney to cock his head around to fix him with a sharp stare. "You know that ain't so," he said, " 'cause me and the boys were in here that night, playin' cards all night."

"Well, that's right," Marvin quickly replied. "You boys were in here all night. You sure were." He didn't ask which night Cheney was referring to—it didn't matter.

"Bring us a bottle over here," Cheney said, then turned and led Shorty and Bull back to their usual table in the corner. He waited for Marvin to set the bottle and glasses on the table and leave them before getting down to discuss this unexpected threat. "Somebody saw us at that house, and one of them two we shot wasn't who we thought he was. We were right about that."

"Well, who the hell was he?" Shorty blurted.

"Don't make no difference," Cheney said, "but we sure know who the hell he wasn't. Beaudry said one of them two gun hands had a scar on his face, and you heard what Marvin said. Some big son of a bitch with a scar on his face was the one that walked in here and shot Worley, and I got a feelin' he ain't gonna be satisfied with just one of us. So we better damn sure get him before he picks off another one of us."

"Where we gonna find him?" Bull asked.

"Shut up and lemme think a minute," Cheney barked. He was trying to recall if Garth Beaudry had told him who lived in the house he sent them to burn, and finally decided that he had not. "I don't know who was livin' in that house. Whoever it was hired those two gun hands for some reason, so the only chance we've got to find the bastards is to watch that house to see if they're still hangin' around there."

Since neither of his two partners had any better suggestions, they decided to ride on up the gulch that afternoon to look around the ruins of Jonah's house in the daylight. Following the dusty road up the hill-side, they paid very little attention to Malcolm Bryant's house as they rode past. A hundred yards shy of the blackened ruins of Jonah's home, Cheney signaled for them to pull up, and he took a long look at the hill still before him. Satisfied there was no one about, he started forward again, constantly scanning left and right, looking for possible places where a man with a rifle might be waiting. In single file, they turned off the road and followed the path up to the front yard.

Twisted and charred, the remains of the house stared out at them like a ghostly monument to their evil accomplishment as they filed by the side of the foundation. "Look here," Bull called to the others. "There's a couple of graves back here."

"That ain't all," Shorty said, and dismounted to look over the remains of Ben's campfire. "Looks to me like somebody's campin' here. These ashes are still warm."

"Well, now," Cheney remarked, "I'd sure like to get a look at whoever it is. I might even be willin' to bet he's got a big ol' scar across his face." His comment caused all three to involuntarily take a quick look all around them.

Noticing the same pine thicket that Ben had spotted earlier, Bull pointed toward it and said, "That looks like the only spot around here where a man could hide to watch this camp. I say we oughta come on back after dark and see if he's the one usin' this place."

Cheney looked at the huge man, surprised that the suggestion had come from such a simple mind. "That ain't a bad idea, Bull. I was just thinkin' 'bout somethin' like that, myself." He looked at Shorty then. "You got any better idea?"

"Nope, sounds as good as any to me," Shorty replied, bringing a wide smile of pride to Bull's face. "It's a while before dark. Let's go on back to the Pair-A-Dice and get a drink."

"He might be back there, lookin' for us," Bull said. "Maybe we oughta go somewhere else."

"Hell, I wish he would come back to the Pair-A-Dice," Cheney said. "But he won't, 'cause he's got a pretty good idea we know what he looks like now, and he knows there'd be three guns on the first scar-faced pecker-head that walks in the door."

It was close to dusk when Ben guided the buckskin carefully down the slope toward the small thicket of young pines. Satisfied that no one was hiding in the thicket, he paused there for a few minutes to look at the ruins of the burned house below him, scanning the hillside all around it, as well as the road in front. There was no place for anyone to hide, so he urged his horse forward, leaving the thicket and descending to the house and the campsite he had left for Cheney and his partners to find.

Gambling that he had sufficient time before hard dark, he built up his fire and roasted some antelope jerky for his supper. As darkness began to settle in, he pulled the saddle off his horse and tethered it opposite the front corner of the foundation of the house, hoping it would be well out of the line of fire if there was any. Then he rolled his blanket and arranged it on his bedroll. After checking his rifle, he stepped into the ruins of the burned-out house, carefully making his way around and over charred timbers that lay in jumbled piles where the roof had collapsed upon the floor. In the middle of the remnants of the kitchen, there were a couple of partially burned ridge poles that had come to rest across the top of the stove, forming a shelter of sorts. This was the spot he picked for his ambush. Down on his hands and knees, he backed up under the poles and situated himself as comfortably as possible. With the iron stove between him and the campfire, he sat and waited.

As the time passed, and the flames from the campfire burned low, leaving only glowing coals, he began to wonder if his wait was in vain on this night. The iron stove before him caused him to recall the last stove he had found in the ruins of a house—his house, and Mary Ellen's stove. Unlike the one here, her stove had been broken almost in two by a much heavier ridge pole than the two smaller ones forming his shelter tonight. The memory brought a moment of melancholy when he was reminded of all he had lost on that fateful day. He reached in his pocket and pulled out the silver chain, squeezing it in his hand until he could feel the heart attached pressing deeply into his palm as the image of Mary Ellen's smiling face came to his mind. *I miss her so damn much*, he thought, and the terrible void her death had left in his life returned to settle over his cramped shoulders. For just a moment, he could not remember how he came to be huddled under these blackened timbers in this dark, deathly place. In the next second, he was jolted back to the present by a sudden explosion of rifle fire from the pine thicket.

Waiting unseen in his cramped ambush, he watched the muzzle flashes from the pines as his blanket and bedroll were pummeled with shot after shot and bullets ricocheted from the hard ground of the hillside. Finally, the fierce volley stopped, and he heard the rustle of horses pushing through the pine thicket. Taking his time, he raised his rifle and steadied the barrel on the top of the stove. Still he waited, as one, then another, and finally the third rider descended to approach the camp and the bullet-riddled blanket cautiously.

"What the hell?" Shorty blurted as Bull pulled up beside him. "There ain't nobody here. It's just an empty blanket."

Crouching in the ruins of the burned house, Ben waited patiently for the two horses to separate and allow him two clear targets, but they remained side by side with Bull's horse and body, covering Shorty's. Beyond them, Cheney walked his horse along the perimeter of the level spot. Ben felt he was quick enough to hit all three before they had a chance to bolt if Shorty and Bull would move apart, but it was almost as if the huge man was purposefully shielding his partner. It seemed to Ben that minutes had passed with the three riders lingering over the empty blanket. In reality, it was only seconds when suddenly Cheney realized the meaning of the deserted camp. "Get the hell outta here!" he shouted, and jerked his horse's head to the side. It was too late for Shorty and Bull, for as soon as they started to run, both men were knocked from their saddles.

As quickly as Ben had gotten off the two fatal shots, it was not quick enough to get a clear shot at Cheney.

"Damn the luck," he cursed, and threw the timbers aside as he ran from the ruins to try to get a shot at the fleeing outlaw. He had no idea which name on his list was the survivor's, but he was able to see a long pony-tail of sandy hair flying as the man slumped low in the saddle, whipping his galloping horse relentlessly. With only a brief glance at the two bodies lying near the graves, he grabbed the saddle horn of Bull's horse and jumped in the saddle. Off through the darkness he rode, urging the horse for all the speed it would give him. After a gallop of about a quarter of a mile, he came to the end of the road and reined the horse up sharply to avoid plunging off a twenty-five-foot drop. Cursing his luck again, he turned the horse back the way he had just come. Evidently, the man had turned off somewhere along the road and disappeared in the darkness. There was no choice but to wait until daylight and hope that he could find a trail to follow. As for now, however, he had to hurry back to get his horse and make his own escape before someone came to investigate the shooting. In the morning, he would search for the trail of the man with the long ponytail.

Back at the campsite, he quickly threw his saddle on the buckskin, then took any weapons and cartridges he could use from the bodies and the horses. He hesitated for a few moments, trying to decide if he should take the horses and saddles. At this stage there was really nothing he could do with them. In fact, he couldn't afford to be caught with them. In the end, he settled for weapons, cartridges, and what money he found on the bodies, knowing he would need that. He pulled the saddles off the two horses and set them free. When he was ready, he climbed aboard the buckskin and started him off up toward the pine thicket. Behind him, he heard excited voices in the dark as someone finally came up to see what the shooting was about.

Sheriff John J. Manning had all he could do to watch over the crippled town of Deadwood amid the chaos following the tragic fire. For this reason, he was not happy to get the report that there were two dead men up at the same site where two were found previously. Bullet holes in them, he was told, plainly a case of murder. He walked from the tent that served as his temporary office to find Malcolm Bryant standing there.

"Two bodies, Sheriff," Malcolm volunteered without waiting to be asked. "Shorty Fagen and Bull Lacey, one bullet each, right through the heart. I found 'em this morning."

"Fagen and Lacey, huh?" Manning responded. "Well, I don't expect there'll be much mourning over the loss of those two. Anything else you can tell me?" He made no attempt to hide his lack of enthusiasm for investigating the report. He had too much on his plate as it was, and no one he knew of would count the elimination of those two as anything less than a blessing.

"Not much," Malcolm replied. "Last night—we'd already gone to bed—this big volley of gunfire woke me up. It sounded like a war right up the hill from my place. You know I've got two women and two small boys at my house now, so I couldn't run off and leave 'em unprotected. So there's not much more I can tell you." There was actually much more that he could tell Manning if he chose, for he had a pretty fair notion who was responsible for the two new corpses at the burned-out house.

"Well, I'll send somebody up there to get the bodies," Manning said, "but I doubt I'll have much to go on for a suspect. Anyway, thank you, Malcolm. I'll see to it."

"Just trying to do my civic duty," Malcolm replied, and went on his way.

"You hear that?" Manning asked his deputy, who was also his brother, Tom, when he returned to the tent. "That happened last night, and nobody said anything about it till this morning. The whole damn town's gone crazy since the fire."

"Yeah, I heard," Tom answered. "Kinda strange, don'cha think? All of a sudden we're getting four murders, right in a bunch. Remember that bulletin we got on that scar-faced fugitive wanted for killing a deputy sheriff in Kansas, just before everything got burnt up in the fire? Wasn't that about the same time that fellow Beaudry came in complaining about some man breaking his nose? He said that man was a stranger with a big scar across his face. Makes you wonder, doesn't it?"

The sheriff had to stop and give that some thought. "Damn, I don't know," he said. "Could be that bastard has showed up here in Deadwood. Couldn't be at a worse time, if it is him. If the telegraph is up again, might be a good idea to wire the marshal's office and let them know what we've got up here. Then if they've got somebody they wanna send up here to help us out, we'd sure as hell appreciate it." He paused for a moment, when a thought occurred. "Whoever it was sure did the town a favor—gettin' rid of those two."

At that moment, the scar-faced fugitive Manning and his brother were discussing was searching for something that would show him where he had lost Cheney the night before. He retraced his ride to the end of the road and the sheer drop-off to make sure the pony-tailed killer had not somehow continued over the edge. There were no tracks, save that of one horse, which he knew were from the horse he rode that night. Watching closely for any sign, he rode slowly back along the road, stopping at a point about one hundred yards from the end of the road. It wasn't much to go on, but it was the only set of tracks plunging off the edge of the road, so he figured they had to be his man's. He descended the steep hillside carefully to keep his horse from sliding until he reached the road below. That was as far as he could rely on tracking, for there were too many tracks on the road, in both directions. He had to make a decision—go right to Lead, or left to Elizabeth Town. Chances were good, he thought, that Ponytail would head back to his regular hangout, so he turned the buckskin toward Elizabeth Town.

He killed a great part of the day looking around Elizabeth Town just on the chance of finding the man, even riding down as far as Montana City. There was no sign of the ponytailed villain, nor did he hold out much hope that there would be, and he wondered if he was in some other part of the ten-mile gulch, looking for him. There was only one other place he could think to look. It might be a dangerous, even foolish, place to return to, but he was becoming more and more desperate to finish this thing he had silently promised Cleve he would do.

Marvin Thompson paid little attention to the dark figure standing just outside the door to scan the patrons in the crowded barroom. A lot of his customers took a cautious look to see who was inside before walking in. When he glanced up to see the man approaching the bar, however, he dropped the glass he was rinsing in the water bucket on the shelf next to him. He had not counted on seeing the scar-faced gunman in his establishment again, and this time he was carrying a Winchester rifle as well as the pistol on his side. Wondering if the grim messenger of bad news was there to eliminate another one of his customers, Marvin backed away from the counter and stood gaping until he spoke.

"Have you seen that feller with the long yellow ponytail lately?" Ben asked.

"Mister," Marvin replied nervously, "Cheney ain't been back since you shot Frank Worley, and I don't expect he'll be back as long as you're in town. He had a room next door, but it's empty."

"Where did he go?"

"I ain't got no idea," Marvin said. "He didn't even tell me he was leavin'—he just went." Thinking that Ben looked annoyed by his answer, he volunteered, "He always bragged about workin' for the Homestake. Maybe he went up that way."

"Much obliged," Ben said, turned, and left the saloon. Outside, he slipped the rifle back in its scabbard and headed for Lead. It was already getting along toward evening, and by the time he reached Deadwood, it was beginning to get dark. He decided he might as well stop for the night while he was close to the stream he had camped at before. Both he and the buckskin could use a little rest. Now he at least knew the name of the man he hunted: Cheney.

Chapter 13

Suddenly feeling very tired, Ben leaned back against the trunk of a tall pine tree and stared down at the black coffee in his cup, setting his mind free to wander. He had never killed a man before this past summer. To take another man's life was something he had always hoped he would never have to do, and now, at this point in his life, he had killed many, both white and red, men. The thing that troubled him most was his lack of remorse for any of the lives he had taken. How could he square things with the Man Upstairs? He gave that question a few moments' thought, and decided there was no way he could be absolved of these sins. Then he thought of Mary Ellen and Danny. Would he see them in another life when this sorry tale was ended? "I doubt it," he concluded aloud, "'cause I'm gonna kill one more son of a bitch before I cash in my chips." He stared at the small fire before him until his eyelids became too heavy to remain open. After a while, the coffee cup dropped from his fingers, spilling his coffee on the ground. He was not aware of it, for he was fast asleep, exhausted, and still sitting with his back against the tree.

She picked up the coffee cup and rinsed it in the stream, moving carefully so as not to wake him. She had brought bacon and biscuits for him, but she decided that it was better to let him sleep. He could eat them cold when he woke up. She then picked up the tattered blanket lying by his saddle and very gently draped it across his shoulders. Satisfied that she had done all she could to let him rest, she sat down beside the tree and kept watch while he slept.

With the first rays of sunlight filtering through the branches of the plum trees by the stream, he suddenly awoke with a start, realizing that it was morning and he had fallen asleep. Startled for a second time, he almost recoiled when he discovered Victoria sitting next to him, breathing heavily in deep slumber. *How the hell . . . ?* he asked himself, trying to remember how she could possibly be there, but he hadn't a clue.

As carefully as he could manage, he struggled to his feet, trying not to wake her, still mystified as to how she happened to be there. Pressed tightly against the tree trunk and hugging herself against the cold, she looked about to start shaking at any moment, so he took the blanket from his shoulders and wrapped it around hers. The weight of it was enough to awaken her. Sleepy eyed and shivering from the chill of the morning, she scrambled to her feet when she realized that she had fallen asleep on her voluntary watch. With a look of alarm, she glanced all around her, looking for signs of danger. With everything apparently all right, her expression immediately changed to one of chagrin, feeling as if she had been caught in a frivolous act.

He waited for her to speak, but when she was apparently at a loss to explain her presence, he asked, "Victoria, what in the world are you doin' here? How long have you been here? How did you know I was here?"

Quickly regaining her composure, she busied herself rekindling the fire while she answered his questions. "It didn't take much thinking to know who killed those two murderers at the house night before last. Malcolm talked to the sheriff yesterday morning, and he sent someone to move the bodies. James was there when they took them. They found a campfire beside the graves and James said they figured the man who killed them had been camping there. I knew it was you and I was afraid you might have come back last night and the sheriff might have been watching for you. So I went there to tell you not to camp there."

"Well, I 'preciate you worryin' about me, but you ought not be stayin' out all night like that. Your mother must be worried sick."

"I told James to tell Mama where I was if I wasn't back by morning."

"Your mama will be fit to be tied," he said.

"Why? I'm with you," she replied, as if it were elementary.

"When I wasn't at the house, how'd you know I was here?"

"Well, I didn't know for sure," she said. "But I thought you might be here, because this is where you always took your horse to water him." She smiled then. "I brought you some biscuits and bacon, but you were asleep. You can have them for breakfast."

With fresh coffee working on the fire, she questioned him while he shared the biscuits and bacon with her. "As soon as we heard the gunshots the other night, I knew you were involved," she said. "Like Malcolm said, why would anybody else be around the place? What are you going to do now?"

"Well, you already know what happened. I got two of 'em, but there's still one on the loose. Just like I figured, they came lookin' for me," he answered matter-of-factly. "But all they killed was that blanket wrapped around your shoulders."

Still alarmed that he would risk his life in such a manner, she said, "Oh, Ben, let this be the end of it. Let the sheriff go after the other one. Malcolm can tell him who the other man is." She closed her eyes momentarily while she shook her head in exasperation. "When I think about you hiding in that burnt-out mess waiting for those murderers—"

"How'd you know I hid in the house?" he interrupted.

"Look at you," she exclaimed. "It wasn't hard to guess. You've got soot smeared all over your clothes and your arms, even some on your face." She reached up and wiped a black smear from his forehead with a corner of the blanket. He immediately drew back, a reflex since the day his face had been transformed into a hideous mask. "Be still," she admonished. "I'm not going to hurt you. You need a bath and some clean clothes."

Becoming a bit impatient with her mothering, he said, "I reckon that ain't the most important thing on my mind right now. Besides, it's too damn cold to jump in this stream."

"If you'll come on back to the house with me, I'll heat some water and you can clean up there."

"I can't do that, Victoria," he said at once. "That feller is probably lookin' for me as hard as I'm lookin' for him. I can't take a chance on leadin' him back to Malcolm's house. I made him a promise that I wouldn't involve him or James, and I sure don't want to drag you and the boy into it. I just hope to hell nobody saw you comin' here."

"No one saw me," she assured him. "And it's a good thing they didn't, because you were fast asleep."

He grimaced, embarrassed to have been reminded of that lapse of vigilance. "Well," he responded, "I'm all caught up now. That ain't likely to happen again. So now I reckon it's time to get on with what I've got to do."

"Can't you just forget about that one last man?" Victoria implored. "I'm sure Papa and Cleve would tell you that they've been avenged enough."

He reached down to help her to her feet. "I can't now," he said. "I started somethin' that the feller with the long ponytail is gonna wanna finish, so I couldn't call it off if I wanted to. I expect you'd best get along back to Malcolm's now, before they start out lookin' for you."

She knew he was right, so she paused to brush off her skirt before leaving him. "James saw the two men you killed, and he said the one that got away is Sam Cheney."

"I know. I just found that out."

She stood gazing at him for a long moment before deciding; then she stepped quickly up to him and kissed him on the cheek. "You take care of yourself,

Ben Cutler," she said, then promptly spun around and left him standing there dumbfounded.

"Much obliged," he mumbled, long after she was out of earshot. Puzzling over the entire surprise visit, and especially the good-bye kiss, he was left to wonder if the young lady actually cared what happened to him. She acted as if she did, he decided. Then his focus returned to the dangerous job ahead. He took the cardboard piece from his pocket and struck a line through two more names, Shorty Fagen and Bull Lacey. That left one, Sam Cheney; then his work would be done. He gathered up what remained of his bedroll and saddled his horse. There was one more message to be delivered.

"Victoria!" her mother exclaimed when her daughter walked into the kitchen. "Praise the good Lord you're safe!" At first registering the relief she felt when seeing her daughter, she quickly furrowed her brow to scold. "James told us where you went. Have you taken leave of your good sense? I didn't get a wink of sleep all night, listening for you to come home," she lied. "And this morning you were still gone. I'd already told Malcolm that we had to search for you." When Victoria casually tossed it off with a shrug, Mary continued. "All night," she exclaimed. "What would self-respecting people say?"

"Oh, Mama," Victoria responded impatiently, "what people? Who cares, anyway? All right, I slept with him. Is that what you're worried about?" Mary clasped her hands together and pressed them to her breast, as if about to have a heart attack. "Oh, Mama, stop it. When I found him last night, he was sitting up against a tree, sound asleep. I sat down and leaned up against the same tree, and I fell asleep. We woke up and had breakfast; then I came home."

Feeling relief once again, Mary chastised her daughter. "You're gonna cause the death of me yet. I declare, I don't think you'll ever get old enough to where I can stop worrying about you." She couldn't help recalling that the last, and only, time a man had taken advantage of her poor plain daughter, it had resulted in the tragic situation they now found themselves in, although, she had to admit, their marriage had produced a fine grandson. Lately she had found herself praying that Caleb had inherited more traits from his mother than he had from his father.

The man who had come to Mary Marple's mind was at that moment drinking coffee in the tiny dining room of Felton Price's Silver Dollar Saloon. Seated to his right, Angel Lopez picked unenthusiastically at a small half-done steak. "When are we going to get out of this dump and go find a real hotel?" she whined.

"When I say so," Garth replied sharply. Then changing his approach, knowing she would punish him later if he was short with her now, he said, "We'll just be here till we can find someplace to start again. This was the best I can do right now."

"This place ain't fit for a lady," she complained. "There's a nice hotel down near Elizabeth Town that don't have bugs."

"Just be patient a little while longer," he said. He wasn't fond of the rooms they were renting upstairs over the saloon, but he deemed it prudent to remain in Lead close to the Homestake Mine since Deadwood was burned out. His only prospect for future success was to stay in close contact with Arnold Freeman at the mine. He was about to explain that to the pouting prostitute when they were interrupted by the arrival of an uninvited guest.

"Damned if you ain't a hard one to find," Sam Cheney announced loudly as he strode over to the table. "I've been lookin' all over Deadwood, what's left of it, anyway, tryin' to run you down. We've got some talkin' to do."

Garth could not prevent the scowl that appeared on his face. "What the hell are you doing here, Cheney? We can't be seen talking together."

Cheney was not in a patient mood. "Is that so?" he replied. "It's all right," he said sarcastically. "I ain't worried 'bout ruinin' my reputation." He pulled out a chair and before he sat down, turned to yell at the one woman who waited tables, "Bring me some of that coffee over here, and a plate of them potatoes he's eatin'." He plopped down in the chair then and reached over to pat Angel on the arm. "Maybe me and you'll have a little tussle after breakfast, honey."

"Keep your dirty hands off me!" Angel spat.

"Keep your hands to yourself, Cheney," Beaudry warned. "Angel has retired from that business."

"Yeah, I'm retired," Angel echoed smugly with a look of contempt for Cheney.

Turning his attention back to Beaudry, Cheney flashed a bitter smile. "Well, I ain't retired, and I've got some crazy bastard tryin' to shoot my ass. He's already done for Shorty, Bull, and Frank, and he damn near got me the other night. And you ain't paid me for that other job."

"I warned you about the two men with Jonah Marple," Garth replied. "If one of them is still alive, then you haven't earned the extra money yet."

"Why, you double-dealin' bastard," Cheney erupted, "the job was to burn that house down and kill them two that was there—and I done that."

"Damn it, Cheney, keep your voice down!" Garth said, looking around to see if they might have been overheard. There was no one else in the dining room but the waitress, and she was at the other end, cleaning off a table.

"I don't suppose you'd be too tickled if I was to tell it around that you was the one that paid Shorty and the others to kill them two fellers up on the hill, would you?" He paused to enjoy the look of alarm on Beaudry's face. "Well, that's just what's gonna happen if I don't get two hundred dollars, gold, to keep that little secret to myself." When Garth started to object, he cut him off. "Now, that's a good deal for you. You promised five hundred for the fire, and eight hundred if we had to kill them two fellers, so you owe three hundred. I'll let you off at a lower price since we didn't get the jasper you wanted, but a killin's a killin', so you owe for it." He glanced over at the bored woman sitting with them and grinned. "You sure you don't wanna change your mind 'bout bein' retired?" She favored him with a look of disgust and turned away.

"By God," Garth replied, ignoring Cheney's comment to Angel, "that's blackmail, and after all the mine business I've thrown your way."

Cheney offered a cantankerous grin in response. "By God, you're right. Blackmail, that's what it is, all right. Maybe you wanna go see Sheriff Mannin' and report it. Or maybe you'd be better off just payin' up what you owe and be done with me." He turned toward the other end of the dining room and yelled, "Where's that damn coffee?"

"How do I know I'll be done with you?" Garth asked. "You might decide you want more later on." He had the money hidden away, gold dust he had confiscated from claims he had been instrumental in acquiring for Homestake, but he didn't care to see it wasted on scum like Sam Cheney. "Most of what I had went up in the fire in Deadwood."

"Now, Mr. Beaudry, don't try to play me for a fool." His malicious grin disappeared, replaced by a threatening sneer. After a moment, the grin reappeared. "You don't have to worry about me comin' back for more. I ain't in the habit of hangin' around places that ain't good for my health, and this place ain't healthy for me no more. I'm fixin' to head back down to Cheyenne as soon as you gimme what I'm due. I got a brother down that way, and I need that two hundred to see me through." He paused when the waitress placed a cup of coffee before him. After giving her a thorough looking-over, he told her, "If I had a mule as slow as you, I swear I'd shoot him."

Beaudry did not reply at once, waiting for the waitress to leave while thinking over his options. There seemed to be only two, pay up or have Cheney taken care of by more permanent means. The problem with the latter choice, which he favored, was that Cheney was the man he always hired to take care of those jobs. *On the other hand*, he thought, *there might be another option after all*. "All right," he said, "I'll give you the money, but I haven't got that much on me. Where are you going to be tonight?"

"Hell, I don't know," Cheney answered. "I ain't goin' back to that place I was stayin' at, next to the Pair-A-Dice."

"You can stay here," Garth suggested. "The rooms upstairs are pretty cheap."

Cheney smiled and winked at Angel. "Yeah, why not?" he said. "But I'll need my money tonight, 'cause I'll be leavin' outta here early in the mornin'.'"

"I'll have it for you by suppertime," Garth said. "Go ahead and get yourself a room."

When Garth and Angel walked into the dining room that evening, they found Cheney already there, seated at a table, well along with his dinner. There were only a few patrons in the room, most of them employees of Homestake. Cheney broke out his standard grin when he saw them. "Well, I was beginnin' to think you mighta forgot where the dinin' room was," he said. "You can set down right here." Then he called out for the waitress, loud enough for everyone to hear, "Hey, woman, get your lazy ass over here."

Beaudry paused by the table for only a moment. "Damn it, it's not good for us to be seen together," he said, almost in a whisper. "We'll sit at another table." When his remark brought a frown to Cheney's face, he hurried to reassure him. "I've got your money. I'll send Angel with it to your room after we've eaten."

"I'll be waitin' for you," he told Angel with a wink. "Now, don't you be too late, 'cause I need to get to bed early." She cast a bored look in his direction, causing him to chuckle in response.

Obviously offended by his boorish behavior, the waitress, a matronly woman of perhaps forty years of age,

arrived at his table in answer to his call. She had really
hoped his earlier visit to the dining room would be his
last, but here he was again, and his offensive manner
was no better than before. "Was there something you
wanted, sir?" she asked.

"Yeah," he replied, "get me some coffee, and make
it quick." He looked around him at the other diners,
enjoying the fact that none would hazard direct eye
contact with him.

He lay on the bed, stripped down to his long johns and
socks, wondering if he was going to have to go looking
for Beaudry after all. He was about to decide that to be
the case when he heard the tap on his door. As a matter of habit, he pulled his .44 from the holster on the
dresser and went to the door. "Who is it?"

"Angel," came the reply. "Open the damn door. I've
got your money."

"Sure 'nough, honey." He turned the key in the lock
and quickly stepped to the side, his gun leveled at the
door and ready to fire. "Come on in. It's unlocked." She
opened the door and walked into the room. He stuck
his head out and took a quick look up and down the
short hallway before closing the door and locking it
again. "Where's the dust?" he asked.

"Put that damn gun away and I'll give it to you,"
she said. When he replaced the weapon in its holster,
she opened a large purse, produced a small pouch, and
placed it on the dresser. "There it is," she said.

With an expectant smile, he opened the pouch and
peered inside. Satisfied that it was of sufficient weight
to be about two hundred dollars, he said, "Now that

you ain't got your daddy lookin' over your shoulder, how'd you like to take a pinch or two of that dust back with you?"

She favored him with a knowing smile. "How big a pinch?" she asked playfully.

"Depends on how good you are," he returned, equally playful.

"All right," she said, "I'll let you decide how much it's worth." She began to unbutton her blouse.

"I knew you'd took a shine to me," he boasted. "Besides, once a whore, always a whore. Ain't that right?"

"I suppose it is. You won't tell Garth, will you? He thinks I'm his property."

"No, ma'am, he ain't ever gonna know, and I might give you a little extra if you really do it right."

She slipped out of her clothes while he stood watching the show with obvious anticipation. When she was undressed, she placed her clothes on the bed and lay down beside them. "Are you coming or not?" she asked, since he was still in his underwear.

"I'll be there, all right, little darlin'." He peeled off his long johns and climbed onto the bed with her.

The transaction proceeded in typical fashion, since both partners had experienced many such couplings. Angel did her part in taking him where he wanted to go. And at what she deemed to be a climactic point in the animalistic struggle, she slipped her hand inside the folds of her skirt beside her and withdrew the dagger hidden there. Seemingly lost in his passion, and oblivious of the stealthy hand, he continued his assault upon her body. Slowly, she raised the dagger above his shoulder and with a grunt of exertion, she brought it down, only to find her wrist ensnared in the viselike grip of his hand.

Breathing heavily from the exertion, he bared his teeth in a sadistic smile. "I ain't as dumb as you and your boyfriend think," he snarled. "You think I'm gonna let you come in here, stab me in the back, and take the gold back to Beaudry?" With eyes filled with contempt, she spat at him. "Now, you shouldn'ta done that," he said, and grabbed her throat with his free hand. Slowly and steadily, he increased the grip on her throat, enjoying the sadistic execution, as she fought for her life, help-lessly flailing and clawing at him. "Say hello to the other whores in hell," he taunted when she began to weaken until the dagger fell from her hand and her arms flopped limp at her sides. Still he clamped down on her throat until he was doubly sure she was dead.

Getting to his feet, he walked to the tiny mirror on the dresser. "Damn bitch," he swore, looking at the marks on his face left by her fingernails. Then he grinned at himself in the mirror. "You gotta get up pretty damn early in the mornin' to get the best of Sam Cheney," he said in smug satisfaction for having antici-pated just such a double cross from Beaudry and his whore. After wiping some of the blood from his face with Angel's blouse, he climbed back into his clothes, put the pouch of gold dust in his saddlebag, and went out the door, headed for the stable to get his horse. Self-satisfied and pleased with the way things had turned out that night, he looked forward to putting Lead, Deadwood, and the scar-faced messenger behind him. "By the time they find that dead whore in my room," he said aloud, "I'll be long gone from this gulch."

Chapter 14

His luck for a random sighting of a man with a long yellow ponytail in Lead was no better than it had been in Elizabeth Town, so he decided to check on a ratty establishment called the Silver Dollar, a saloon with a dining room in back and rooms to let upstairs. At least he figured he could get something to eat in the dining room, reasoning that no one was looking for a scar-faced man except Cheney. As usual, conversation ceased when he walked into the dining room, and it remained silent until he sat down at a table with his back to the wall.

"My stars," Pearl Cotton exclaimed when she got her first glimpse of the man seated at the table in the corner, his rifle propped against the wall behind him. She turned to the cook and said, "Maybe you'd like to go and tell him about our policy of no weapons in the dining room, George."

George walked to the kitchen door to see who she was referring to. "No, thanks," he said, almost in a whisper. "That ain't my job."

"I get to do all the dirty jobs around here," Pearl said, and headed toward the table. "You want coffee or water?" she asked.

"I'd like to have some coffee, please, ma'am," Ben replied, "and whatever you're servin' for supper."

Pearl was somewhat startled by his polite response. She had expected something more in keeping with his image. It emboldened her to inform him of the rule. "I guess this is your first time in here, so I expect you couldn't know that the owner don't like to have no fire-arms in the dining room. It upsets the other customers." She took a step backward, pointed to a small table beside the door, and waited for his reaction.

"Sorry, ma'am. I didn't take notice," he said. He had walked in with his eyes on the rest of the diners, so he didn't even glance at the table. Everything seemed peaceful enough in the small dining room, but he didn't like the idea of giving up his weapons in case Cheney walked in the door and caught him sitting there unarmed. "I can understand your concern," he said. "Mind if I ask you a question first?" She nodded, and he continued. "I'm lookin' for a man and I wonder if he mighta been in here. His name's Sam Cheney. Does he ever come in here?"

"I don't know," Pearl replied. "I don't know anybody by that name."

"He's kind of a rough-lookin' man—has a long yellow ponytail hangin' down his back."

"Him!" she replied, quickly recalling the rude man who had been in the night before. "I've seen him, all right. You a friend of his?"

"Not exactly," he replied.

"I'm glad to hear it. That man you're talking about

was here last night. He killed a woman in one of the rooms upstairs." She studied Ben's face as he heard the news. It prompted her to ask a question. "Sheriff Manning was in here this morning. You're not a lawman, are you?"

"No, I'm just tryin' to catch up with him." His voice was soft but determined. "I've got a message for him from a friend of mine." He paused for a few moments to think over this latest development. "Well, I reckon he's long gone now," he said, knowing he had no idea where next to hunt.

"Well, I can tell you what he was talking about with Garth Beaudry and that prostitute when they were eating here last night," Pearl said. "Him and his big mouth were loud enough for everybody to hear." She paused then, confused by the sudden stony expression on his menacing face. "If you're interested," she added.

"I'm interested," he said softly, his mind almost stopped by her mention of Beaudry's name.

"Evidently, Beaudry owed him some money for some job—burning something, it sounded like. I couldn't hear all that for sure. I had to take some dishes to the kitchen, but that man with the ponytail was plenty hot about it for a while. I guess they got it straightened out."

Ben was now sure that his speculations on the events that had taken place over the last few days were accurate, speculations that drew Garth Beaudry into the dirty business that took so many lives. "If I knew where to look for him," he murmured, deep in thought and not realizing that he had uttered it aloud.

"Maybe I can help you," Pearl said. "I heard him tell Beaudry that he was going to Cheyenne." She watched his reaction, pleased by what she saw. "I'd tell you more if I could."

"Lady, you've helped me a'plenty." He pushed his chair back from the table and started to get up.

"Ain't you gonna eat?"

"I ain't got time now," he said. "I'll get me and my firearms outta here, so I don't break no rules."

"If you'll wait a minute, I can have George put a couple of slices of ham between some bread and you can take it with you." He sat back down, and she hurried to the kitchen. In half a minute, she was back with a cup of coffee. "Won't be but a minute," she promised.

"I sure do appreciate your help, ma'am. I was wantin' this cup of coffee pretty bad." In a few minutes, George came from the kitchen, carrying his sandwich wrapped in a cloth. He handed it to Ben, then stood there watching with a grin on his face. "Much obliged," Ben said. "How much do I owe you?"

"Nothing," Pearl replied before George had a chance to. "And I hope you catch that loudmouthed murdering son of a bitch."

Still grinning, George said, "He ain't gonna be too happy to see you comin' after him." He hesitated then. "No offense."

"I might not be able to bring your cloth back anytime soon," Ben said.

"You're welcome to it," Pearl said.

"Much obliged," Ben said, and drained his coffee cup. Still somewhat astonished by their generosity, he nodded his thanks to each of them and, with his supper in one hand, and his rifle in the other, took his leave.

George walked to the door to watch him ride away, standing there until he disappeared into the growing dusk. Turning back to Pearl, he commented, "That looks like a whole heap of bad news comin' ol' Pony-tail's way."

"He said he had a message for him," Pearl said with a chuckle. "Ol' Ponytail better hope the sheriff catches him before that fellow does."

George's face registered surprise that Pearl hadn't heard that Manning wasn't going after Cheney. "Mr. Thompson said this mornin' that the sheriff wasn't gonna chase that feller. He said he's got his hands full right now, and as long as Ponytail hightailed it outta the gulch, that was gonna have to do. He was leavin' it up to the federal marshals to track him down."

Deputy Marshal Ike Gibbs stood at the front of the coach as the train pulled into the Cheyenne depot, ready to step down as soon as it came to a stop. He picked up his saddle and headed straight for the stage station to find out when the next stagecoach was scheduled to leave for Fort Laramie. Still amazed to find himself sent on this assignment, he neverthe-less endeavored to see to its swift completion. He was operating far out of his jurisdiction, but circumstances dictated an unusual attempt to apprehend a special fugitive. It was important that a message be sent to the lawless emphasizing the fact that anyone killing a U.S. marshal would be hunted down and punished. Ike was sure the job would have been assigned to another marshal's office, had it not been for the reputation of Graham Barrett, and the high esteem he'd enjoyed in the Topeka office. There was a strong tradition of tak-ing care of your own in the marshal service, and Ike couldn't say that he disagreed with it.

He had been sorry to hear about the disappearance of Barrett; they had been partners for quite a few years. He and Barrett had not been close friends. No one he knew of was really a friend of Barrett's, but Barrett tolerated Ike, more so than any of the other deputies. Ike was sure that had a lot to do with sending him to Deadwood to follow up on reports of a man answering Ben Cutler's description there, and his possible involvement in several murders. It was a helluva long way out of his usual territory, but his boss had gotten very little help from the marshal in Dakota Territory. In the first place, he had been told, the Black Hills were still officially Indian Territory by treaty, so a U.S. marshal had no jurisdiction there. It was suggested that they turn the matter of their missing deputy over to the army. Ike's boss would have none of that. He was convinced that Barrett was killed by the fugitive, Cutler, and now he was continuing his killing rampage in Deadwood. So on a chilly fall day, Ike found himself hoofing it to the stage station in Cheyenne, lugging his saddle on his shoulder.

He would have preferred to bring his horse along on the train, but it was much quicker to take the stage from Cheyenne instead of going horseback. The government had built a road from Cheyenne to Deadwood, following the Chugwater and Laramie rivers, passing through Fort Laramie, and on up into Indian Territory to Custer City and Deadwood. Road ranches, or swing stations, were all along the road about every ten miles, making it much faster to make the trip in a big Concord coach with a six-horse team than a man could travel horseback—about two and a half days, compared to about seven and a half days.

Maybe he shouldn't have left Barrett on that afternoon north of Ogallala. Barrett might be alive now if he hadn't, but he felt no guilt in his decision to turn back. If he had to assign blame, he might put it on Barrett himself for being so damned determined to bring Cutler in. Even now, Ike wasn't convinced that Cutler was a conscienceless killer, and nobody knew what had actually happened to Barrett because his body had never been found. It was probably no more than a wasted trip, Ike figured. *But what the hell*, he thought, *as long as I'm being paid to do it?*

With nothing more to go on, Ben started out for Cheyenne, hoping that the information given him by Pearl Cotton was accurate, and aware that as each day passed, his odds of catching up to Sam Cheney went up. He thought about Cleve as he left Custer City, following the stage road. If Cleve was still alive, he would no doubt have led them to shortcuts through canyons and valleys the surveyors hadn't known about. Since he didn't possess Cleve's knowledge of the country, however, he would stick to the road laid out by the engineers. He could only assume that Cheney had taken the same road. Even though he was keeping the buckskin to a steady, ground-eating pace, he was unlikely to overtake him on the trail unless Cheney decided to stop over awhile at one of the stage swing stations. The stage ranches, as some were called, were generally spaced approximately ten miles apart, so the rapid pace of the six-horse teams could be maintained. As he approached each one, Ben looked it over carefully before asking the operators if they had seen a man with a long yellow ponytail. He was treated with suspicion each time, and received no confirmation that Cheney had been there. It was on his fourth stop at the Cheyenne River crossing that he gained assurance that he was on the right trail.

"The name's Wilcox," the man stated before asking Ben what he could do for him. As the others before, he studied Ben's face closely, wondering if he would be better off with his shotgun in hand.

"I'm tryin' to catch up with a friend of mine," Ben said. "At least, I thought he was a friend of mine, till he ran off and left me." Wilcox seemed to relax a little then, although the guarded expression remained on his face. "I reckon I had a little too much to drink at a saloon back yonder in Custer City," Ben went on, "and I woke up this mornin' in the alley behind it. When I went back to our camp, damned if Cheney hadn't took off without me."

A smile broke Wilcox's worried expression. "I can't say that couldn't happen to me if I was to get off without my wife sometime. What'd you say your friend's name was?"

"Cheney," Ben repeated. "Wears his hair in a long ponytail down his back."

"Oh, him," Wilcox said. "Yeah, matter of fact he *was* in here—stopped in for supper last night."

"Well, I reckon I'm not that far behind him at that," Ben said. "I 'preciate the help. Maybe I'll get a little somethin' to eat while I'm here. I need to rest my horse."

"Maggie can fix you up with a plate of catch-as-can stew," Wilcox said. "That's the special for today. It's best if you don't ask what's in it." He chuckled as he pointed to the long table behind him. "But I've been eatin' it for twenty years and I'm still here."

"I'll risk it," Ben said, "if there's coffee to go with it."

"Coffee as black as the inside of a mortal sin," Wilcox responded. "You're lucky to get it while it's fresh brewed. We'll have a stagecoach pullin' in here before long, so you'll get ahead of the passengers."

The stew was well worth the seventy-five cents Maggie charged for it. As Wilcox had said, it appeared that she had thrown about everything she could find into the pot. He enjoyed the luxury of not having to fix supper for himself, but he reminded himself that he should not spend the balance of Shep, as he referred to the money he had saved in the small grave beside Mary Ellen and Danny, on too many fancy suppers.

When he left, Maggie came from the kitchen to stand by her husband as he watched Ben step up in the stirrup and throw a leg over. "I declare," she opined, "that is one evil-lookin' man."

"Yeah," Wilcox replied, "I was kinda nervous about him when he walked in, but once you get to talkin' to him, he seems like a nice feller. He said that other feller was a friend of his, but I got a feelin' he ain't the kind of friend ol' Ponytail is gonna be glad to see."

He had ridden over five miles when he saw the stage to Deadwood approaching, a team of six well-matched horses thundering along the hard ground at top speed, hauling a brightly painted yellow Concord coach. *That catch-as-can stew is going to be pretty old by the time you folks get to the Cheyenne River,* Ben thought. He pulled his hat down low on his forehead and cocked it to one side, a habit he had acquired in an effort to hide as much of his face as possible.

Slim Yates cracked his whip a couple of times to

keep the lead horses' minds on their business. Beside him on the seat, Ike Gibbs held on when the coach rumbled over a rough set of dried ruts. "I don't often get the chance to have a U.S. marshal ridin' shotgun," Slim yelled over the noise of the coach, "and I ain't even carryin' no gold on this run."

"I'd be ridin' in style inside if you didn't charge so damn much," Ike said. It was cheaper beside the driver, at five dollars, compared to ten dollars inside. And that was for a middle seat. It was fifteen for a window seat. "Rider up ahead, heading towards us," he said as the coach cleared the mouth of a wide ravine.

"Looks like he's by hisself," Slim commented as the distance between the coach and the rider decreased. It was not the usual occurrence to meet a lone rider this far above Fort Laramie on the road. From habit, Slim took a critical look at the terrain on both sides and up ahead, then decided there was no indication of a holdup about to be sprung. For emphasis, he cracked his whip over the lead horses, and the coach rumbled on. When the two met, the rider pulled off to the side, well out of the way of the charging horses, and doffed his hat to answer Slim's yelled greeting and wave.

Ike waved as well with no more than a casual glance at the man on horseback. Something triggered a thought in his mind as the stage rattled past, however. *He was riding a buckskin horse.* A lot of men rode buckskin horses, but it was enough to cause him to turn in the seat and crawl back on the top of the stage to try to get another look. When the rider had taken his hat off and waved it, the wide brim had actually hidden his face. There was only an instant in which Ike caught a glimpse of the scarred face. *Damn! It couldn't be!* Already the distance between the racing coach and the rider was almost one hundred yards, and rapidly increasing. Frozen with indecision, he couldn't react at once. What were the odds he would pass the man he was going after on the road to Deadwood? The rider was getting farther and farther away while Ike hesitated. Finally, he could no longer ignore the feeling he had that he had just waved to Ben Cutler. Scrambling back to the seat then, he exclaimed, "Stop! Stop this damn thing!"

Slim looked at him as if he had lost his mind. "Stop, hell. I'm about five hours late reachin' the Cheyenne crossin' now."

"Damn it, you've got to stop this damn stage," Ike shouted. "We just passed the man I've come all the way out here to find!"

"The hell you say?" Slim replied, all the while making no move to even slow his horses. "How do you know that? I thought you said you'd never seen the feller."

"I saw enough to know. We've got to turn back, so I can know for sure."

"Turn back?" Slim blurted incredulously. "I can't turn back. This stage line ain't in the business of chasin' outlaws. Look inside that coach. I can't risk the lives of my passengers for you to go huntin' for murderers and such. I'm riskin' my own life if I don't make up some of this lost time." Seeing the look of alarm in the marshal's eyes, he reconsidered. "I reckon I can stop long enough for you to get off if you wanna do that."

"Are you crazy?" Ike fumed. In the time they had argued, the coach had already covered at least a mile, not counting the distance traveled by the man on the horse. "I can't go after him on foot."

"Maybe he'll stop to make camp before too long,"

Slim suggested, "and you can catch up to him then." The look of astonishment on the deputy's face told him that was out. "I reckon you'll just have to wait till we make Cheyenne crossin', and buy you a horse from Wilcox. That's the best you can do."

Ike sat down hard on the seat, almost blinded by his frustration, convinced beyond a doubt now that the man he had just seen was in fact Ben Cutler. It was just so damned ridiculous that it had to be so, and here they were, going in opposite directions just as fast as they could. At that point, they were only a couple more miles from the station, but it seemed like double that before the coach actually pulled into the yard. Ike was off the box before the coach came to a stop. Wasting no time, he pulled his saddle off the top and headed toward the house as fast as he could walk.

"I can't give you none of your fare back," Slim called after him. "I don't handle none of the money." When Ike didn't bother to even look back at him, he added, "Good luck, though."

"Where's the owner?" Ike demanded as soon as he burst into the room. "What's his name? Wilcox? Where's Mr. Wilcox?" Immediately alarmed by his obviously agitated state, Maggie Wilcox backed away a step, not sure she wanted to tell the man where her husband was. Realizing at once the cause of her concern, Ike pulled his coat aside, far enough to display the badge on his vest. "I'm a U.S. deputy marshal, ma'am, and I need to buy a horse just as fast as I can." They both had to step inside the door then to get out of the way of the passengers streaming in, heading for the dinner table.

"My husband's outside, hooking up the fresh team of horses on the stage, I suppose," Maggie said, relieved that she had not been about to be robbed. Ike spun on his heel and charged back out the door without so much as a thank-you. Maggie sighed in tired indifference before turning and seeing to her duties as hostess.

"You don't say?" Wilcox responded when Ike explained his predicament. "That man was an outlaw, after all. I'll tell you, he sure looked like one. I was afraid he had come in to rob us or somethin', but once you got to talkin' to him, he—" That was as far as he got before Ike interrupted him.

"Mister, I need a horse, and I need it in a hurry," Ike blurted impatiently. "Have you got some stock that's saddle broke? And I don't mean any ol' fleabag you're fixin' to put down. You'll be paid by the federal marshal service."

"Well, yeah," Wilcox said, somewhat hesitantly, "I've got some good saddle-broke horses. I guess I could part with one of 'em. Ain't you got any cash money on you? I don't know how the federal government is gonna pay me."

Ike was trying hard to hold on to his temper, but it was getting more difficult as he thought of Cutler getting farther and farther away while he stood there bickering with Wilcox. He was already considering stealing one of the man's horses if he didn't get down to business pretty soon. "You don't have to worry about the money," he said. "I'll see to it that you get it."

"How they gonna do that?" Wilcox persisted. "There ain't no bank or post office around here. You ride off on one of my horses, chances are I'll never see you or the horse again. Then where's my money?"

"Jesus, man!" Ike fairly exploded. "They'll wire the money to Cheyenne, and you'll get it on the stage. Now, are you ready to sell me a horse? Or had you rather I take the damn horse at gunpoint?"

"There ain't no call for you to get testy about it," Wilcox said. "I just want to make sure I get paid. Come on, I'll show you what I've got." He turned and led the way to the corral. There were about fifteen horses there, not counting the tired team just unhitched. "There's about three good saddle horses in that bunch. That little mare is a good'un for a ridin' horse," he suggested. "I could let you have her for fifty dollars."

Ike looked the bunch over quickly, then brought his eye back to the gray mare Wilcox had pointed out. "She mighta been, before she got so old she can hardly stand up," he said curtly. "I ain't in the market for some old nag to ride the children around the yard. How 'bout that sorrel in the corner there?"

"I see you got a good eye," Wilcox said. "That's a good horse, all right. That's the horse I ride if I gotta go somewhere. I'd have to have two hundred dollars for that horse."

Ike didn't flinch, he just gazed dead-eyed at Wilcox for a long moment before responding. "The government will give you one hundred dollars for that horse, and that's probably twenty-five more than he's worth." He didn't wait for Wilcox's answer, but immediately took a coil of rope from the saddle at his feet and climbed over the fence. "Write your full name and whatever address you use on a piece of paper, and I'll see you get your money."

"Well, I reckon that's a fair price," Wilcox called out helplessly while Ike threw a noose on the sorrel and led it to the corral gate. "I ain't got no paper or pen."

Ike pulled a piece of paper and a pencil from his

saddlebag and handed it to Wilcox. Then he slipped his bridle over the sorrel's head and set the bit in its mouth. The horse did not fight it, so Ike threw his saddle on and tightened the cinch. He took the paper and pencil from Wilcox and put them in the saddlebag, then stepped up in the saddle. The sorrel bucked two times before settling down. "He ain't been rode in a while," Wilcox offered as explanation. Then when Ike reached down and opened the corral gate, he asked, "Ain't you gonna go in and eat?"

"I ain't got time to eat," Ike said, and nudged the horse with his heels.

Wilcox stood watching him until he loped out to the road and turned back the way the stage had just come. Wilcox returned to the stagecoach then, just to check to make sure the new team was hooked up properly. Satisfied that everything was in order, he started toward the house. *I knew that fellow with the scar was an outlaw, first time I set eyes on him,* he thought. "Wait till I tell Maggie I finally got rid of that cross-tempered ol' sorrel." He smiled at the thought. "And for a hundred dollars," he added. As he stepped up on the front porch, another thought occurred to him. *I wonder if I should have told that lawman that the scar-faced fellow was chasing ol' Ponytail.*

"What do you want?" Garth Beaudry demanded brusquely when he glanced up to see Floyd Trask in the doorway. Taking a second look at the unimposing young man, he asked, "When did you start wearing a gun?"

Floyd ignored the question. "I thought you'd be at the funeral," he said. In effect, it had not really been much of a funeral. There had been no one in attendance but Floyd, two gravediggers, and the undertaker when Angel Lopez's body had been committed to the ground.

"Hell," Garth replied irritably, "I had to pay for the damn thing. That was enough." He was still in an irritable mood, caused by Angel's failure to do the job he had sent her to do.

"She was a beautiful lady before she took up with you," Floyd said. "And now she's dead because of you. You didn't deserve a lady like Angel."

Alerted then to the change in the usually subservient nature of the simple young man, Garth didn't like the direction the conversation was heading. "I don't know what you're thinking," he said. "But you don't need to let this business put crazy thoughts in your head. Angel was just another whore whose number was up. I advise you to let it go at that."

Floyd shook his head sadly. "You didn't even care enough to go to her funeral."

"No!" Garth screamed. "Don't!" He knocked his chair over in jumping to his feet when Floyd unhurriedly pulled the revolver from his holster and pointed it at him. "Wait!" he begged as Floyd deliberately aimed the weapon at his chest. The few patrons in the dining room, having been alerted when Garth knocked over the chair, ran for the door when they saw the drawn pistol. Behind them, the report of the revolver cracked sharply, the sound amplified by the smallness of the room. Garth Beaudry crumbled to the floor, a bullet through his heart. Floyd turned and walked out of the room behind the frightened diners, who parted to make a path for him.

Chapter 15

Ben held the buckskin to a steady pace, one the sturdy gelding was capable of maintaining for hours without rest. His entire plan was dependent upon a great deal of luck, but there was very little choice available. Just as he would, he reckoned Cheney naturally veered off the road when he decided to make camp at night. None but a few of the stage swing stations served the passengers meals, so there was little reason for Cheney to stop overnight at one of these stations. The others changed the horses, and the coach moved on right away, allowing passengers time to get out and stretch while it was being done, but little else. So in the event that he overtook Cheney, he had to keep an eye on likely places to leave the trail to make camp. He would be more careful tomorrow in this regard, for he knew he was too far behind to be concerned at this point. Come sunup, he didn't plan to be this far behind the ponytailed murderer, because he intended to ride on through the night until his horse demanded a rest. If Cheney wasn't in as big a hurry as he, then he should be able to close the distance between them considerably.

His ride was made easier with the help of a full moon that lit the road ahead of him. He rode on through the night until he deemed it due time to rest the buckskin. The moon was dropping closer to the hills before him, and he decided that he needed some rest himself. So he left the road when he came to a narrow stream, and followed it up a ravine for about a hundred yards or so. There were no trees along the stream, but there were thickets of berry bushes that were thick enough to provide a screen for his fire, and plenty of grass for his horse. He pulled the saddle off and hobbled the horse, so it could graze while he built a fire and roasted a little venison to go with the coffee he always had to have. After he had satisfied his hunger, he brought his horse closer in and tied it to a bush while he got a couple of hours of sleep.

On his way again at sunup, he rode into a land of endless prairie, with the Black Hills still visible behind him. High grass and rocky defiles with no trees as far as he could see, it was a forbidding country. There was no place to hide, and throughout the morning he constantly scanned the horizon all around him, searching for some sign of another rider. He was alone, it seemed, no one else on the endless prairie but himself, and a seemingly never-ending wind that blew cold in his face. The possibility that Cheney had changed his mind about Cheyenne, and might even now be off in another direction, persisted in worrying him. It was then that he was startled by the sound of a rifle, somewhere in the distance, and he pulled the buckskin up to listen. There were no more shots, only the one, and as best he could determine, it came from the direction he was heading. *Cheney? Maybe.* One shot could mean he had killed an animal of some kind, an antelope possibly. There was also the distinct possibility that it was not Cheney, but an Indian instead. No matter which, Ben was bound to find out. His concern, however, was how to get close enough without being seen from a mile away, and he could see no possibility of that as he gazed out across the empty land. Too bad it was early in the day, instead of evening when he could use the cover of darkness. In the end, there was no decision to make. If he was going to honor his promise to Cleve, he had to overtake Cheney.

Congratulating himself for bringing down the antelope with a shot that had to have been at a distance of one hundred and fifty yards, maybe more, Cheney smiled in anticipation of some fresh roasted meat as he carved up his kill. As soon as he cut a few strips off the carcass, he secured them on a couple of branches from a large bush by the stream that meandered down through a grassy draw. After he placed the makeshift spits over the fire, he went to the stream to rinse the blood from his hands. He had had no intention of stopping this early in the day, but a man had to take the opportunity for fresh meat when it was presented. Already, he could smell the aroma of roasted meat, and the thought occurred to him, *I wonder if there's anyone around that might have heard that shot.* Just to satisfy himself that he had not attracted a Sioux hunting party, he climbed up to a rocky table jutting up out of the north side of the draw and looked back over the way he had come. The wind sweeping across the prairie grass was the only living thing he could see as he sat there for a few minutes. Just about to return to tend the meat roasting on the fire, he suddenly caught movement out of the corner of his eye, and he jerked his head around to focus his gaze upon it. *Antelope?* Possibly, but he could tell now that it was a single object, and it would be unlikely there was just one antelope without some others close by, so he waited.

Closer now, he could see that it was a man on a horse, and apparently not an Indian, judging by the hat and what looked to be a stock saddle. "Well, well," he chortled. "Looks like I've got company for breakfast." He hurried back down to his horse and took his rifle and a pair of field glasses from his saddlebag, then scrambled back up to the rocks. His visitor looked to be about three hundred yards away at this point as he trained the field glasses on him. "Scar-faced son of a bitch!" he blurted involuntarily when he recognized the rider. His initial reaction was panic, but he quickly recovered when he realized that Ben was following the Cheyenne road, and might not even be trailing him. He quickly discarded that thought when he thought about Shorty and the others. *The bastard's after me! How the hell did he know I was heading to Cheyenne?* That question disturbed him the most because it conjured eerie images of a man who seemed half demon. "I don't care if he's the devil himself," he announced in an effort to bolster his determination. He told himself that the advantage was his. The menacing messenger that had killed his three partners could not know that he was waiting for him, so he could not be aware that he was riding into an ambush. "Come on, then," Cheney urged. "I'll be ready for you." He looked around him, quickly evaluating his position, and decided right away that he was already in the best place to bushwhack the unsuspecting rider. If he continued on the same track, he would follow the road through a ravine that would put him some thirty feet below Cheney's perch on the rocky table.

Watching Ben's progress through the field glasses, Cheney planned to take no chances on letting him get away. He would hold his fire until the dreaded hunter was too close to miss. When his target advanced to within one hundred yards, he aimed his rifle at him, but did not pull the trigger as he trained the weapon along Ben's path, waiting for him to ride down into the ravine. He picked a spot on the trail below, just beyond a stone ledge that would block his view for only a few seconds. He aimed his rifle at that spot and waited for Ben to reappear from behind the rocks. When the buckskin's head appeared, he rested his finger on the trigger, poised to squeeze it, but held up suddenly when the horse came out of the ravine with an empty saddle. At once, his panic returned and he looked all around him frantically to see if he was about to be attacked. Seeing no one, he fled from his perch, scrambling down the side of the draw, too fast, for he stumbled and went head over heels to land at the bottom. He wasted no time to see if he was injured, but staggered to his feet and ran for his horse.

Ben made his way up toward the rocky ledge, half walking, half crawling at the steepest part near the top. Minutes before, when approaching the point where the road dipped through a ravine, he had suddenly been startled by a flash of light. Moments later, he had seen the same light again, but this time he was able to pinpoint the location, and realized that it was the sun's reflection off a glass. And whoever was watching him through it looked to be in an ideal ambush position. He had noticed that there would be one point on the road where vision would be blocked by a huge outcropping of rock, and chances were that neither of them could see the other. When he reached it, he had slid off his horse and given it a slap on the rump, while he scurried along a gully that led up to a rock ledge. Upon reaching the top, he was in time to see a man running for his horse, a long yellow ponytail bouncing back and forth as he ran. *Cheney!* he thought, and got off one quick shot that caught the gunman in the leg, causing him to fall and his horse to bolt.

Caught in the open then, Cheney was lucky that Ben could not scramble over the rocky shelf in time to take advantage of his vulnerability. In only seconds, Cheney managed to crawl to the stream and roll over behind the low bank with a couple of shots from Ben's Winchester kicking up dirt beside him. In the next several minutes, a dozen or more shots were exchanged before both men realized they were wasting cartridges in a standoff. An empty lull settled over the ravine as both men considered their options, each wondering if it would be wise to dig in and wait for the other to make a move.

Lying flat behind the low cover of the stream bank, Cheney tried to determine how badly he was wounded, while still unable to understand how Ben knew he was there. It only added to the fear he held for the man with the horrible scar across his face. He couldn't help thinking back to the ambush that took the lives of Bull and Shorty, and how the scar-faced demon seemed to rise out of the ashes of the burned-out house. *Well, he won't seem so damn scary when he shows himself from behind those rocks*, he told himself in an effort to bolster his courage. The numbness that had seized his leg when he was first hit had now given way to a throbbing pain, and he could feel a pool of blood welling up in his trouser leg, causing a new fear that he might bleed to death. Lying flat to keep from exposing any part of him to the rifle fire from the out-cropping at the upper edge of the ravine, he pulled a large bandanna from his coat pocket and tied it tightly around his leg, just above the knee. When the bandanna failed to stop the flow of blood completely, he began to panic, and thoughts of bravado gave way to cold fear and the urgency to run for his life.

Rolling over on his stomach, he started to crawl as best he could toward a thicket of bullberry bushes that hung over the edge of the stream, thinking that if he reached them, they might afford enough cover for him to stand up and look to see where his horse had fled to. He cursed himself for not tying the animal by the stream, as he pulled himself laboriously along the rocky streambed, leaving a trail of red water behind him. It occurred to him that there had been no shots from the rocks for some time. Encouraged by this, for he pictured his adversary lying behind the outcropping, keeping his head down, he kept struggling until at last he gained the clump of bushes.

With the thick bushes between him and the point from where Ben's rifle fire had come, Cheney slowly raised himself high enough to expose his head and shoulders over the bank of the stream. When there was still no fire from the mound of rocks, he got to his feet. He was acutely aware of a trickle of blood as the pool that had welled up in his trousers emptied to run into his boot. Carefully pulling a few of the branches apart, he peered through at the rocks on the side of the ravine. There was no sign of anyone. *He's keeping his head down*, he thought, further encouraged by the lack of any shots in his direction after leaving the stream. Shifting his gaze a little, he spotted his horse, patiently grazing on the top of a low ridge approximately fifty yards distant. *I can make that before the bastard finds out I'm not pinned down behind the bank anymore*, he thought. Concealing himself as long as possible, he inched his way along the bushes to the end of the thicket. Then he worked his way around it, to stop dead in his tracks when he came face-to-face with the scar-faced executioner, his rifle held ready to fire and aimed at his belly. Panic-stricken, he froze, unable to react.

"I've got a message for you from Cleve Goganis," the grim avenger said calmly. "He's waitin' for you in hell."

Cheney finally made a move. Almost paralyzed by what he knew was sudden death, he tried to raise his rifle, but was cut down before he could bring it past knee-high. He slumped to the ground, dead, but to be absolutely certain, Ben pumped three more rounds into the body before turning away. "That's the last of 'em, Cleve," he said, and took the piece of cardboard from his pocket and crossed out Cheney's name. He tore it up then, symbolically putting an end to his passion for vengeance. As he watched the pieces flutter to the ground, scattered by the cold wind, he suddenly felt very tired.

He had taken a hell of a chance, guessing that

Cheney was crawling along the streambed, and would be unable to see him run across a two-hundred-yard clearing to cut him off. At the time, he didn't pause to consider the certain consequences if he had guessed wrong. He just wanted it over and done with. He stood there, looking down at the corpse with the long sandy ponytail for a few minutes more before relieving it of its rifle and gun belt, and suddenly he realized there was nothing left to drive him on. Cleve was gone. Mary, Victoria, and the boy were settled for the time being with Malcolm. Maybe he could be of some help to them, but he didn't suppose they really welcomed it, since he was a wanted criminal. *I guess I'll decide what I'm gonna do after I've thought about it some.* Then, with the extra gun belt over his shoulder, and a rifle in each hand, he went in search of the buckskin. Coming from behind the thicket of berry bushes, he was startled to find his horse standing there, with the barrel of a Winchester lying across the saddle, looking at him.

"Lookin' for your horse?" Ike Gibbs asked. When Ben dropped Cheney's rifle and started to react, Ike warned him. "Don't even think about it. I'll cut you down before you can cock it, and I know you ain't cocked it after your last shot. I pay attention to things like that. Besides, you'd just shoot your horse full of holes. So drop that other rifle and let that gun belt slide off to the ground." Ben realized that he had no choice; the man had been smart enough to use the buckskin for cover, so he did as he was told, still wondering what the man's intentions were. He should have guessed.

"My name's Gibbs," Ike went on. "I'm a U.S. deputy marshal. That marshal you killed was my partner, so if you don't wanna get shot in the head, you'd best behave yourself and do like I tell you."

"I didn't kill your partner," Ben stated unemotionally.

"Well, now, all I've got is your word on that. Ain't that right? And, Mr. Ben Cutler, with the string of men you've killed, there won't be nothin' left but women in the territory if you ain't stopped. And that's what I'm here for. So let me tell you what the plan is. I'm intendin' to take you back to Deadwood right now, since the sheriff there was the one that telegraphed for help in catchin' you. We'll see if we can't get the straight on what happened there with them three men you shot." He shook his head as if perplexed. "I swear, Mr. Ben Cutler, you have been one busy son of a bitch. Maybe you can start by tellin' me who this poor jasper is you just shot back there in the bushes."

Ben didn't answer at once, still in a state of indecision over whether he gave a damn about being in the hands of the law again. He considered the lanky deputy waiting patiently for an answer to his question, his eyes showing no evidence of fear or even excitement as he held his rifle trained on him. Ben decided at that moment that Ike wouldn't hesitate to cut him down at the slightest provocation. "His name's Sam Cheney," Ben finally answered. "Since you seem to have watched the whole thing, maybe you noticed that he was hid back there, fixin' to bushwhack me."

"Is that so?" Ike responded. "Now, why do you suppose he'da wanted to do that?"

" 'Cause he knew I was comin' to get him for killin' two friends of mine," Ben replied honestly.

"Who might that be?" Ike asked.

"Cleve Goganis and Jonah Marple," Ben answered. His gaze shifted briefly to the weapons lying at his feet.

"Best you forget about those guns," Ike warned him. "My orders are to bring you in, dead or alive. Don't make much difference to me which way you choose, but I'm kinda interested in hearin' your side of the story—a helluva long story at that, with a string of dead people left behind. Then if you're still feelin' lucky, you can make your move after we're done talkin', and I'll shoot your ass and tell ever'body 'bout how you nearly got the jump on me." Ben almost had to smile.

"All right," Ben said, "here's my side of it. That piece of shit over there, and his three partners, shot my friends, Cleve Goganis, and Jonah Marple, set Jonah's house on fire, and threw their bodies in the middle of it."

"Why would they wanna do that?"

"They were paid to do it by Garth Beaudry," Ben replied. "But I ain't got no proof about that part of it, just what a lady overheard 'em talkin' about."

"How do you know it was those four that actually did it?"

"Eyewitness saw 'em when they done it."

Ike studied the scarred face intently as Ben stated his case in simple phrases, with no embellishment and no evasion. Ike was convinced that these were the facts as Ben believed them to be. He had to remind himself that his prisoner was a one-man death squad—judge and jury—and one might be inclined to forgive him for the executions of all of them, except one. And that one was the bone that was sticking in Ike's craw, deputy marshal Graham Barrett. "How'd you happen to get the drop on Barrett?" he suddenly asked.

"I didn't kill Barrett," was Ben's sober reply.

"Graham Barrett was the best in the marshal service," Ike pressed, hoping to trip Ben on his own ego. "It'd be a helluva good man to get the drop on Barrett."

"I didn't kill Barrett. Sioux Injuns got him, northwest of Ogallala, near the Niobrara River," Ben said, again without emotion.

Ike shook his head, perplexed by Ben's somber responses. "To hear you tell it, you've just been ridin' the territory and punishin' them that needs punishin'."

Ben thought for a brief second before replying, "That's about the size of it."

Realizing that he wasn't going to get anything more from his prisoner, Ike instructed him to sit down, cross-legged, beside the berry bushes. Once he was settled, Ike came out from behind the buckskin, and with the rifle still trained on Ben, he walked a few paces back to grab the reins of his horse and led it back to stop before Ben. He pulled a pair of manacles from his saddlebag and tossed them to Ben. "Here," he said, "put these on." As soon as they were secured and locked on his wrists, he told Ben to get on his feet and turn around. Moving around behind Ben's back, he locked a set of leg irons around his boots. "I need a little time to think about what I'm gonna do with you," he stated. "We're a lot closer to Deadwood than we are to Cheyenne. I expect I'll go ahead and take you back there, but first we're gonna eat. That feller you shot—what did you say his name was? Cheney?—well, he left a good supply of fresh meat back downstream, some of it still cookin' on the fire. That is, if you ain't in any particular hurry."

Ben didn't reply, but he thought back about the treatment he had received while in the custody of Graham Barrett. It was a sharp contrast to the style of Ike Gibbs. *So far*, he hastened to remind himself. He shuffled along in his leg irons back downstream where Cheney had been busy butchering his antelope. Ike walked along behind him, leading the two horses, with Cheney's horse following at a distance of around forty yards, apparently undecided about joining the party. As if reading Ben's thoughts, Ike volunteered, "I expect I'll catch that other feller's horse and see if it ain't a little better than this damn sorrel I just bought to come after you. He ain't that bad a horse, but he's got an irritatin' habit of tryin' to take a nip outta your leg when he thinks you ain't payin' attention. It's already cost him a couple of lumps on his head."

"I swear, that's good eatin', ain't it?" Ike remarked. "That ol' boy shot a nice tender young doe. I wonder if he got a taste of it before you came along." When Ben made no reply, Ike continued to ramble on. "I sure as hell ain't gonna take the time to pack all this meat with us, so you might as well eat till you can't. I'd rather have you with your belly full and sleepy, anyway. Keeps you from gettin' too many ideas 'bout runnin'.'" He was still making up his mind about Ben Cutler. Thinking back to recall the way the folks of Crooked Fork had talked about him, one would think they'd elect him mayor, instead of hanging him for murder. He studied the brutally scarred face as Ben sat across the fire from him, chewing on a strip of antelope. "Accordin' to what that sheriff in Crooked Fork said, his deputy—the one you shot down in the saloon—done that to your face with a sawed-off sword. Is that a fact? Is that the reason you shot him?"

Ben stopped chewing and looked Ike straight in the eye. "I shot him because he murdered my wife and my son, left me for dead, and burned my house down. Ain't that reason enough?"

"Well, maybe," Ike replied. "Course you coulda let the law handle it."

"He *was* the law," Ben said.

Ike didn't reply to that, but he took a moment to think about it, still remembering Sheriff Jubal Creed's failure to support his late deputy, Eli Gentry. *Maybe I'm getting soft in the head*, he thought, concerned that he was being taken in by Cutler's story. *It would be easier to believe the man was no more than a victim of circumstance if he didn't look so damn capable of thoughtless murder.* He continued to dig. "And you still say you didn't kill Barrett. Some Injuns done it, you said."

"That's right," Ben said.

Ike cocked his head to one side and frowned. "See, that's where your story turns to gristle. There ain't no way to prove that one way or the other, and that's what's gonna cause a judge to hang you." He watched Ben's face closely for his reaction, but there was none. "Here, let's finish this pot of coffee," he said. "Then we'll mount up and get goin'." He filled the two cups and poured the last few drops on the fire. "You know, we're just talkin' here, but I'd take it as a favor if you'd tell me how Barrett got killed." Ben shrugged indifferently. Aside from the fact that his hands and feet were in chains, there was almost a casual air about his arrest. So he related the incident, including the fact that he had used Barrett's body for cover while firing at the Sioux warriors. "Well," Ike commented when he had finished, "I believe the part about Barrett slammin' you in the head with his rifle. I've seen him do that to other prisoners. I'd like to believe the whole story, but I'd have to see Barrett's body before I could. Yes, sir, I'd sure like to see ol' Barrett's body."

"I reckon that would be kinda difficult," Ben said. "With wolves, coyotes, buzzards, and everythin' else, I doubt it's still there."

"You know where it happened, though. Right?"

"Well"—Ben hesitated—"not exactly. I might know the place if I rode through that part of the country again." He was trying to recall the events leading up to the attack by the Sioux warriors. "We were somewhere just south of the Niobrara; then we turned almost due west, and that's when they hit us, after we made camp. I can't tell you much more than that. It was my first time in that part of the country."

Ike thought about it for a moment, trying to pinpoint the general area. "He was takin' you to Fort Laramie," he decided.

"Maybe," Ben said. "I couldn't say. He didn't mention where he was takin' me, just that it was a day's ride to get there."

Ike found himself wanting to believe Ben's story—a situation that could prove fatal for him, he cautioned. This was no time to get careless, but he realized that he wanted to try to find Barrett's remains to somehow prove Ben's version of the deputy's death. It was perplexing to him, for he had never faced this predicament before in all his years of service. Possibly, it was inspired by a desire to prove Graham Barrett wrong for once. Maybe, and more likely, he was reluctant to send Ben to prison, or the gallows, for the crime of being unlucky. He thought about Ben's comment that it was unlikely Barrett's body was still there, and he couldn't agree more. *But damn it,* he thought, *if I could find that body with just one arrow sticking in it, I might begin to believe this fellow is telling the truth.* His boss back in Topeka would be mad as a hornet if he knew the decision he was about to make, but Ike decided he was going to take a hell of a chance. "I wanna see that place where the Injuns jumped you and Barrett," he announced. "That is, if you ain't in any particular hurry to get to jail. But that's an awful lot of territory to look in if all you know is you were south of the Niobrara. God knows how long that river is."

Giving it more thought now, Ben tried to picture the country in his mind, eager to help since it would give him more opportunity to escape. "All I can tell you is we camped on the river near two big hills that Cleve said was full of bones of old Indians and animals."

The comment caused a gleam of discovery in Ike's eyes. "A day's ride from Laramie," he exclaimed. "Hell, I know the place." His brain was already working on the direction and the approximate distance from where they now stood, even as he battled his better senses over what he was about to do. "That place on the river where you saw them two hills is about a day and a half's ride from here, so maybe we oughta pack up a little bit more of this meat, after all. It'll keep for a day or two, cold as it is." He studied Ben's face for a few moments more before he made his final decision. "We're goin' to see if we can find Barrett's remains.

Just so you know, you ain't no better off than you were thirty minutes ago. You're still under arrest, and I'll still put a bullet in your head if I see the first sign of trouble outta you. Are you clear on that?"

"I reckon," Ben answered.

"I don't trust you no farther than the end of my rifle barrel," Ike said, "and I'll be keepin' a sharp eye on you all the time." *And I hope I ain't making the biggest mistake of my life,* he thought.

Chapter 16

Ike's estimate of the distance to the spot where Ben had seen the two lone hills was accurate within a few hours' ride at just under a full day and a half. In spite of the fact that he made the trip with his hands cuffed the whole time, and his legs shackled when not in the saddle, Ben could not complain about his treatment. It was late in the morning when they reached the banks of the Niobrara, and they rested the horses while Ben looked around to determine where he and Barrett had crossed, heading south. He was not certain of the exact spot, and to make matters more difficult, there were many tracks along the riverbank, most of them new, and all of them from unshod horses. "Lot of Injun activity," Ike commented, not at all happy about it. "We'd best keep a sharp eye."

They rode slowly along the river while Ben searched for the crossing. Finally, he came to a wide gully leading down to the water with many tracks, both horses and deer, and he remembered it as the place where

Barrett had led him down into the water. "This is it," he said, looking toward the other side. "We stopped right under that bank yonder while the horses drank."

Once across, Ben had a general idea of the direction they had set out on from that point on, but he had to admit that he could be off by a few degrees either way. Ike dismounted to look for tracks that could narrow it down. As on the other side, there were many tracks, most of them unshod. After a close search, he was rewarded by the discovery of a hoofprint from a shod horse. "Climb down off that horse," he said, "and help me find another print." With both of them searching the ground leading away from the water's edge, it was still another twenty minutes before a second shod print was distinguished from the multitude of unshod. "That way," Ike declared after sighting a line that ran through both prints. "And you say you rode on this line until you stopped to make camp, and that was where the Injuns jumped you?"

"That's right," Ben replied, as things began to look familiar, and details of the ride came back to remind him. "Couple hours' ride," he said. "Then look for a tree where there ought not be one—a big cottonwood by a little stream." He recalled every detail then, and just as anxious to find the campsite as Ike now, he pointed toward a line of ridges more to the west than their present course. "Toward that notch," he said, pointing. "There's a little valley on the far side of those ridges with a stream, and one tree."

"You sound mighty sure," Ike said as he set his horse's nose on the notch in the distant hills. "But I reckon you oughta know." He had already seen enough to believe that Ben wanted to find Barrett's body as much as he, hoping to prove his innocence.

It was as Ben had remembered it. Once they passed through the notch in the ridge line, they discovered a shallow valley below them with a stream flowing freely down through the center. About a quarter of a mile from where they struck the stream, the tall cotton-wood was easily seen, a lone sentinel against a cloud-less sky, looking remarkably out of place. As the two riders reached the cottonwood, Ike looked all around him at the rough terrain. "Damned if I don't believe I coulda picked a better place to camp," he said, noticing the many gullies that offered concealment to anyone with a notion to sneak up on an unsuspecting camp. "Especially with all the damn hostile raidin' parties in this part of the territory this year," he added.

"He didn't seem to be worried about it," Ben said with a shrug. "Turned out, he shoulda been, I reckon." Following Ike's orders, he did his best to reset the scene accurately. "I was here by the fire when he hit me with his rifle. I don't remember if I went down the first time or not, but I went flat on my face the next time. That's when he got hit with the first arrow." Ben went on to recount the entire episode while Ike listened with intense interest.

When he had finished, Ike stood silently while his mind replayed the entire incident. Then he began examining the ground around the ashes of the fire for some evidence to substantiate Ben's story. There was very little to be found in the grassy bank of the stream, but eventually he came across some scuff marks in one of the bare gullies that could have been made by a heavy object being dragged across it. Barrett's body was a heavy object, Ike reasoned. Ben said he'd left the body lying where Barrett fell, but maybe the Indians came back afterward and moved the body. It was easy to imagine the Indians dragging Barrett's body behind a horse to desecrate and defile it, probably after scalping him. "We'll start making circles around this spot," Ike said. "Maybe we can turn up somethin'. I'll ride and lead your horse and the other'n, and you can walk—just in case you get the urge to leave without me."

It was later in the afternoon when Ben sang out, "Here's what you're lookin' for!" Standing on a knoll in grass knee-deep, he waited for Ike to come to him. "Here's what's left of him." He gestured toward a skeleton, partially covered with ragged pieces of material, all that the scavengers left of the deputy marshal. Ike got down from his horse to examine the bones more carefully. There was a prominent crack in the skull and there were bones broken in many places, especially the ribs and pelvis, which Ben attributed to the many rounds pumped into the body when he was using it for cover.

"I expect that's Barrett, all right," Ike allowed. "Be pretty unlikely it was anybody else." A few black feathers lying in the grass testified to the squabble among the buzzards attending the banquet, vying for the choice parts. Of particular interest were the two broken arrow shafts lying among the ribs, no doubt dislodged when the flesh and sinew that held them firm had been eaten. They were sufficient evidence for Ike to again feel a strong inclination to believe Ben's claims of innocence, not only of Barrett's murder, but of the prior charges before that. Still, it was difficult for him to make a decision that would go against his strong belief that his job was not to judge guilt or innocence, only to bring the accused in to trial. As he continued to stare down at the skull of his onetime partner, Barrett seemed to mock him for his softness. *You go to hell,* he thought, *if you ain't there already.* Suddenly struck with a feeling of urgency, he looked up to tell Ben it was time to get out of this place, but it was already too late. The look of alarm on the scarred face told him that Ben had the same sudden feeling he was experiencing. They had both ignored the whinnying of two of the horses. "Let's get the hell outta here!" Ike exclaimed.

Ben took a running jump for the stirrup and galloped after Ike, amid a swarm of arrows, as the Sioux warriors rose from the tall grass at the base of the knoll. They had been caught with their senses down, allowing a half dozen Lakota hostiles to advance on foot to within range of their bows. Holding on to the saddle horn with both hands, since Ike was still leading his horse as well as the sorrel, Ben bent low in the saddle. Coming off the knoll, they saw several more warriors on horses, riding to cut them off. Ike swung his horse around and headed for the first cover he could see, a deep depression that looked to be an old buffalo trap. With the first shots from the warriors' rifles flying around them, they rode down into the basin and came out of the saddle. "Lead 'em down to the bottom!" Ike yelled. The defile was not deep enough to give the horses complete cover. He figured the Indians would not purposely shoot the horses, but he wanted to take away the risk of an accidental shooting.

"Get me loose!" Ben exclaimed, holding his cuffed wrists up. "Hurry up, damn it!" he complained when Ike fumbled in his pocket for the key. When Ike finally produced the key, and Ben was free, he took the horses' reins and led them to the end of the defile. Then drawing his Winchester from the saddle sling, he ran back to take a position opposite Ike at the edge of the basin. He was not a moment too soon, sliding to a stop against the lip as the hostiles charged down upon them. With no choice but to ignore the bullets kicking up dirt around him, he took careful aim and knocked one of them off his pony. Taking care not to rush his shots and waste cartridges, he methodically ejected the shell and repeated the procedure, separating another warrior from his pony. Ike accounted for two of his own, and the immediate loss of four of the warriors was enough to call for a change in strategy on the part of their assailants.

"They're fallin' back!" Ike said. "They've gotta think twice 'bout chargin' us."

"I figure they're gonna wait for the rest of 'em that were hidin' in the grass back there," Ben replied. "Then I guess they're gonna try to surround us and see if they can get lucky with a couple of shots."

"Yeah," Ike said, "and they can wait us out till we're out of water, but I don't think they'll have that much patience." He ducked behind the edge of the basin when a couple of shots kicked up dirt between them. "That's just to let us know they're still there."

Ben looked back over his shoulder at the sun settling down close to the distant horizon. "I don't know how you feel about it, but I'm thinkin' that when it gets good and dark, that bunch could pour in this hole and settle our bacon before we got more than one or two of them."

"I'm thinkin' the same thing," Ike said. "So the only chance we've got is to make a run for it as soon as that sun sets. If we're lucky, maybe we can outrun 'em, and get to Fort Laramie. It ain't but about thirty miles from here—that way," he added and pointed slightly south-west, remembering that Ben said he didn't know the country. "Course, if we get separated, I'll expect you to report to prison on your own," he joked.

"You can count on it," Ben said, facetiously. They settled down to wait, watching for any sign of move-ment that would suggest another attack.

The time ticked slowly by as the sun seemed reluc-tant to drop below the horizon. Straining to see in the gentle glow of evening, they sat back to back a few yards apart with rifles ready. "You know," Ike said, "it occurred to me that you could shoot me in the back and make a run for it on your own."

"Yeah," Ben replied, "it occurred to me, too."

"You still say you didn't shoot ol' Barrett?"

"I still say it."

"It will be dark soon," Wolf Kill said to Red Sky. "They will regret jumping into that hole. If we are careful, we can shoot them before they know we are upon them."

"If we are careful," Red Sky echoed. "We were not so careful before and we lost four brave warriors. Both of the white men have the new repeating rifles, and they are both good shots. Are you sure one of them is the scar-faced man who wounded you and killed Dead Man?"

"Yes," Wolf Kill said. "I saw him when he and the

other one crossed the river near the sacred hills. It's him. No other man has a face like that."

"You were wise to come back to our camp for help. I think this scar-face has strong medicine, and I don't know if he can be killed."

"I will kill him," Wolf Kill replied. "I don't fear his medicine. He has killed too many of our warriors, and he must not get away again. I think his medicine is nothing without the gun that shoots many times."

"We will see," Red Sky said. "Already there will be crying in four lodges tonight. I hope we can avenge our brothers who have fallen today."

"I reckon it's about time," Ike said. "You ready?"

"Reckon so," Ben answered. "You gonna keep leadin' that sorrel? It might slow you down some if it turns out we're in a race with those Indian ponies."

"You might be right," Ike said. "The damn horse has got a mean streak, anyway. Might serve them Injuns right if they catch him. We'll take what we can use off him and leave him." They checked their weapons and their saddles in preparation to move out of the basin. "In case you forget in the excitement that's fixin' to happen, you're still under arrest."

"I'll keep it in mind," Ben said.

It was too dark now to see if they were being stalked or not, so there was nothing to do but climb in the saddle and ride like hell. Up out of the defile they charged with Ike leading the way. Their flight was immediately discovered and a loud cry of alarm filled the air behind them as the warriors scrambled for their horses to give chase. They were able to gain a sizable lead because of the time it took for Red Sky and Wolf Kill to gather their warriors from both sides of the basin. Galloping recklessly across the prairie, ignoring the possible dangers of prairie dog holes and weathered gullies, they used the dark forms of some distant hills as a guide with the sound of Sioux war cries growing stronger behind them.

"We can't outrun those damn Injun ponies," Ike yelled as they descended the side of a wide ravine. "We'd best look for a place to stop and slow 'em up." Ben nodded his agreement as they rode up the other side of the ravine.

The race continued until the Sioux ponies had closed the gap enough to get within range of their rifles, and shots began to zip by the two white men. "Up ahead!" Ben yelled, and pointed to a low stand of bushes that indicated water of some kind. Ike yelled back his okay and they held the two tiring horses to a hard gallop, their hooves thundering across the prairie grass, in an effort to reach the safety of the creek banks. With bullets whining all around them, they slid from their saddles and led the horses back behind some of the thicker bushes. Then they quickly scrambled back to the edge of the creek bank with their rifles and cartridge belts, prepared to thin out the ranks of their assailants.

Red Sky paid dearly for his continued assault upon the two white men with Winchester rifles, as Ben and Ike methodically picked off one warrior after another, until the hostiles were forced to break off their attack and scatter for cover out of rifle range. Red Sky looked around him in frantic despair to discover the number of missing warriors. "This is no good," he said to Wolf Kill. "I have already lost too many." He turned so all could hear him. "This is not a good day to fight. We have lost many warriors. Their weapons are too much for us, so we must let them go before we lose any more of our brothers."

"No!" Wolf Kill responded. "We must kill the scarface or he will continue to kill our people. We must not turn back now when we are this close."

"I will go back to mourn our dead," Red Sky said, knowing that this defeat would weaken his medicine and cost him his status as a war chief. "Wolf Kill must listen to his own heart, and each of you must decide what your heart tells you. That is all I have to say."

"Who will follow me and kill this white devil?" Wolf Kill challenged, his pony stepping from side to side nervously as a cold wind spun tiny eddies of fine snow to dance around them. It was not a good sign for the warriors. "No one?" Wolf Kill exclaimed. "Then I will go alone."

"I believe that stopped 'em," Ike said, straining to see the remaining warriors who had now come together several hundred yards away. "They've lost too many men. They're thinkin' now that their medicine ain't right tonight. I expect it'd be a good idea to sneak on outta here now and get a little more distance between us, in case they change their minds and come at us again."

Hoping their retreat would not be noticed in the dark, they waded the creek, leading their horses slowly up the opposite bank. Ben stroked the buckskin's neck and face. "I'm sorry, boy," he uttered, knowing the horse was nearing exhaustion. Because of this, they continued to walk, leading the horses, as long as there was no outcry of discovery from the gathering of warriors. So far, there was no indication that they had been seen as they led their tired horses across the prairie.

"Hell," Ike commented, "I can't believe they ain't seen us. Pretty soon we'll be out of sight in the dark. We might just walk the rest of the way to Laramie." He had no sooner said it than a shrill war cry was heard behind them. They looked back to see a warrior charging after them at a gallop. "Shit!" Ike uttered, thinking the lone rider was leading the whole pack after them again. "Let's get goin'!" he shouted, and climbed up in the saddle.

Ben, still on foot, heard the impact of the rifle slug that caught Ike in the back a split second before the report of the carbine. Ike slumped forward on his horse's neck as the gelding sprang into flight. Ben yanked his rifle from the scabbard and turned to meet the charging Indian. He saw only one, so he dropped to his knee and brought the front sight to bear on the rider's chest. As soon as he pulled the trigger, the Indian recoiled with the shot and threw both hands in the air, but did not fall from the saddle. The horse continued to gallop toward Ben, forcing him to jump out of the way to avoid being run over. Several dozen yards past him the Indian pony came to a stop and his rider keeled slowly over and fell to the ground. Ben took a quick look back toward the dark prairie. There were no other riders following the lone Indian. He didn't take the time to wonder why. Instead he jumped in the saddle and took off after Ike, whose horse was still running, but wandering off to the south.

Within a few minutes' time, he caught up to the

errant horse and took hold of the bridle. Ike looked to be barely holding on. "Can you hang on till I find someplace to help you?" Ben asked.

"I'll hang on," Ike responded painfully, his speech slow and labored. "I think I'm hurt pretty bad, but I'll stay on this damn horse."

"There wasn't but one of 'em and I got him. I don't think the others are comin' after us, but I'll look for a place to hide, in case I'm wrong." He took Ike's reins then and led his horse back to the course that Ike had originally set. Constantly looking over his shoulder for signs of pursuit, he held the horses to a gentle lope, hoping to gain more ground before having to rest them. When it became clear that the Indians were not coming after them, he began searching for a place to rest and try to tend to Ike's wound. Moving up into a more hilly country now, he finally came to a small stream that wound its way down a narrow ravine. *This looks as good as we'll likely find*, he thought, and led the horses up the stream toward the head of the ravine.

Once he got Ike off his horse and settled on a blanket on the ground, he soaked a bandanna in the stream, intending to clean the blood around the wound. As soon as he got his shirt off, however, he realized that Ike was hurt worse than he had hoped, and there was very little he could do for him. The bullet had lodged deep in his chest, and there was no amount of probing he could do to extract it without killing him for sure. "You need a doctor," he told him. "There ain't nothin' I can do for you. That bullet's deep inside you."

"I'm freezin'," Ike complained, between spasms of stinging pain. "Dumb son of a bitch," he muttered as he gasped for breath. "I got careless—dumb son of a bitch."

"I can't build you a fire," Ben said. "I ain't got nothin' to build it with. We don't wanna take a chance on anybody seeing a fire, anyway." He was at a loss, not sure what to do for the wounded man, and he was trying not to reveal his indecision in his tone. He only thought on it for a moment, however, before deciding. "We ain't stayin' here, anyway. I'm takin' you to the doctor at Fort Laramie."

"I don't know, partner," Ike gasped, his breathing becoming more and more difficult. "I believe I finally found the bullet with my name on it. I don't think I can make it to Laramie."

"I'll be damned . . . ," Ben replied sharply. "You'll make it. I don't intend to have another dead lawman on my hands. You'll make it, or I swear, I'll put another hole in you." He took his extra shirt from his saddlebag and cut it up to make bandages to try to stop the bleeding, placing them over the wound in Ike's back. With what was left of the shoulders and sleeves of the shirt, he held the bandage in place, tying the sleeves around Ike's chest. Then he pulled Ike's shirt back over his head and wrapped the blanket over his shoulders. "You said back yonder at the Niobrara that Fort Laramie wasn't more'n thirty miles from there, so we've got maybe twenty or twenty-five from here now. You can make that, Ike. Hell, you can make twenty miles standing on your head. So don't talk to me no more about dyin'. I'm gonna put you back on that horse and we're goin' to Laramie—if you told me the right way to go. If you didn't, you deserve to die."

Ike tried to laugh, but choked on it and coughed instead, each cough causing him to wince with the pain. "All right, partner, I'll try."

As soon as he could get Ike settled on his horse, they set out for Fort Laramie. The wounded deputy marshal tried to sit upright in the saddle at first, but soon slumped over to lie again on his horse's neck. Ben checked on him frequently, encouraging, even daring him to hang on as they made their way toward the hills to the west. In the wee hours of the morning, they struck a road that led to the fort, and Ben followed it past the first signs of settlement until at last the buildings of Fort Laramie came into view. "You still with me, Gibbs?" Ben asked anxiously.

"I don't know," Ike rasped painfully. "I reckon so."

"You hang on, damn it, 'cause we made it. You got just a little bit more to go."

Approaching the parade ground, they encountered a sentry who issued a challenge. "Halt! Who goes there?" Ben explained that he had a critically wounded U.S. deputy marshal who needed medical attention right away, and the soldier directed him to the hospital with no further delay. Ben stood by while two hospital orderlies carried Ike inside, then one of them ran to rouse the doctor out of bed. By this time, the Officer of the Day had been alerted and had come to investigate. He was naturally interested in hearing any details of a hostile Indian attack. When Ben told him the route they had traveled, the lieutenant commented, "Probably Red Sky's band. He's been raiding north and east of here." He paused to study the sinister face of the stranger, then had to ask, "You both deputy marshals?"

"Ah, no, sir," Ben answered, "just him. I just brought him to the doctor."

"What was he doing out in that territory? Where was he going?"

Ben shook his head thoughtfully. "I reckon you'd have to ask him. I just happened along."

"Well, I guess he'll tell us more after the doctor sees him," the lieutenant said. "You're probably tired and hungry after what you've been through. The mess hall will be open for breakfast in about thirty minutes. You can get something to eat there if you want. I'll tell the mess sergeant."

"'Preciate it," Ben said. "I expect I'd better take his horse to the stable first, if you could point the way." As tempting as coffee and breakfast sounded, he had no intention of lingering any longer than he had to. He was thinking about wanted papers and what Ike might say when they asked him who the man was who brought him in, so it was healthier for him to leave Fort Laramie and head for parts unknown.

The morning stable detail had not reported for duty when Ben took Ike's horse to the barn. There was no one there except the soldier on guard duty. Ben explained the reason for his being there to the indifferent guard, then unsaddled Ike's horse and let it out in the corral with the others. When that was done, he climbed in the saddle and headed the buckskin north, eager to put Fort Laramie behind him. He only traveled far enough to ensure a little distance between him and the fort before finding a place to camp. His horse was already near exhaustion and he felt an intense need for coffee and some sleep afterward, so the quiet little stream lined with cottonwoods looked extremely inviting. And this close to the fort, he felt he was relatively safe from trouble with any more Indians. So after taking care of his horse and building a fire to boil coffee to complement his dried jerky, he spread his blanket and went to sleep.

His sleep was deep and filled with dreams that made no sense, about Cleve and Ike, Jonah and Victoria, and hostile Indians. When he awoke, it was already past noon. Still drowsy and reluctant to move quickly, he revived his fire and boiled more coffee. Then he sat by the fire and tried to decide what he should do, for he was now free of all the obligations he had set for himself, except one—Garth Beaudry. He had accounted for those who had pulled the triggers that took Cleve's and Jonah's lives, but not the one responsible for ordering them to do so. "Damn!" he suddenly swore, sick of this trail of vengeance, but the need to punish all those who were part of the murder of the people he cared about weighed heavily upon his head.

Thoughts of Beaudry brought thoughts of Victoria, and he suddenly found himself wondering how she was handling the loss of her father. He tried to picture her plain, friendly face, and found he could not, more easily remembering her soft voice and her easy way. *She'll probably marry again*, he thought. The ratio of men to women in Deadwood was so much heavier on the males' side; she would no doubt be swamped with proposals. *That ain't for me to concern myself with*, he thought. *It ain't got nothing to do with me.* He remembered how obviously frightened she was by him when she had met him for the first time. "I hope she finds a good one this time," he announced to the buckskin. "She deserves it. She's a fine woman."

Undecided on whether or not to return to Deadwood right away to finish the business with Garth Beaudry, he turned his attention to the state of his existence. There was still the matter of being wanted by the law, and the scar that made him so easily identifiable would always be there. So where could he go? He longed for a peaceful life, but how far would he have to go to have a chance for one? In the end, he decided to go back to the Black Hills. There were plenty of places for a man to hide in those mountains and plenty of game to hunt. After all he had been through in the past weeks, he still had his weapons and most of the money from Shep. He could afford to outfit himself pretty well. He would think some more about settling with Beaudry. Part of his hesitation was the fact that he would be taking the life of Victoria's husband. Even with his despicable treatment of her, she might still feel something for the father of her son, and Ben could not bring himself to do anything that would alienate her feelings for him. One decision he didn't hesitate on, however, was the necessity to change his name. There had to be plenty of men sporting scars in this untamed country. He'd just be one of them.

Chapter 17

Lieutenant Robert W. Shufeldt, post surgeon, came to stand beside the bed of the patient admitted two days earlier. "Well, I'm glad to see you're still with us," he said when Ike opened his eyes and looked up at him.

"Damn, Doc," Ike managed, "I ain't so sure I'm glad I made it or not."

"You're lucky to be here. If that bullet had been half an inch closer to the left, you wouldn't be. You're gonna be in a lot of pain for a while yet. I'm sorry we can't make you more comfortable."

"What about the feller that brought me in?" Ike asked.

"I don't know," Lieutenant Shufeldt said. "I'm told he took your horse to the stable, but never came back." They were joined then by another officer and Shufeldt introduced him. "Mr. Gibbs, this is Lieutenant Chambers. He wants to ask you some questions about the attack and also about the man who came with you—if you're up to it."

"I reckon I'm up to it," Ike said.

He gave Chambers all the information he could about the Sioux war party that attacked them near the Niobrara, the number they had killed, how well they were armed, and how they had managed to escape. The lieutenant listened attentively, and when Ike had finished, he had one more question. "Who was the man that brought you in here?"

"Him?" Ike replied. "Oh, he ain't nobody special. He just happened to come along in time to save my ass from them Injuns."

"The reason I asked is we got a wanted notice in the adjutant's office about a man named Ben Cutler, wanted for murder, and he's said to have a serious scar across his face. And from what I've heard from the Officer of the Day on that morning, this fellow who brought you in had the nastiest scar he's ever seen. Any chance this might be the same man?"

"Ben Cutler?" Ike replied. "No, that man ain't Cutler— Cutler's dead, killed in a gunfight on the Deadwood road, just south of Custer City. That feller that brought me in was just one of them gold miners from up Custer City way. I don't know his name. I think it's Fred somethin'. Too bad he didn't hang around long enough for me to thank him for haulin' me over here."

"From what Lieutenant Shufeldt tells me, you owe him a lot," Chambers said.

"I reckon I do," Ike said. "Maybe I can figure out some way to pay him back."

It was the first real snow of the season, about four inches, and it was not even really winter yet. Oblivious of the snow, Ben knelt in the pines that formed a thick belt around the mountain, watching a small gathering of deer as they made their way down the slope toward the stream below. Having already selected a young doe as his target, he patiently waited for the deer to emerge from the thick pines before taking the shot. Cartridges were precious and he did not intend to spend more than one for his kill. Many random thoughts crossed his mind while he waited. He was glad to have finished his hut before the current snowfall, and he was confident that it would serve him well throughout the coming winter. Thoughts of Victoria often found their way into his musings, and he was reminded of a promise he had made to Malcolm Bryant that he would supply him with fresh meat from time to time. It was the night he had left Malcolm's house to go after Sam Cheney's gang of murderers. *I didn't get much chance to go hunting,* he thought. *Maybe I could take them some fresh venison now. I expect they'd be glad to get it.*

He had to admit to himself that it had been difficult to stay away from Deadwood during these last few weeks since he had left Ike Gibbs in the hospital. It would have been foolhardy to chance being seen in Deadwood, since he had escaped Ike's custody. On several occasions he had ridden in close to the gulch, just to see if the town was totally dead because of the damage the fire had done. He had been surprised to see the determination of the people to rebuild the town, with new construction already well under way. *I ought to check on Victoria and her mother, and Caleb,* he told himself, still trying to convince himself that the only reason was to see if they needed help in case they found it necessary to leave Malcolm's house to find a place of their own. They had no source of income that he knew of. *I'd best see if they're all right.* The decision made, he raised his rifle and dropped the unsuspecting deer. *Then I'll settle with Garth Beaudry.*

It was late afternoon when he guided the buckskin up the street carved into the hillside overlooking Deadwood Gulch, unable to ignore the excitement he felt from the prospect of seeing Victoria again. He reminded himself that he had told Malcolm he'd be back to get Barrett's horse, so there was reason enough for his visit. His thoughts were interrupted when he approached Malcolm's house, for there were a couple of buggies and several horses gathered in the front yard. Undecided then as to whether or not he should continue, he pulled his horse to a halt while he thought it over. In a few seconds, a man came out of the house, climbed aboard his horse, and proceeded down the hill toward Ben. Ben guided his horse to the side to give the man approaching room to pass.

"Howdy, neighbor," Ben called out when the man was beside him, trying to sound as cordial as he could and knowing he would get the usual startled look in return.

"Howdy," the man returned, his face reflecting the shocked expression Ben had anticipated.

"What's the trouble up at Malcolm's house?" Ben asked.

"No trouble, at least not yet," the man replied. "They're having a wedding."

"A weddin'?"

"Yep, a wedding," he replied. "There was bound

to be one before much longer, as scarce as women are around here." He chuckled at his remark. "Well, I've got to get back to my store. If you hurry up, you might get there before the food's all eaten up."

Ben sat stunned for a few minutes after the man rode away. He had been telling himself all along that she would most likely marry, but now that it had happened, it struck him like a blow from a hammer. She had always complained about her lack of beauty, but Ben knew that all women in Deadwood were beautiful, no matter how plain they were. *I wish her well*, he thought, and turned his horse around. Victoria, her mother, and Caleb were obviously doing well and were in no need of his help.

He started back down the hill, nudging the buckskin into a lope, then drew back on the reins. "They're friends of mine," he announced. "I at least oughta wish 'em the best of luck." Turning his horse again, he rode on up to the yard and dismounted, where he again had second thoughts about proceeding. The house looked to be full of guests, and he wondered if he should risk an appearance. He didn't want to spoil Victoria's big day. In the anguish caused by the unexpected wedding, the venison he carried had been forgotten. Remembering then, he considered staying long enough to contribute that to the party. Then he could pick up Garrett's horse and be out of everyone's way. Crestfallen, he changed his mind again. "I've got no business here." He stepped up in the saddle and turned the buckskin back toward the street.

"Ben?"

The voice came from behind him and he recognized

it at once. He turned to see Victoria coming down the porch steps. "I thought that was you. Where are you going? Aren't you coming in?"

"I didn't wanna spoil the weddin'," he explained.

"Nonsense," she said. "You're not going to spoil anything. I'm so glad to see you. We were worried about you. We didn't know if you were all right or not. But I can see that you are, so we can all quit worrying now."

"Well, I won't stay," he said. "I don't wanna keep you from your guests. I just wanted to wish you the best of luck. You deserve it."

"Why, thank you. I appreciate that," she said, while favoring him with a look of astonishment. Then it occurred to her. "Ben, I'm not getting married. Mama and Malcolm are." She watched in amazement to see the transformation that took place in the scarred face. Smiling then at the message she read there, she said, "I planned some time ago that I was going to marry you, whenever you got over that scar on your face and got around to asking me. I think it would be the best thing for both of us. And Caleb practically worships you, so what do you think?"

"I think I must be dreamin'," he sputtered. "I mean, yes, hell yes." Then he remembered the job that he had resigned himself to do, and he wasn't sure if Victoria was even aware of the role her husband had played in the murders of her father and Cleve. "There's some unfinished business with Garth Beaudry that has to be done."

Again she looked puzzled. "Well, it's too late to do anything about Garth," she said. "Garth's dead. He was shot by a young man who worked for him."

It was the second time he had been stunned in the last few minutes. "Then I reckon there ain't nothin' else to attend to."

"Are you going to get down off that horse so I can hug you?" she asked. There was no necessity to repeat the question. "You know, the parson's still inside."

Read on for an excerpt from the
next thrilling historical novel
by Charles G. West,

OUTLAW PASS

Available now from Berkley.

"Mose said you were lookin' for me," Adam Blaine said when he met his father coming from the barn. "If you're still worryin' about those missin' cows over on the north range, I found 'em this mornin' holed up in a ravine near the creek."

"No," Nathan Blaine replied. "I figured you'd find 'em. I knew they wouldn't be far. Mose always blames the Indians when we've got cattle missin'. I keep tellin' him that if there's one or two missin', then it might be hungry Injuns cuttin' out some of the stock—but not when we're talkin' about twenty or thirty at a time."

Adam smiled, picturing the worried face of the old Indian scout. Mose Stebbins had come to work for Adam's father when his eyesight began to fail him and he no longer trusted himself to lead a cavalry scouting party. The old man had gone on many a hunting trip with Adam in the mountains to the north and the Absarokas to the south. Now his eyes were no longer sharp enough to be accurate on shots of any distance. Never one to admit to this weakness, he always tended to give

Adam the longer shot, saying the young man needed the practice.

"I counted thirty-two head," Adam said, "all bunched up together."

"I figured," his father repeated. "That ain't why I sent Mose to find you, though." He waited for Adam to step down from the saddle. "I think it's time you went to look for your brother."

"Yessir," Adam replied without emotion. Jake, three years his junior, had been away from home for more than a year. That in itself was not cause for concern for Adam and his father. Jake had sent a message that he was planning to leave Bannack and head for home that very day. Now, two weeks later, Jake had failed to show up from what should have been a five-day ride at most. There was no concern on his father's part for the first week. Jake was always his free-spirited son, prone to drift with the wind, and Nathan was not surprised when he didn't show when he was supposed to. Never content to work at raising cattle, Jake had hurried off to join the horde of other dreamers when news of a major gold discovery in Bannack reached their little settlement on the Yellowstone. Adam had to smile when he remembered Jake's promise on the day he left: "I'll find enough gold to buy all the stock we need to make the Triple-B the biggest cattle spread in the Gallatin Valley."

His father had responded with the statement that the Triple-B was already the biggest. "But if you have to chase your tail in a circle around Bannack, go to hell on. When you run outta grub, come on home."

Nathan's claim was not an exaggeration. The Triple-B *was* the largest, because it was the only cattle ranch in the valley. He had built it up from its simple start as a small herd he had driven up from his home in Briscoe County, Texas. The old man was now fully aware that his was a situation that was bound to change soon.

More and more settlers were showing up on the trail that led from Fort Laramie to the gold strikes in Bannack and the more recent one in Virginia City. These were not the folks that worried Nathan; they were just passing through. It was the people looking for space to build new homes that concerned him, and the fertile land of the Gallatin Valley was a strong attraction to many of these farm families. Nathan knew the fences would come, and his free range would shrink with each new arrival. John Bozeman, along with Daniel Rouse and William Beall, was already rumored to be thinking about laying out a town. For now, there was room for everybody, but how long would that be the case? These were the issues Nathan would deal with in the not-too-distant future. His concern on this day, however, was for his son and what trouble he might have gotten himself into in the mining camps.

In sharp contrast to Jake, Adam was as steady as a granite cliff. Taller by a couple of inches and with a powerful frame, Adam was truly Jake's big brother, and Nathan was confident that his elder son would ensure the continued success of his ranch long after he was gone. Adam had been getting his younger brother out of scrapes since they were boys, so it was not unusual that Nathan was sending him to find Jake once again.

It was all the same to Adam. Unlike his brother, he never crowded his mind with thoughts of places he had not been. To him, life was what you made it, with whatever tools or weapons were at your disposal. He didn't fault Jake for being a dreamer. That was just the way Jake was. In fact, Adam sometimes envied his younger brother's longing to see the valley beyond the next mountain or to follow the river to its beginning. Jake often teased his brother about his emotionless approach to each new day and the work that was waiting to be done. But he knew and appreciated the fact that the rock that was Adam was always there to lean on. Mose said Adam was soulful, born without a funny bone, but Nathan suspected his son's serious approach to just about everything was due to his mother's early death and the subsequent burden that had fallen upon him to look after his younger brother while doing a man's share of the ranch work. It was Adam who had convinced his father to let Jake follow the prospectors to the gold fields. "He'll get it out of his system pretty quick," Adam had predicted, "when he finds out all his hard work won't result in much more than a little grub money." As it turned out, however, Jake had evidently stuck with it longer than Adam had figured. And according to the message he sent, he was coming home with a little more than "grub money." Adam wasn't surprised in one respect, knowing how important it was to Jake to prove that he was his own man and was not dependent upon his father or Adam to make his mark. Still, it was hard to picture Jake with a pick or shovel in his hand. No matter what he did, though, Jake was always going to be Jake—wild, sometimes to the extent of recklessness—and that was more than likely the reason for his failure to arrive when he said he would. Maybe he had encountered a saloon along the way that had tempted him to risk some of his fortune on cards and women. It wouldn't be the first time. *I wouldn't be surprised*, Adam thought. *Well, I'll go see if I can find him.*

"I figured you'd be ridin' Bucky," Nathan Blaine remarked when he walked into the barn, where Adam was securing his saddlebags on a red roan named Brownie. Bucky was Adam's favorite horse and almost always his first choice when considering a ride of any length.

In response to his father's comment, Adam turned to

gaze at the big bay gelding in the corral. "I decided it'd be best to let Bucky rest for a few days," he said. "He's tryin' to get a split hoof on his left front, and I'm hopin' it'll heal on its own, given a little time. Tell Mose and Doc not to work him till I get back."

"I will," Nathan responded. "Here," he said, and handed Adam a roll of bills. "You might need some extra money in case you have to bail your brother out of jail or somethin'." Then he gave him a small pouch. "There's three gold double eagles in here. That ain't but sixty dollars, but you might need it in case they won't take any paper money in that damn place." Adam nodded, took the money, and put it away in one of his saddlebags. Nathan stepped back while his son climbed up in the saddle. "You be careful, Adam."

"I will, Pa," Adam said, and slid his Henry rifle into the saddle scabbard. With no further words of parting than this, Adam wheeled the roan and set him on a southwest course toward the Yellowstone. His father spun on his heel and returned to the house, confident that Adam would find his brother. Passing the back corner of the corral, Adam saw Mose and Doc replacing a broken rail. He pulled up when he was hailed by Mose, who walked out to meet him.

"Boy," Mose addressed him—he always called him "boy." Adam figured the old man would always think of him and Jake as the two scrappy little fellows in their childhood. "You be damn careful, you hear? There's a lot of wild, godless outlaws preyin' on the hardworkin' folks around them diggin's. You mind your back."

"I will, Mose. I'll find Jake and be back here before you know I'm gone."

Mose remained there for several minutes, hands on hips, watching Adam until he turned Brownie toward the river. Of Nathan Blaine's two sons, he admitted to himself that Adam was his favorite. Maybe it was because Adam had always been interested in learning everything Mose had offered to teach him, whether it was stalking and killing an elk or knowing a horse's mind. Unlike Jake, who openly flaunted his self-reliance, Adam seemed secure in a quiet confidence that he was prepared to handle whatever confronted him. In spite of their differences, Mose had to concede that the two brothers were close. He attributed that to Adam's maturity and the fact that he had more or less watched over his younger brother since their mother died. His thoughts were interrupted by the sound of Nathan Blaine calling for him from the house. *I don't know how long this place would survive without me to take care of everything*, he thought as he turned and started toward the back door of the house.

Adam arrived at the bank of the Madison River at the end of the second day's travel, his first day having been shortened considerably by his late departure from the Triple-B. He made his camp a hundred yards up a stream that emptied into the river, where the light from his fire might not be noticed by anyone passing by. After an uneventful night, he was out of his blanket at first light and saddling the roan, preparing to ride for ten or twelve miles along the river before stopping to rest his horse and have his breakfast. Following an already well-traveled road, the roan maintained a steady pace, so much so that Adam decided to push on until Brownie showed signs of getting tired. Consequently, it was close to noon when he decided that the horse had earned a good rest.

While he sat by his small fire, drinking a cup of coffee and gnawing on a strip of jerky, he watched idly as the red roan nosed around in a patch of green lilies at the water's edge. There had never been any reason for him to travel to Alder Gulch, so all he knew about

Virginia City, Nevada City, and the other towns along that gulch was what he had heard—that they were wide-open and lawless towns with thousands of new people streaming in every day. Based on these stories, he had halfway expected to meet other travelers on the road along the Madison, but so far, he was the only traffic. Back in the saddle, he continued his journey.

Leaving the river, he followed the road up into the hills for another nine or ten miles before sundown once again called for him to make camp. Virginia City couldn't have been more than another half day's ride, he figured, and Bannack was supposed to be about sixty miles beyond Virginia City. And although Jake was supposed to be in Bannack, Adam planned to start looking for his brother in the saloons and bawdy houses in Alder Gulch and Daylight Gulch before moving on to Bannack. If he was lucky, he might find him holed up there, delayed by a run of luck at the poker table or a "fancy lady" who happened to catch his eye. He shook his head and sighed, much like a harried parent thinking about a rambunctious child, as he guided the roan toward a stand of cottonwood trees that suggested the presence of some form of water. Sure enough, he found a small stream cutting a shallow gully between the trees. In short order, he had his horse taken care of and a fire glowing cheerfully. With his coffeepot bubbling on the edge of the fire, he broke out his frying pan and started to prepare some more of the jerky he had brought. It was then he noticed the ears perking up on the roan grazing nearby, followed a few seconds later by an inquisitive nicker. Knowing it could have been a mountain lion or a bear out in the darkness that had caused the horse to inquire, he nevertheless casually rolled away from the firelight, drawing his rifle from the saddle behind him.

"Hello the camp," called a voice a few minutes later.

"Saw your fire back there. Mind if we come in? There's just the two of us."

Adam's first thought was that he hadn't hidden his camp very well, but there was nothing to remedy that now. "Come on in," he called back while edging his way a little farther from the firelight until his back was against the trunk of a cottonwood.

In a few moments, two riders approached the fire, slow-walking their horses through the trees beside the stream and leading a packhorse. Pulling up in the small clearing, they looked right and left before sighting Adam sitting with his back to the tree. "Howdy," one of the men said. "Don't blame you for bein' careful. There's a helluva lot of road agents ridin' these trails around here. We all have to be careful."

"That's what I hear," Adam replied and got to his feet, his rifle still in hand. "You're welcome to some coffee. I don't have much food to offer but some jerky I was fixin' to fry when you rode up."

"'Preciate it," the rider said. "Me and Jim here would love some of that coffee, but we've got plenty of fresh-kilt deer meat that needs to be et before it starts to turn. Jim shot a young buck a few hours ago right when it was crossin' the river. So if you'll furnish the coffee, we'll furnish the meat."

"That sounds like a fair deal to me," Adam said, still watching his visitors with a cautious eye.

The two dismounted then. "My name's Rob Hawkins," the one doing all the talking said. "My partner here is Jim Highsmith. We're headin' to Virginia City. Which way are you headin'?"

"Adam Blaine," Adam said. "I'm goin' the same way you are."

"You headin' to the diggin's to try your luck at prospectin'?" Highsmith asked, speaking for the first time.

"Nope," Adam replied. "I'm lookin' for my brother.

He's the prospector in the family. I don't know much about it, to tell you the truth." He continued to watch the men carefully as they tied their horses near the stream, taking special note that they left their rifles in the saddle boots. In a show of equal trust, he walked back over to his saddle on the ground and slipped his rifle back in the sling.

The gesture did not go unnoticed by his guests. Rob smiled and unbuckled his gun belt. "Why don't we just hang our handguns on our saddles, so we don't have to keep an eye on each other, and cook up some of this meat?" His remark served to clear the tension from the air, and all three chuckled as Jim and Adam followed his example. "Matter of fact, I might pull off my boots and pants. They still ain't dry." He went on to relate the encounter with the deer at the river. "If Jim had waited till the damn deer climbed up on the bank, I wouldn'ta had to go in the river after him. I swear, he shot him when he was right in the middle, and he was about to wash downstream with the current."

Jim shrugged and replied in defense of his actions, "How was I to know if he was gonna come on across or turn and go to the other bank? You'da got your ass wet either way."

"Oughta made you go in after him," Rob groused. "You were the one that shot him."

Adam recharged his coffeepot to accommodate the new arrivals while Rob carved off some of the fresh venison. There was no need to conserve. The meat wouldn't keep much longer with the weather as warm as it was, so everyone ate his fill. By the time a state of satisfaction was reached, the three men felt at ease with one another, and the talk turned to prospecting. Rob, sitting by the fire in his underwear, complained that he and Jim were too late in arriving at the diggings, but decided they had nothing better to do. "There's always some little spot that nobody found, and that might be the place we hit it big."

"Maybe so," Adam said. "You sound like my brother. The only difference is my brother ain't much for hard work. He'll likely look for some way to have somebody else do the diggin'." He studied his two visitors without the sense of suspicion he had applied at first. They were an interesting pair. Rob was tall and lanky, and his face wore an expression of carefree indifference. His partner, Jim, was a study in contrast. Short and stocky, his face reflected a sense of constant worry. He walked with a slight limp, the result of having been born with one leg considerably shorter than the other, according to him. Before the evening was over, Adam invited them to unsaddle their horses and ride on in to Virginia City with him in the morning.

The conversation eventually got around to the many rumors of gangs of road agents that preyed upon the trails between the gold fields and Salt Lake City and the lack of law enforcement to protect stagecoaches and freighters. "Bannack, Virginia City, and all the other little towns along those gulches are wide-open for outlaws," Rob said. "And since you say you ain't ever been to any of them places, you'd best beware of who you talk to, especially if you're carryin' any money on you."

"Well, I reckon I don't have anythin' to worry about," Adam lied, "'cause I'm dead broke. But I 'preciate the warnin'. Like I said, I'm just lookin' for my brother, and as soon as I find him, the outlaws are welcome to Alder Gulch and Daylight Gulch, too."

"Still ain't a bad idea to sleep with your six-shooter handy, though," Rob said, and that was what all three did when it was time to turn in.